g but thoroughly compelling new stories
...d High Witches of thrilling YA. This is a
...bling cauldron of mystery, mischievousness and
...A as it should be – dangerous, dark and daring. I

C.J. Skuse

...eply compelling dark tales that twist and snare the
...tion. Three tales of love, loss, heartache and page-
mystery.'

Jenn, www.jenniely.com

...girl": what a tingling, winter storm of a story! Nia and
...e and sunlight, loss and finding, the fragile flame of
...hlight hope, and the music that holds them all … it's
...'

Hilary McKay

...sterious, intriguing and chilling. This is a fab collection
...anyone who likes their tales just a little bit twisted…
...hree Strikes is perfect reading for long winter-evenings.'

Elen Caldecott

'"The Darkness": A raw tale, reminiscent of *Black Mirror*,
with compelling characters stranded in a stark landscape, all
bound together in gritty, gripping writing.'

Joanna Nadin

Three Strikes

Dark and Chilling Tales

Firefly

Lucy Christopher is the British/ Australian author of *Stolen*, which won the Branford Boase Award, the Gold Inky, and a Printz Honor Award. Her other books include *Flyaway*, *The Killing Woods* and *Storm-wake*. Lucy is senior lecturer in creative writing at Bath Spa University where she received her PhD in Creative Writing.

Kat Ellis is the author of *Blackfin Sky* (Firefly, 2014) and *Purge* (Firefly, 2016) in the UK and *Blackfin Sky* and *Breaker* in the US (Running Press Kids). She lives in Rhyl in North Wales.

Rhian Ivory is the author of four YA titles with Bloomsbury, *The Boy Who Drew the Future* (Firefly, 2015), which was nominated for the Carnegie Medal, and *Hope* (Firefly, 2017).

Three Strikes

The Darkness
Lucy Christopher

The Twins of Blackfin
Kat Ellis

Matchgirl
Rhian Ivory

Firefly

First published in 2018
by Firefly Press
25 Gabalfa Road, Llandaff North, Cardiff, CF14 2JJ
www.fireflypress.co.uk

ISBN 9781910080863
ebook ISBN 9781910080870

*This book has been published with the support of
the Welsh Books Council.*

Printed and bound by Pulsio Sarl

The Darkness

Lucy Christopher

> *HEY! Want to get away? Escape?*
> *Something bad happen to you*
> *that you can't deal with yet?*
> *Join*
> ***THE TRIBE***
> *An immersive psychological programme.*
> *Through group work, therapy, and tailored psychological*
> *tasks, we'll help you to overcome*
> *your own personal darkness.*
> *Best of all, escape to a tropical African*
> *island paradise as you do...*

There! I stuck it in. The advert. Kept it, see? Found it folded up in a back pocket. Not that long ago, I read it every day.

For a while, it was the only note I wanted to read.

For a while, it was a good thing.

Mum left a note for me too, the night everything happened. I found it later, after the police had gone and I was alone at the kitchen table waiting for Dieter. Back when it was dark as killers' eyes outside.

Tonight I'm catching the black cat.

3

All she wrote.

Mum was odd like that. You'll see.

But maybe I'm getting ahead of myself.

So…

The first thing I remember about being here? That's something Lily wanted me to write about.

I guess it was the heat, slamming into me with a force that took my breath. People talk about walls of heat, but this felt like a whole mountain. It stopped me moving, made me unwilling to ever move again. I was sweating instantly, standing at the top of those rickety plane steps and staring out at the darkness. Long, black, endless darkness. That seemed appropriate, at least.

After the bright lights of the plane, the black was impenetrable, like there was nothing else beyond the end of the runway: the lights stopped and the world stopped too. There could've been a gigantic cliff there and we'd never have known it. They could've marched us straight towards it. That darkness was alive, too – full of screeching creatures, rustling movement. But there was no sound of water. No beach.

'Some island,' I said.

Sam was pushing me. 'Come on, the rest of us want to see too.'

The steps wiggled, so I grabbed hard onto the flimsy banister until I found the tarmac below. Heat seeped up through my trainers. If my feet had been bare, I'd have been hopping. I thought it was crazy that tarmac could be so hot when it was night-time – how boiling did it get during the day? Could that tarmac melt and become a sticky river?

I turned to say this to Sam, but he was no longer right behind me. Instead, he was walking away from the plane with Nyall. They were chatting about one of the films that'd been on, something cheery about earthquakes and the end of the world. Nyall nodded seriously, not smiling at all, while Sam laughed and joked. Maybe Nyall was just bricking it to finally be here, like I was.

When Pete came over, I bet he was bricking it too, under his tough-guy look. But he slapped Nyall and Sam on the back like they were all comrades – a team about to embark on a dangerous mission.

Wanker.

I turned away and found the other girl, Annie, at my shoulder, pressing me to keep going. I stepped away from the plane. The camera was there, even then: George in front of our faces with a little hand-held, asking us *leading questions* about ourselves and how we were feeling.

'What's it all like? First impressions? What can you hear and taste and smell…?'

I can remember the smell: the shock of it. It was sweet, sort of, and wet. Like a mixture of damp school jumpers and the cheap flowery perfume one of my therapists had worn. I'd been expecting the sea. Something like salt-and-vinegary chips, maybe. I'd thought there'd be a breeze.

'It smells like a slug,' I said.

5

Sam was too busy chatting with his new best friend to hear me. Annie was still there, though, with her face screwed up, smelling it too.

'It smells like hot knickers,' she said, right to the camera.

I laughed. I didn't think she could be funny. The camera caught it all.

Where's that footage now?

Annie moved away from me then, away from the camera and George and out across the tarmac. I followed, still watching the darkness. Was it all just trees? Maybe it was like the woods on the mountain back home. And maybe the smell was a bit like bracken and moss, like the stuff Mum and I collected one autumn for one of her art projects. We had spent days doing that; I'd had dirt under my fingernails for weeks. I closed my eyes to stop thinking about it, but the noise of the place jolted them open again: the shrieks and rustles and calls. It was like we were stepping out into a zoo. When I caught up with Sam his cheeks were hot, red as cherries and almost bitable.

'I told you this would be good,' he said. He was looking at Annie, at her long blonde hair. He was breathing in the night.

'We haven't even got there yet, not properly,' I said.

There was a gnawing feeling in my stomach, the one that had started the very first day I'd agreed to do this thing with him, that'd been eating away at me ever since. The one I still have now.

But it wasn't the day when I said *yes* to *The Tribe* that really

6

started that feeling, not if I truly think about it. And *this* is what Lily actually wants me to write about – the beginning, my journey to being here. What started my own personal tip to the dark.

So maybe it starts here: when Sam asked me out.

I liked that. A lot. At the time.

I liked how Sam didn't even care that he was in the middle of our English classroom and there were people all around us. I liked how he kept holding my gaze. I liked how his cheeks went marshmallow pink, too. And he was grinning at me, knowing my answer. I liked that best of all.

'Tonight, after dark, we'll take her car,' he said. 'I know how.'

He'd been talking about doing it for ages. Just me, him and Mum's old banger at the end of the street. I'd thought it was all a joke, one of Sam's crazy ideas that never happened.

He scrunched his fingers into a fist, flicked his eyes from where Brandon was eavesdropping, and back to me. 'What do you think?'

And I looked at how wide and brown his eyes were, how cute his lips looked when he chewed them at the corner, and I said,

'Yes.'

…even though I had something else to do that night. Even though I knew what he was planning was unbelievably stupid and probably illegal. Even though Mum would hate it.

Sam punched the air, then immediately looked around the classroom to check who'd seen. I almost started to laugh. Sam was so rubbish at trying to play cool. He shrugged it off.

''bout ten? Earlier?'

I shrugged back, looked out the window to the playground.

'Sure, whatever.'

Unlike him, I could do *nonchalant*. It was a skill I'd perfected being round Mum. She could get so excited over nothing, she needed *nonchalant* to bring her down to earth. Needed me to bring her down, too. (Needed that more than I care to think about.)

I need *nonchalant* out here as well; it gives me a mask. Sam and the others, they don't seem to need anything.

But none of them

! NONE OF THEM !

But

none of them

killed

There. I wrote it.

Happy?

I didn't write all of it though. Not

quite.

Not the whole story.

Not yet.

(And, actually, I don't know for sure that none of them have killed. Pete's probably done over a few.)

Since I wrote that stuff above, I've watched a flock of parrots zigzag across the sky. They stopped in a tree opposite our huts and made the branches shake. I didn't look at this page the whole time they were there. Little distractions. I'm good at them.

I feel funny. I'm not sure writing this is a good idea. I don't want to do it, even though a part of me thinks I should.

But waiting like the others are – just sitting around and talking about nothing and pretending – that's the worst thing ever. And Sam thinks writing this might be worth it.

'Lily will like it,' he said. 'And that's good, right?'

But I'm not sure I give a fuck about what Lily likes (and if you're reading this, Lily, you might as well know it), I just want to get us out of here.

And this was a Task after all. My task.

Keep a Group Journal of everything that brought you to this point.

Lily's words. She even talked about burning the journal afterwards in some elaborate *Letting Go* ceremony, probably complete with joss sticks and hippy dancing around a fire.

I don't see Sam writing. He's sitting with the others. Perhaps he just told me to do this so I'd be out of the way. I don't think so though. I know if I go over there, he'll try and hug me and expect me to be a part of things. I'd rather be by myself. Even if it means thinking about why we're here … how it started. That day.

'Start with the day everything changed,' Lily told me when she gave this out.

Did she give anything to the other guys, or just this journal to me? My mind is already starting to forget things. It's the air of this place, the smell. It's the drugs I'm sure Lily and George are smoking, seeping into me too.

So…

It's a long while ago now, but out here I have a lot of time to count things like this. For example, there are 12 parrots flitting between the trees in front of me – 12 I can see, anyway. I am 5,804 days old. Sam is 5,821. We've been here 15 days, but I've been *here*, on the steps of this hut writing this, for 1.

The other important numbers are these:

It's 390 days since Sam asked me out.

And 389 days since Mum died.

There.

I wrote it again.

Most days I try not to think about this last set of numbers … that there are only a few hours between the two. But today, sitting here in the heat and the dirt, I dunno…

Sam thinks it will get us out, writing this stuff. I'm not sure about that, but writing this gives me A REASON not to sit with the others.

Until we find out what's happening.

Until we find out when they're coming back.

That's another number I can write down, actually.

29

29 hours since we saw Lily and George. Since they disappeared.

I don't know how many numbers until they return.

If they do.

Maybe they just want to freak us out. Make us think we're alone. Fuck with our minds. I can't be the only one of us who's thinking it. Perhaps it'll go all *Lord of the Flies*, or *Hunger Games,* and we'll start killing each other. Perhaps they're watching for it right now. Waiting for us to crack. It's what makes good telly after all. Good psychological drama.

Are we living up to their expectations?

Experiential psychology

Immersive healing

The Tribe

What a joke! How did I ever think that a month with these nut jobs would cure anything?

But I did, didn't I? I chose to come and begged the money off Dieter to do it. I shouldn't forget that. I told him that if he gave it to me, he could go off with Cynthia, or whatever she's called, to Corfu, or Crete, or wherever. I told him it would help.

Take some responsibility – isn't that what we're always being told?

I just gave a *hard stare* (as Mum would call it) to the trees. I still see the red lights in there, blinking.

Sometimes I think they're eyes. Sometimes cameras. Sometimes, when I go looking for either, I find nothing.

But they're watching, aren't they?

(*You're* watching aren't you, Lily?)

I feel it. The eyes. The stare.

Something's tracking us. Some … one.

Maybe.

I want to draw a cat.

Paw prints.

I want those paw prints to cover this page. These words.

I want scratch marks in my arm.

Claws.

Paw prints in my skin.

Claws could rip up a page like this.

Sam's wrong if he thinks I'm writing down everyone's stories. I don't care about them. They can write their own; they can stay here forever and I won't care. Anyway, I don't want to know anything about them. But me and, yes, even Sam … I want us to get out. That's why I'm starting with that day, because it's not just the beginning of my story; it's Sam's too.

There are 200 pages in this notebook. Too thick. My story's not big enough to fill that. But I'll write what I can. Though I'd rather have a knife in my hand. I bet I could find one too. In the main cabin, there's all sorts of things that hurt.

A pen is less useful than a knife but maybe it just stabs differently. And every scratch I make in this paper is an effort. Maybe both require a kind of courage to use.

The pages of this thing are damp and soft, a little bit like skin … like they've sweated, too. When I run my fingers over them, it's like touching the soft insides of my elbows, the places the sun doesn't hit. When I think about it like that, I want to mark these pages. Perhaps these words can be the new marks I make.

Yeah.

I like that.

Claw-marked words.

Lily would be happy with my poetic philosophising, at least.

Thinking about her smiling at me, all satisfied-like, makes me want to stab this paper with my pen and a knife and pretend that it's her skin I'm digging into.

• • •

There. Can you see them, Lily? Stab marks?

It doesn't make me feel any better though.

• • • •   • • • • •

OK.

Maybe a little.

• • • • • • • • • • • • • • • •

• • • • • • • • • • • • • • • •

The night Lily gave me this journal seems ages ago now: the jolty four-wheel drive with us all crammed inside, going through the dark for hours, the feel of Sam's hot arm juddering against mine.

So many bumps.

Ruts.

Smells.

And then, spinning this notebook through the hot air. The pages fluttering in the wind like wings: a paper dove. I watched it flip away and almost wanted to flip out of the window after it.

Which I did, I guess. Lily made me go back for it. It was on the track, a couple of metres back. I could see it in the red beam of the brake lights, its blank pages fallen open, still flicking. And I picked it up and stood there, my back to the vehicle, looking out at the dark. It was thick and heavy and endless, the blackest thing I'd ever seen, darker than the mountain behind our house back home. But it wasn't solid or still. This dark was boiling with creatures, filled with blinking eyes that caught the glint of the car's lights. What would happen if I stepped beyond the red beam? How quickly could that darkness eat me up?

Is that how I might escape?

Then … I'd never come back to Dieter, or what's left of Mum, or to the mountain behind our house. I'd become someone new. I'd change my name from Kasha to Kate. I could do it.

But something stopped me from running – the dank,

muddy smell, again, maybe? Where was the sea, or the sweet tropical flowers? Maybe I should've realised then that this place wasn't how it'd looked from the leaflet. Wasn't anything like it.

So I went back to the car and climbed in beside Sam. Lily even turned around in the passenger seat and gave me a lecture about throwing this. I didn't say anything. What was the point? It was my choice, being here. They'd told us before we left: *whatever happens, remember you've decided this.* So I just put this notebook in my pack – at the very bottom of my pack – leant my head against Sam and shut my eyes.

Then I forgot about it.

Finding it today – the first time I've really looked at any of the stuff they gave us at the start – well, it makes me think. It – almost – makes me want to understand.

And it's something to occupy my fingers.

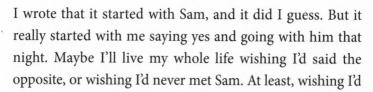

I wrote that it started with Sam, and it did I guess. But it really started with me saying yes and going with him that night. Maybe I'll live my whole life wishing I'd said the opposite, or wishing I'd never met Sam. At least, wishing I'd never liked him. Not like that.

I feel bad for writing that. But going with Sam that night killed Mum. Isn't that the real truth?

I'd known Sam almost four years by then – 1,451 days, including a leap year. Which I guess is a long time when you're 5,415 days old. We'd lived opposite him and his mum and his brother since Mum and I moved there from the city; after Dieter decided he needed to get away from Mum's craziness and go off with a woman half his age, which seemed just as crazy as Mum's craziness to me.

And, I know … cliché, right?

Sam's room was opposite mine, only the small street separating us. I could see him always: getting out of the shower with a towel round his waist; getting changed for school. I saw him on his computer for hours.

He might have seen me do the same. Might have seen me dancing to music when times were better with Mum. My silent disco. My own crazy.

We had a kind of Morse code, Sam and me:

Three double arm waves = come out to the cubby in my garden.

Thumbs up = OK.

Arms crossed in an x = no.

There were other signs too. Maybe I could fill these pages with pictures of them all. Maybe I could make up some more – signs that we could use out here. Might be easier than talking.

I liked Sam from the start. No point lying about that.

Turns out Sam's family had been in the city too and his mum was also separated from her husband. At the beginning, while she and my mum talked at each other in the street, Sam and I would escape into the cubby house in my garden. We'd draw on the walls, play hangman on them. Sometimes, when we didn't see each other for a few days, we'd write notes and leave them folded up tiny in the cracks between the wooden planks for the other one to discover later.

Sam and I could do that here too, leave notes – we could fit whole novels in the cracks in these walls. These cracks are big enough to contain someone's life story. They certainly contain spiders. I've seen them at night, crawling out from the darkness like they're feeling their way into new skins. I don't mind them that much, they're company, and they haven't jumped on me yet. The light brown one who lives above the door I've called Lily. With her skinny legs and arms, the real Lily looks like a spider too, only she's a small deadly one: the kind who'd eat her mate just after she's had sex with him. Spiders do that, don't they, some of them? They get what they want then destroy after. Maybe that's what it's all about: wanting things, destroying them after. Maybe life's just a never-ending cycle of wanting and destruction. When you think of it like that, why does anyone bother?

Now I'm imagining Lily sleeping with George. She's so little, and he's so big; I don't know how they'd fit. Maybe they do it like animals do, quickly or doggy-style. Maybe they don't do it at all. Maybe I'm wrong in thinking they're a couple. I bet Lily looks weird with no clothes on though, like a sapling, or an alien. George would look alright. He's had his top off round camp; he's tanned as leather, and he's got way more muscles than Sam. Everyone was looking, even the guys. But I guess if you're round here all the time – chopping wood, making things – that's just what happens.

17

There's no fat in nature.

I think Mum said that once. And she was skinny as a straw at the end, paler than milk.

I've just gone into the cabin I slept in last night; the cabin Sam and I slept in. It feels hotter in here than outside, and smells like mouse shit and mothballs. There's something shuffling somewhere, in a corner. But it's more private than out there with everyone looking over every few minutes. I can't handle that. It's like they're waiting for me to walk over and show them what I'm writing. I know Sam wants that. I'd rather burn this journal in a hippy ceremony than show them anything. The only person who can see this is Lily, and even then I won't let her read it. Not unless she makes me. I just want her to see that I've done it – written the words and talked about this stuff – then we can move on to the next task.

When she comes back.

If she comes back.

I'm lying on a thin camp bed. There's a spring sticking up into my stomach, and I can almost see the mattress crawling beneath me, but I'm getting used to that now. The bedbugs aren't as bad as they were. I think they've even stopped biting me. They've realised what I've known all along – I'm sour inside, no sweetness left. And this mattress is better than the one I had in the other cabin. At least it's not ripped or stained. At least it doesn't look like someone died on it.

I won't tell Sam, but I'm glad we did this: moved everyone around last night, changed where we all slept. Annie hated sleeping with me as I much as I hated sleeping with her, so it worked out in that sense. Sam and I took this cabin, the one the boys have been in, with the three small beds and the rotten cupboard that none of us want to open in case there's something horrible inside. Nyall and Annie pushed the four beds together in the other cabin to make a huge, gappy double bed. Pete chose the main cabin – the cane couch near the dining table to be precise – on the other side of the clearing. He said he didn't mind sleeping by himself, said it was better than with snorers. Not that he would say if he did mind. He likes to pretend he's the toughest: the one who can deal with anything. Sometimes I wonder how he wound up here, his reasons. He's more 'lone wolf' than 'Tribe member'. Maybe more like me.

It was darker, last night, without the fire torches around. I almost said yes when Sam asked me to sleep in his bed with him.

'There's enough room,' he said. 'Not as lonely. Not as cold.'

I almost saw his smile through the near dark. I certainly felt it. I felt his eyes too, searching for me.

'But it's boiling,' I said. 'Not cold!'

It was hotter than a furnace in here last night: a black, dark hole of an oven. My skin cooked in the sheets. But that wasn't the only reason I said no.

'But Annie and Ny…' he began.

'They're different. They're more than just friends.'

That shut him up. I could sense him sulking after that. I

19

know he wants us to have Ny and Annie's easy relationship of kisses and cuddles. Wants the sex too.

I'm surprised, though, that he still tries so hard. It's been months since I touched him. And the only time I do is when he hugs me first, or tries to. Sometimes he'll try to tease me about the girls who want him at school.

'Half the girls in our year would kill for this,' he says, flicking up his shirt so I can see his flat, brown stomach.

He's joking, course. I know that by the way he only grins with half his mouth and how his eyes sparkle. But he knows I hate it. What he doesn't know is that later, at night, when I think about that stomach again, I want to hurt myself. I want to make myself forget it. Forget him.

He's kissed other girls. I've seen it. He's probably done other things with them too. Loads of the girls in our year, and some of the ones above, probably would kill to be in a bed with him, even if it did have bedbugs and was in the middle of a stinky rainforest.

Not this girl. Not now. Sometimes I think Sam hates that most of all.

Last night, he turned about in his bed for ages, sighing like a little kid who wasn't allowed to play with his toys … wanting me to say something about why I would sleep in the same room, but not the same bed.

'C'mon, Kash,' he murmured.

But I was quieter than a dead person. It was ages before he went quiet, too.

I listened to the rustle and scratch of tiny claws on the roof;

the smash of leaves as creatures jumped through trees; the screeching and howling of the night. It's never quiet outside the cabins, not even at night. Especially not then.

When Sam's breathing got deeper and slower, I lay on my back and focused on the cracks in the wall. I could see the starlit sky through some of them, the swaying of branches through others, and through some I saw nothing but dark.

There was a crack opening up inside me too, bigger than any in these wooden walls. In that crack whole worlds could disappear, memories and thoughts and people all could fall over its edge.

I flinched when legs scuttled over my cheek: a gecko, pale and softer than the sheets, with feet smaller than fingernails. It crawled over my mattress and down to the floor. I turned over and watched it disappear, then I stretched down and felt where it went, ran my fingers over a smooth-edged crack in the boards. I wanted to follow it, disappear into the darkness the other side. Maybe there, with dust on my skin and feet smaller than fingernails, I'd find Mum. I could cuddle up to her like I used to as a little girl, and there'd be no need to say anything at all.

I'd told Mum a few of us were going to the cinema, that night. It wasn't worth telling her I was going with Sam. Lately, she'd got funny even about Sam; said I was too young to be hanging around with him so much.

But even when I said I was going out with girls, not boys

– not Sam at all – she didn't like it. 'I'll go to the cinema with you,' she said, trying to smile. 'If you really want to go.'

'It's not that, Mum,' I said.

But she didn't get it. She never did. She just got worse at being left alone, got worse at me doing stuff without her.

'Tell me then,' she tried again. 'Tell me how the cinema is better than being on the mountain and looking for the black cat? Maybe we can start a new art project?'

But what could I say? That anything was better than being cold and wet and bored on the mountain? That everything was better when I didn't have to worry about her? These were reasons Mum wouldn't understand, might get angry about. So I lied.

'We want to watch a girly film,' I said. 'You know, talk about girl stuff.'

Mum didn't like that either. She pursed her lips into a straight line. 'But I can do that, Kasha,' she said, all sing-song and innocent sounding. 'What girl stuff?'

That threw me. She never asked about things like this. My knowledge of periods and bras and sex had come from my friends, not her. But she was serious. I saw that in her eyes. I laughed and threw my hands in the air, trying to brush off her question.

'Just stuff,' I said, keeping my tone light. 'You wouldn't want to know about it.'

Mum could never be brushed off, not when she really wanted something. I should have known that by then.

'You mean, like boys?' she said softly, firmly.

I laughed again, couldn't help it. The sound came out all breathy. I thought about Sam, waiting across the road for me.

'Not really boys,' I said, thinking too much about Sam to answer Mum properly. Stupid mistake.

'Not *really*?' she said, eyebrows raised. As she watched me, she crossed her hands across her chest.

It made me so mad, the way she could stand there in the middle of the kitchen and expect to own it all: me, my time, the people I saw.

'I'm almost sixteen,' I said quietly. 'Everyone else…'

I stopped myself. The look on Mum's face made me wish I hadn't spoken at all. She strode towards me and put her hands on my shoulders, heavy as rocks.

'You're a baby,' she whispered. '*My* baby. You're too young for boys. Boys only ever make things worse.'

I turned my face from her sour breath, looked out at the garden and the darkness of the woods beyond. *Not every boy is like Dieter* – that's what I wanted to scream – *not every boy leaves.*

In the moonlight, the cubby house was glittering. I knew it was just the dew, but in the spots where the moon touched it, the wood had diamonds threaded through. I focused on the cracking paint around the windows, the door slightly off its hinges. I was almost twelve when we moved in, too old for cubby houses, but Mum had been thrilled about it.

'A perfect little place for Kasha to play,' she'd told the agent.

Perhaps I should have realised then that she wasn't right

23

in the head. That Dieter's leaving had made something leave inside her, too.

Mum moved to stand next to me, also looking out of the window. She made a little whimpering sound as she cleared her throat.

'You know what boys want,' she said. 'One thing, Kasha, only one thing. Then they leave you for the next one.'

I kept looking at the garden, keeping my face blank. Sam didn't want that one thing. Sam was better than that.

She took a deep breath, as she did when she was trying to keep calm. She was waiting for me to talk, but I wouldn't. I thought about Sam. Was he looking across at our house? Was he thinking about that *one thing*? I didn't believe it. Sam was other things too. He was also about fixing cars and being in the rugby team and being shyly good at science. There was more to him than Mum thought.

'You're too young for all that,' she said. 'Only a couple of years ago you were playing in that cubby.'

I rolled my eyes, but carefully, in a way Mum couldn't see. The last time I'd been in the cubby I went to do my homework in peace, away from her. I'd drawn faces on the walls, practising shading for Art. I'd written KF 4 SW in one corner. My stomach tightened. Had Mum seen those letters? Maybe that was the reason for all this fuss.

'I've told Sam he's not to talk to you.'

'What?' I turned to her and stared at the serious, sensible expression she was trying to give me. 'Why would you do that?'

24

Her eyebrows rose. 'I told you,' she said, calmly. 'You're too young for boys. Even Sam wants…'

'Sam just wants to be my friend,' I said, louder than I meant to.

Mum smiled this really horrible, knowing smile, like she was the one who knew everything about this stuff and I was just an idiot. But Mum hadn't had sex with anyone for years; not since Dieter, and even then probably not very often.

'Sam wants what all fifteen-year-old boys want,' she said, still acting like the teen-sexpert she wasn't.

My hands went into fists and I wanted to hurt her. Wanted to push my fists into her smug, sensible expression. Wanted to push her off the mountain she loved so much. Wanted the cat to get her. I turned away. I don't think I'd ever been so mad, so close to not caring whether I was sending her over the edge. I think I actually wanted her to flip.

She took a deep breath. 'I'm not going to bend on this. No boys. Not until you're an adult. No Sam either. I'll make you promise if I have to.'

'But he's my friend,' I hissed. 'My *best* friend.'

'He's still a boy.' Mum glared, hating that I was challenging her. She was completely serious, unbendable as iron. She waited for me to agree.

Every fibre in my body wanted to shout at her, but I knew what would happen if I did. The more I pushed, the more Mum resisted: Mum was always right, I'd learnt that enough times. The more I argued anything, the more she stood firm.

Plus, if I kept fighting, she wouldn't even let me leave the house. Not that night, anyway.

And it had to be that night. I'd promised Sam.

I wanted it to be that night.

If it wasn't that night, it might never happen.

So I changed tack. 'Fine, no boys,' I said dismissively. 'Not until I'm eighteen.'

It sounded ridiculous to me, but Mum bought it. I guess she just wanted so much to believe it.

'Good,' she said. She was happy now, happy enough even to give me a small smile. As a kid, Mum's smiles had felt like gifts. Right then, this one felt like something slimy. She took my hands, her mood already completely changed, and squeezed them gently before letting them go. She was so much like a child herself!

She grabbed a coil of rope from the top of the fridge. 'Let's go to the mountain instead! I've got a new trap we can try out – we can make it the next project.'

I shook my head quickly. Too quickly, maybe. 'I can't let the girls down.'

Mum started to frown again so I tried to smile back, make the mood lighter somehow.

'It's just girls, Mum, I already told you. I can't spend all my time with you, surely?'

She thought about this. After a moment, she nodded, reluctantly. It was the first step out of there. I kept talking.

'And anyway, Abby really wants to see this new film with…'

I struggled to think of a film star Mum would know; I

26

tried to think of a film star who wasn't a boy. I couldn't think. In the end I just said,

'…with me.'

It sounded pathetic; too much like a lie. I talked quickly to cover it.

'I can make you dinner before I go,' I said. 'I'll even go down to the corner shop and get you a bottle of wine.'

This was a big thing, and she knew it.

'Red, or white?' I continued. 'Ramen's working tonight, isn't he, so he'll sell it to me if I say it's for you? I'll grab it before the film.'

She nodded slowly. I saw something like gratitude flicker over her eyes. I'd got her! I opened the freezer and took out a pie before she could say anything. I slapped it on the bench.

'15 minutes at 220.'

I even turned the oven on.

Mum didn't look at the pie. Just watched me with her best stay-with-me-please look, her eyes wide in the I-need-you way she was so good at, the look Dieter hated. She didn't dare try to bribe me by saying I could have a glass or two with her; she'd tried that tactic before and I'd thrown the whole bottle out. Even so, I knew what was coming next: the guilt tactic.

'Without you the world falls apart,' she said, so quietly. 'I miss you too much.'

She widened her eyes, big enough to cry. Dieter called them her 'stupid big cow eyes'.

'The world's fine without me,' I said.

I was angry at Dieter too then; that he'd escaped and left me alone with her; that he didn't ever come back and help. That the only time he ever called was Christmas and birthdays.

Mum turned back to the window. 'What if the cat comes, and you're not there? What if nobody sees?'

I said as calmly as I could, 'Nothing's going to happen without me. It never does.'

'But I need you to help me work the trap.'

'You don't.'

She nodded but didn't believe me … not really. In her world, a huge black cat roamed across the mountain beside our town. In her world, she'd catch it one day and take an amazing photograph: make everyone believe her that it really did exist. Make art like that, and fame. But everyone knew that wouldn't happen. In reality she'd probably just heard a story about an escaped panther from a zoo and convinced herself it lived here.

'You don't need me.' I stood on my toes and kissed her flushed cheek. 'You'll be alright.'

She grunted. Her skin smelt like Marlboro. I hesitated.

'You're smoking again.'

I was more surprised that anything. She'd said she'd given it up when Dr Phillips told her it was bad for her anxiety. But Mum was always lying about something. I wrinkled my nose against the stale smell. Mum saw and moved away, turning back to the window. Her jaw went hard and nasty.

'Piss off out then,' she said.

She didn't mean it. She was just saying it because she was angry at me and didn't want me to go.

But they were the last words she ever said to me.

'Hope the fucking cat eats you,' I said back. Quietly. But probably not quietly enough.

The last words I ever said to her.

I turned and walked. Stuff her wine. And her. I was out.

I was so relieved I'd got out that I forgot to check Mum's pills like I normally did. I checked my own pockets instead for lip gloss, polo mints, mascara to put on in the park. I smiled as I slammed the front door. I'd done it! If Mum had known what I was really doing, she wouldn't have let me past the kitchen. It felt like the biggest victory.

I stood on the step and texted Sam. *Meet you in the park, see you soon.*

And I was out of there. From inside my coat pocket, I even stuck my finger up and aimed it back at the house. Mum was an idiot if she thought she was going to stop me.

This morning, when it was grey-dark and closer to night than day and not yet hot, Sam spoke to me. His voice came from his bed, but he sounded close enough to be in mine. I opened my eyes to check he wasn't, and looked over at the lump that was his body, lying on top of his sheets, still and sprawled. I hadn't even known he was awake.

'Tell me a story,' he said, hoarsely. 'Like you used to.'

His voice was fragile and unsure, still half in a dream. I kicked the sheets off my legs and turned to him. In the soft light I could almost make out the features of his face, though not his expression.

'You're sleeping,' I said. 'You're dreaming.'

'Make me.'

I was quiet. I was thinking he might go back to sleep, but after a while I could see his eyelids, blinking now and then. Waiting. I thought about the stories Mum used to tell me, the stories I'd repeated to Sam before. I hadn't thought about those stories for a long time, hadn't let myself. But it was dark and quiet, and talking with Sam like that was almost like how it used to be, back when we could say anything to each other.

'Go on,' Sam said.

So I opened my mouth, and there the words were.

'There once was a dark, craggy mountain,' I began. 'A place where trees, at its base, grew taller than buildings … and there were as many animals on that mountain as it was possible to imagine.'

The words felt strange in my mouth. Wrong. Like they were made up of sharp edges digging into my cheeks, piercing my throat. These were Mum's words, not mine. My voice made a mockery of them.

'I remember this,' Sam said.

I focused on the lump in the bed opposite until I saw where Sam's chest rose and fell. I spoke slowly and calmly, the way Mum once spoke to me when she was trying to get me to sleep.

'In the dark, craggy mountain there were a thousand shades of green, two thousand of brown, a million more of grey…'

Sam's breathing slowed, just like mine used to. I told him how each colour in the mountains had a different smell; how walking up there was like entering the world's most amazing sweetshop.

Trees rustled outside the cabin as I spoke, animals jumping around us, things waking and stretching. I stopped to listen. It was kind of like Mum's craggy mountain out there, too. Only there were more animals than I could ever know the words for. Mum would've had a field day making art here, making traps and taking photos.

'And right in the middle of those mountains lived a huge black cat,' I whispered.

I stopped. I couldn't describe the image in my head. Not to Sam. Not to anyone. The black cat in my mind was bigger and stronger and more vibrant than could ever actually exist. It trembled with life. There weren't enough words. Maybe that's why Mum'd always had to draw it instead – make art to represent it. It was just too fierce.

Perhaps I could do that too. Make that cat come to life here with dark, deep scratches from this biro?

I can't draw it like Mum did, though.

When I first told Sam about Mum's Black Cat we were in the cubby. I'd spoken the story slowly, loving the way I could make Sam's eyes widen as I repeated Mum's tale.

'The cat was enormous,' I'd told him. 'And she was staring right back at Mum. Mum swears the cat could've killed her right then on the top of the mountain. But the cat chose not to. Instead, she prowled on silent feet around the edge of the trees, considering. After that, Mum always knew that cat was watching her, somewhere. Whenever she went up the mountain, she had a feeling that this would be the day the cat would finally pounce.'

I'd pounced my hands onto Sam's shoulders to make him jump. He'd laughed and said, 'Go on.'

'But no one else ever saw the cat,' I'd said. 'Not even me. And Mum couldn't trap her, no matter how hard she tried – could never even take a photo of her. But she saw paw prints now and then – she put them in her paintings. She saw how the cat parted bushes after she'd pushed her shoulders through. Mum found her black hairs on trees. Maybe … she still does. Maybe, she always will.'

I'd laughed. I wasn't being serious about any of it.

⎯⎯⎯⎯⎯▪

Day is almost here. The forest heating's turned on. The volume of its radio cranking up.

My mosquito net has rips. Six. Maybe I should patch them. Getting malaria on top of everything else is all I need right now. But the cracks of sunlight coming through those rips make me smile.

Already there's the familiar feeling of sweat on my spine. Perhaps this is the day Lily and George return. Or they set another task. They never actually told us the exact day when we go home.

That'll be up to you.
Only when you've completed all your tasks.
Then you get your bags and your passports back.

What if they never come back?
Will we still leave in a month?
Should I escape before? Take Sam?
Can we leave without passports?

I turn to watch him. When he breathes out, the hair that's fallen across his cheek moves a little. Occasionally his top lip twitches. What's running through his dreams … are there any black cats pouncing? Does he dream of escaping too? Would he come with me, if I asked?

With the day coming, I see the freckles on him. Scattered across his nose, all the way to the darker freckle above his top lip. So many times I've wanted to touch that. Only once I have.

I don't want to wake him, even if I can hear the others moving about outside. I just want to watch his peace. Imagine what it might be like to lie beside him.

I have a memory from last night, though I'm not sure if it really happened or if I just dreamt it. I heard a noise. I got up out of bed and parted the frayed thin curtains across the window. And – *there!* – for a moment I thought I saw it. At the edge of the trees. Big and dark. Moving smooth as water, low to the ground … as low as something so big can get. I haven't told Sam yet, but…

…it could be a cat, couldn't it?

Cats in a jungle isn't a crazy thought, is it?

The others are annoyed with waiting. It's the end of the day now. Thirty-five hours gone. How long are Lily and George going to leave it? It's like there's an unspoken sentence hanging between us, holding us together somehow.

They're coming back, aren't they?

The question circles around us, keeps us out of the trees. So far.

Pete asked the others about going looking for them. No one replied. Nyall and Annie are city kids, Pete too I'm guessing – not sure they'd have the guts to go anywhere through those trees.

I would, though.

But I think it's a trick, anyway.

It all just seems too easy – forcing us together and seeing what we'll do. Exactly like something Lily and George would try: make us fend for ourselves. A psychological experiment. They have the cameras' eyes in the trees watching. Why do they need to be here as well?

So, what do I really think? They're not coming back. Least

not for a while. They've got something else planned. We just have to wait and watch.

I just stood up and looked around the clearing, trying to count the red lights I can see. When it gets dark, it's easier to imagine eyes there instead.

Demon eyes. Cat's eyes.

This place could send someone mad. Maybe that's the idea. Maybe that's what they want. That, at least, might make a good documentary.

Either way, I'm sure they've left us on purpose. Why else would they have stacked a couple of days' worth of tinned food on the camp table? And what about the rope and knives lying about? Maybe they want us to catch our food – *hunt*. Either that or they want us to kill each other. Nothing about this place would surprise me.

Sometimes I wonder if Lily and George are pretending about the whole psychology-camp-to-make-you-better thing: *The Tribe*. Maybe we're just here to make a few bucks out of, and they'll send all this footage off to some TV company to do something weird with. Maybe we're already being broadcast across thousands of screens on some odd reality TV programme. I've seen the sort.

Teenage Bootcamp.

Screwed-up Teenagers Communicate with Animals.

Brat Camp.

The Tribe.

Or maybe it's something sicker. Some kinky snuff film. Maybe they'll market us as *Hunger Games* meets *Love*

Island meets *Battle Royale*. Only we're not as attractive as Hollywood wannabes, or as fucked up as a Japanese horror film (surprising, I know!). And none of us have died … yet.

Maybe there's a tag line: *You need to get lost to find yourself.* Or: *You need to die to live.* A voiceover talking about how we're coping.

It's the kind of programme Mum would have watched, glass of wine in hand and cackling like a hyena. It's the kind of programme we would've laughed at together.

I've just been over to look at the stuff Lily and George left. There was a three-inch knife, a serrated one, a small filleting knife … no big knives, but maybe the others took them before I got there. I took the filleting knife – sharp as a razor, and fits easily in my shorts' pocket. I can feel it now: small, hard, metallic. It's so tempting to touch it, to hold it against the tips of my fingers and dig in until my skin goes red. I want the pain, badly, exactly like how I used to want Sam. But I'm good at saying no to things, now.

There is lots of rope, too. Wire. Even nails. I was expecting a machete to cut branches down. I mean, how are we supposed to get through a jungle with just filleting knives? Lily and George might as well have left art materials! Cotton wool!

It would be easy to build an animal trap from all that stuff, though. I can think of at least three different types without even trying. The others don't know I can make traps; only Sam, and maybe he's forgotten. Or perhaps he's deliberately not mentioning it. But there's only so long we can survive on tins of baked beans and chickpeas, and the bread's run out entirely.

Annie's yelling at us from the kitchen area. 'Does anyone want to make anything?'

We talked about it this afternoon, whether someone should take over on cooking duties. No one volunteered. I guess Nyall and Annie never had any need to cook, living on the streets. Sam's mum is the best cook I've ever met, so why would he learn? And Pete. He's too much of a dick to stand still long enough to boil peas.

And me? Yeah, I suppose I can cook some, but I haven't told them this and I don't want to look after any of them. Besides, my specialities aren't anything they'd want to eat. Thanks to Mum and our time on the mountain, I can cook rabbits and rats on a campfire. I can skin them too. My other speciality is heating frozen food.

Maybe in the morning I'll look in the chest that has the books. There are field guides in there, information about plants. I'd trust those words more than the crash course on bushfood George gave us before he disappeared.

But they're watching me for this. They're waiting for me to use the skills they know I have – waiting for the psychological breakthrough from my *meaningful interaction* with nature.

When I first met Lily and George, I saw dirt in their skin. I knew they'd spent time outdoors, that was part of what drew me to them, I guess. They stooped, crouched forward, were always on alert. And I thought – these are shifty people: people who slip through cracks. Like Mum. Like me.

Sam's just come over.

'Pete wants to make a plan for the morning,' he said. 'Maybe we'll try and find Lily and George's camp, where they're staying?'

I shuffled over on the tree stump to make room for him, but he sat on the grass instead. The crickets all shut up for a second as he crossed his legs. Maybe he squashed them. He picked at a grass stalk and didn't look at me. I think he's still annoyed I didn't sleep in his bed.

I watched him in the gloom, pulling strips off the stalk. 'Is that what you want?'

He shrugged. 'I'm sick of waiting. Nothing else to do, is there?'

Fireflies were lighting up around him. Tiny, orange, flickering beams. Like the smallest campfires in the world. When I reached to touch one, it went out.

I could think of lots of other things to do.

We could leave this place, go find our own way home. We could run away forever into the dark. I could reach out and throw my arms around Sam.

He sighed, looking between me and this journal. 'Annie's making some sort of stew, do you want some?'

I shook my head. 'Good luck with that.'

He got up and paused for a moment behind me. I held my breath. 'You have to eat,' he said. 'I won't feed you.' Then he moved on, went back to the main cabin.

It's getting too dark to write now. I'm using my torch, but it's making insects land on my face, and land on the page too.

I can feel legs on the back of my neck, scrabbling on my skin. Plus, I don't want to use up my batteries.

It's strange, I guess, but none of us have talked properly about the other possibility: that Lily and George aren't coming back at all. That they've left us like this forever. That it's up to us now to find our way out. That something's … *happened*.

We all heard them, after all: the shots.

The second night without L and G. It feels hotter somehow – *louder*. I'm writing with my head torch strapped to my forehead. Tomorrow we're leaving, it seems. The others have packed day bags ready. It's decided!

I haven't done mine yet. When Sam asked me, I told him I hadn't and he went off to bed in a huff. I'm not sure if he's still awake – or if I'm keeping him awake with this light – but I don't think so. Sam and sleeping go together like bread and cheese.

Mmm.

Bread. Cheese.

If only we weren't stuck a million miles from a shop.

Maybe that's an advantage in looking for the other camp. There might be bread there – cheese! – and it might not be mouldy.

But I can't move yet. There's a new horrible-sickie-sinking feeling inside me…

What if Lily and George disappearing wasn't a joke? What if whatever – *whoever* – took them is now waiting out there for us? What if when we leave…

Bang!

Us too.

'That's anxiety talking,' Pete said when I told him. 'You need to get a handle on that – it's hereditary, you know, anxiety.'

And I wondered … had Sam told him about Mum? That thought made me dig nails into my palm. Another reason, maybe, why I haven't packed my day pack yet. Maybe I don't have to go with them.

I can escape. Just go.

Later I heard Pete saying to the others what I'd said to him about the shots. 'Perhaps it was soldiers,' he said. 'Or warring tribes. What if it's no joke?'

I can't sleep.

Just turned the torch off and then on again. Everything feels … uncertain. I mean, we don't even know where we are, not really. An island off the west coast of Africa they said… There must be hundreds of them, right? Maybe thousands.

Did Lily and George tell Dieter the details like they said they would? Does he, at least, know where we are? Does Sam's mum? Anyone?

There's a huge, wild, wide-open panic attack building inside me. I feel it like a tsunami. It could crash down at any moment. It would flood this whole camp if I let it. I'd be sobbing.

I want to crawl in with Sam. I want to kiss him. Want to do more than this.

Want. Want.

Want!

The knife is on the floor, still in the pocket of my balled-up shorts. I want to use that, too. It wouldn't take much: my hand out from under this mosquito net, one slit. Then, maybe, one more.

I'll keep writing so I don't do either. No cutting. No fucking. I can handle that, can't I? If I keep writing, can I make my fingers too tired from words?

So…
So…
That night…

I was jumpy in the park, waiting for Sam. It got dark and cold. Almost like snow would come, even though it was already late spring. I thought about texting Sam again and telling him to hurry up, but what if Mum hadn't gone to the mountain yet? If she saw Sam leaving his house and heading in the same direction as me, she might start to suspect. She might even come after him. In the mood she was in, who knew?

My fingers turned rigid around the swing chains and I had to get up and walk around, down near the stand of oaks that separated the park from the rubbish dump. All the time, my body felt stiff enough to snap. I was watching for Sam, for Mum … anyone really. Every sound was like a footstep behind me. I thought about walking on to town and meeting Sam there. I hadn't realised how creepy it was in the park at night, way creepier than up on the mountain. In the park, anyone could come along. Up the mountain, it was just Mum and an imaginary cat.

I kicked at soggy pieces of a cardboard box and sent an empty plastic milk carton flying across a ditch. I wondered if Mum would light a fire on the summit, whether she'd cook something on it. I stuck another Polo in my mouth, wishing I'd brought something more substantial. I could go on to town and bring chips back, but Sam would smell them on my breath and feel the grease on my hands. He would if things went the right way, anyway. I sucked on the Polos, timing how long I could make each one last.

Eventually, I saw Sam's tall, gangly figure loping towards me. He had one of his brother Jake's skater hoodies on, too big for him, with some symbol scrawled across the front. The beanie he always wore was shoved down over his ears and hair. I'd never been so glad to see anyone in my life. But I tried to keep it cool.

'Alright?' I said.

I was breathing mint fumes from all the Polos. He laughed at the way I was bouncing from one foot to the other, trying to keep warm.

'How long you been here for?'

I shrugged. 'Mum went up the mountain, so I thought I may as well leave too.'

Sam nodded. He knew about Mum and the mountain.

'What did you tell *your* mum you were doing?' I asked.

'Going to the cinema, same as you. Had to make up some shit about what we were going to watch.' His eyes held mine, laughing at me. 'Said it was some car-chase film.'

I swallowed the last Polo. 'You said it was *us* going, you and me?'

'Why not? Mum likes you. She's always liked you.'

I thought about it, wondered if Mum would find out from Sam's mum that I'd lied about the group of friends I was meeting. Considering Mum hardly talked to Sam's mum anymore, it was unlikely.

Sam shook his head. 'Don't worry, I told her not to say anything; she understood. She's told me before she thinks your mum's too controlling.'

There was a silence then. I was trying to work out whether I could tell Sam about the argument I'd just had with Mum. I wanted to. It wasn't long ago that I'd told him everything like that. But something had shifted lately and I didn't know where we stood. And anyway I didn't know what Mum had actually said to Sam about not wanting him to see me. Mum could have been lying about it, just saying it to scare me – it wouldn't be the first time she'd done something like that. But she might've really done it too.

Sam was watching me think, reading my mind again. 'Your mum alright?'

I nodded, but I must have looked a bit funny because Sam came right up to me and gave me a hug.

'You're colder than an ice pack.' His arms were so tight and warm around me and, even though his jumper smelt like Jake's roll-up cigarettes, I wanted him to keep hugging, but instead he pulled back and took off his beanie. He tugged it down over my head. 'That help?'

I nodded again, grateful. The red wool felt damp over my ears, and smelt slightly doggy. Without it, Sam's hair bounced up like a nest. He ran his hand over it, flattening the dark curls. Then he leant over to tuck a strand of my hair back up under the beanie. I felt the rough, cold pads of his fingertips against my skin. He lingered them there for a moment. I wanted to turn my cheek and kiss them.

'So, we doing this thing?' he said.

'It's too friggin' cold to do anything else.'

He grinned at that, chucked an arm around my shoulder. I leant my shoulder into him, hoping his body warmth would jump across to me. He sort of swaggered as I did. He was getting so confident lately, like he'd grown so much older than me as well as so much taller. All that working in his dad's garage had made him strong too. I felt it in his arms as he gripped me around the shoulders and half lifted me across the playground. He tried tripping me up over the slide, pushing his long legs against mine to make me fall, but I held onto his waist and wouldn't let him.

'You're like a monkey,' he said. 'Tiny, gripping fingers.'

'If I fall, you fall too.'

He laughed at that, corrected me. 'If you fall, you get squashed.'

I imagined us falling over the slide, landing in the woodchips the other side, him on top. It didn't sound so bad. But Sam pulled us on. A group of girls was watching us as they came through the main gates. Sam leant in close to my ear, not even looking at them. That was something else that had happened to Sam lately, he got noticed. Girls no longer ignored him when he passed.

'Let's cover our bases,' he said. 'Go the long way round.'

He took his arm back and grabbed my hand instead. His was warm now and huge around mine. I suddenly had the sharpest flash of memory of walking exactly like this when Sam must have been half his height. We were following along behind his mum, walking to our first day of high school. Weird that we were holding hands; we were old enough not to be. Weird he never became my boyfriend then either. I chewed on my lip. Neither of us had ever said the words before to each other: *boyfriend, girlfriend*. But we were inseparable at school. I sent more text messages to Sam than to everyone else put together. And then, *this*. Surely this is what it all meant: where it was all going.

Sam led the way through the smaller side-gate of the park. Then he doubled back, walked past the pub on the corner, and up the last dead-end street before where the mountain path began, until we got to Mum's old car.

I don't know why she'd left it there, in that dead-end street ... just the park on one side and the mountain on the other. It was like she wanted someone to steal it! For months now she hadn't even been out of town. She seemed to have forgotten she even had a car. Must've been a year, at least, since she'd been inside it.

Sam hadn't forgotten though.

'I'm having that,' he'd said, one evening as we walked past it.

Now he crouched down beside the driver's door, his back to the mountain. He didn't care that I hadn't managed to find the key, said it was better this way.

'This way, she'll never suspect us,' he said. 'And I know how to get into a car.'

I went on lookout. But really I was watching the curve of Sam's back as he hunched over his backpack, his long fingers digging around inside it for tools. It was so much colder without his arm around me. I guess I'd dressed pretty stupidly, too bothered about wanting Sam to look at me. I think Sam liked it though. It gave him a chance to play the hero and keep me warm.

He took out a screwdriver and a piece of flat blue plastic. I tried not to listen as Sam made the door groan and bend open, instead thinking about where Mum and I used to go in this car. To the city. To Dieter. To shopping trips in other places. Once to the airport, where we parked it and went on holiday to Tenerife.

There was a hollow thud as the door opened.

'We're in.' Sam chucked the backpack inside the car then turned to me. 'You first.'

I crawled across the driver's seat and into the passenger one, my skirt getting caught on the gear stick. Old bits of rubbish made crinkling noises beneath me. Then Sam got in and shut the door quietly. It was weird, the smell in there. It was all Mum's hairspray and perfume, back when she was trying to get a job and impress Dieter again.

'You alright?'

Sam's eyes were shining in the dark, waiting for approval. But for me, right then, it was enough just to sit there. I wasn't sure I even wanted to move the car anymore. I remembered being small, in the back, late at night when Dieter was driving and Mum was asleep beside him.

Sam reached for the backpack, dug around in it and took out a small bunch of keys. I leant my head against the window and pretended I was still on lookout. I was worried those girls from the park would come around the corner and spot Sam instantly. But the street was empty. Too cold, I guess. Perhaps the girls had gone home.

'I took the skeleton keys from the garage,' Sam said. 'One of them should work on a car like this.'

He was proud of all he'd learnt with his dad. He was always talking about it, and he always had engine oil on his skin, even at school. He jiggled first one key then the next in the ignition.

'Course, even if we get a key that fits, there's no guarantee it will start,' he said.

But it did. First go.

Until then, I wasn't really thinking we'd do it. It was just something fun: a chance to sit in a dark, enclosed space with Sam, a chance of it meaning something more than just friends. But when the car started, I felt different. We were breaking the law. There was no going back, then.

That was the moment, I guess.

The moment I could have stopped it all. That was the 'pause moment' as Lily called it in those first strange therapy sessions: the place I could rewind my life to, and stop for a while to assess. Freeze-frame on Sam with his mouth open, two hands on the wheel, eyes on me. Freeze on me looking back, not sure whether to smile or scream.

The moment where everything shifted – *changed* – where the world went up a gear.

And things could have changed. If I'd got out of the car and gone back to Mum, if I'd said I'd changed my mind about the cinema and wanted to go up the mountain with her instead, or watch some crappy TV show, I wouldn't be here. Sam wouldn't be either. It would be some other poor fuckers.

And Mum?

She'd be somewhere, too.

But we know what happens. It's so stupidly obvious. *I'm* so stupidly obvious. I didn't stop to think, didn't pause anything. Back then I didn't even want slow motion. Wasn't looking for anything other than fast forward. I wriggled across my seat so that my mouth rested against Sam's ear lobe and I whispered, 'Let's go.'

I felt him shiver as I did.

Sam woke me this morning. Guess I did manage to send myself to sleep by writing after all. I checked my arms. No cuts. By the look on Sam's face, I hadn't kissed him in my sleep either. No cuts, no fucks.

'We've got a plan,' he said. 'Going to walk down the main track, past the shower area, see where it leads. Lily and George's camp can't be too far.'

I was still bleary from dreams. 'All of us?'

Sam frowned. 'You want to stay here?'

He glanced out of the door, away from me, to where the others were getting ready. I could hear them talking and chucking stuff about. The thought of Sam leaving with them, without me, even only for a few hours, was painful.

'I'll go,' I said.

He nodded, didn't even look that pleased. 'Better get dressed then.'

By the time I got out and joined the others, they were all ready, day packs and sleeping bags on their backs. I stared at them. 'How long you planning on going for?'

'Got to plan for anything,' Pete answered. 'Remember George said this island isn't safe.'

I shrugged. 'Seems fine to me.' I was starting to hate the way Pete always assumed he was in control.

'Have you forgotten two days ago?' Pete said. 'The gunshots?'

I glared at him, then I went back into the cabin, grabbed a water bottle, a hat, this book, and stuck them in a small bag. I checked the filleting knife was in my pocket, and came back out. 'OK, I'm ready.'

'You don't have much.' Pete looked doubtful, but Sam pushed him towards the track to get going, turning him from me.

'Let's do it,' Sam said, but he looked back at me sadly.

I glanced around the clearing before we left, looking again for the camera lights. I scanned either side of the track as we started walking down it. Couldn't see anything, but Lily and George would've hidden the cameras well, in plants and between stalks of bamboo, deep in that thick undergrowth.

No one spoke much. Pete led, of course. Then Nyall and Annie, walking really close to each other, practically on the same bit of track. Then Sam. Then me. I'm surprised Pete let me go last actually. Everyone knows it's where the next most capable person goes. Perhaps he thought that since Sam was back there too it didn't matter.

The track led downhill. We passed the small path to the toilet, then the smaller path to the lean-to shower, then the hut that had the generator in it. Then we were on virgin territory. For us, anyway.

After only a few minutes sweat was pouring down my face, soaking my shirt. I was glad I hadn't brought a heavy bag, though wished I'd brought more water, a little food. My head was spinning from the heat. Occasionally we heard the crash of seed pods dropping to the ground, or animals leaping through the trees. Each sound made Pete jump – I saw it – they made us all jump.

How many days ago was it when George had gathered us around the campfire to tell us there were fighting tribes nearby? Four days? Five? He told us to never go beyond the immediate trees of our camp without him, said we could get hurt. It seems like a lifetime ago. I hadn't believed him, didn't think any of us had. I'd thought it was another trick to fuck with us.

But as we walked down that track, I knew what we were all listening out for: more gunshots.

I just stopped writing to peer out at this new set of trees. Still nothing. Still so loud. How can something be so full and so empty at exactly the same time? So dark and rich.

Maybe the shots we heard are something to do with George and Lily's disappearance. I mean, why else would both of those things happen on the same day?

The others didn't believe Pete at first, when he'd said they were shots. Though I knew the sound. There's that unmistakable crack and echo that only comes from a gun.

We'd stopped, still as the trees, stiller, listening. Two shots. Then – *maybe* – a grumble of engines, trucks or something. Then nothing. Silence. After a moment, I was aware of Sam breathing hard. And Annie's breath coming back to her in a rush. Then the forest started to screech and shuffle, and everything was as it'd been.

'What the hell was that?' Sam whispered.

Nyall scooped his arm around Annie and looked up at the trees.

'Guns,' Pete said.

'Someone hunting,' I'd suggested. 'There are probably poachers here.'

So we'd decided not to plant the flag on the summit behind the camp (the only place George had ever let us walk) even though it was one of our tasks. We'd started off down the hill again instead. We didn't speak as we'd walked, not even when Annie slipped a couple of metres down the slope. We just offered our arms towards her and she grabbed them, and we pulled her up. I could sense everyone getting slower as we got closer to camp. We didn't know what we'd find.

Still don't.

But there was nothing to find then.

Least not in our camp.

'Do you think we'll be in trouble for not doing the task?'
Annie had said.

The first time I saw a gun I was about six years old. This was
back when we still lived in the city with Dieter. Mum'd been
sitting on their huge double bed, cleaning it, and I'd come in
to find her. It was a shotgun, I think, still saved from when
she grew up on the farm with Gran and Gramps – it's
probably still in her studio at our house now.

I'd padded into the room in my red reindeer slippers and
the look on her face stopped me in the doorway. I'd caught
her before she'd seen me. Her eyes were half closed as she
wiped down the gun, and she was humming something softly.
She looked so calm – maybe that's how I look when I use the
knife on my skin. Perhaps it's kind of the same thing?

I watched her for a while, methodically snapping open the
middle and working a bristly stick that looked like a mini
toilet brush down the barrel. She polished until the lights of
the room glinted in its wooden handle and bounced back
onto her face. After a while she stopped humming, and held
the clean gun out in front of her. She stayed like that for ages,

just looking at it, turning it over in her hands. Then, quickly, she pressed something to make it click. It sounded so loud in the quiet of the bedroom it made me jump, but Mum didn't see my movement. Instead she put the end of the barrel under her chin and held it there. Then she stared straight ahead at the mirror with the gun motionless against her jaw.

I watched. I didn't know what it meant, this movement. I didn't know why she was staring so intently at her reflection, or why she sat there for so long. All I know is that when the doorbell went suddenly, she jumped as if she'd been punched. And there was this noise, louder than anything, crashing all around me, echoing off the walls. I slammed my hands over my ears and collapsed onto the floor.

It took me ages to look up again. I saw Mum's shoes first, on the carpet in front of me. Then I felt her fingers, brushing my hair. When I looked up at her, she was standing over me, shaking her head very slowly like she did when she didn't want me to tell Dieter something. And there, behind her, was a jagged hole in the ceiling.

Perhaps that's when Dieter started plotting to leave us. Perhaps that's when I should have started plotting to leave, too.

I should write more about what's happened today.

There's been so much, but somehow my head's still stuck in the past, still wanting to get all that out first.

Maybe Lily's right about writing the past down, that it helps.

Or maybe I just don't want to cut myself. Or fuck Sam. And when I'm writing, I can't do either.

There! That's a kind of progress at least – doing something positive with my fingers.

Or maybe... Maybe I'm even starting to like this writing thing. Lily would really feel smug then.

So, we found another track. That was the first thing.

It's a bigger track than the one that leads up to our camp, wide enough for vehicles. There were recent tyre marks on it too.

'C'mon then, mountain girl,' Pete said, glancing at me. 'Which way are they going?'

I glared at him. 'How am I supposed to know?'

He smiled, nastily. 'Thought you knew things like that?'

'Fuck off. They're tracks on a bit of dirt. How's anyone supposed to know?'

I threw a glare at Sam. Only he could have told Pete about Mum's mountain. I wondered what else he'd said. Sam just stepped out into the track and looked slowly in both directions.

'Their camp can't be far,' Pete said. He made us take a vote, and we went left. We hadn't walked for long before the tracks were more churned up.

'This is it,' he said. 'Getting closer.'

The forest was eerily quiet, and we walked slower. I knew

it was just because it was getting to midday and things always seem to shut off around that time out here, but the sudden silence still creeped me out. Annie and Nyall walked as if they were practically glued to each other, glancing up at the trees as if something was going to drop on them. I found myself listening for shuffles and shrieks even more than usual.

I remembered that black cat in the trees from two nights before, seen from the cabin while Sam slept. Had I seen it, really? Or was it just an overhanging dream? Perhaps I was going mad, hallucinating? Last night Sam had smoked some of the weed Lily and George had left lying about, perhaps some of it had got into my brain too … perhaps Pete stuck some in my food. Another reason not to eat.

'Why's it so muddy and still so hot?' Annie said, leaping together with Nyall over the ruts.

Pete shushed her.

Then there were buildings up ahead.

I saw their straight, solid edges through the trees. Pete stopped and turned back to us with two fingers on his lips. The way he did it was almost comical, like he was acting out an old war film, like the kind my gramps used to watch.

'Think this is their camp?' he whispered.

Nyall nodded. 'Has to be.'

'Maybe we should circle it and approach from the back?' Sam suggested.

'I think we should just walk straight in,' I said.

Sam looked at me quickly. 'But if something bad's happened there, that's not very smart. The gunshots, remember?'

Even though I was still mad at Sam from what he must have told Pete, I still liked how he was asking me about what to do, *asking me, not Pete*. I pointed at the thick vegetation to our right. 'We could go through there then, try and get a better look first?'

Pete stepped towards the bushes immediately. 'I was just thinking that.'

Annie sighed. 'I think we should go straight in. Lily and George are probably sitting in the middle, laughing at us all. Like Kasha said earlier, maybe it's just another test.'

I nodded. 'It's possible.'

Pete scowled at us. 'You know what George told us, there's fighting near here – warring tribes. We need to be careful.'

I stared back. 'Do you really believe either of them about anything? And *warring tribes*, really?'

Pete looked at me coolly. 'Who else do we have to believe? Anyway, we heard the shots.'

'We're on an island, Pete,' I reminded him. 'No space for warring tribes.'

He turned back to the bushes. Sam followed him straight into the undergrowth. Clearly Annie and I were the only ones willing to consider my idea of this all being a test because after a moment even Nyall ignored us and followed the other two. Annie shrugged and went after him. Again I came last.

Pete moved excruciatingly slowly through the vegetation. Even so, we creaked and crushed branches, making enough noise to wake half the forest. I felt sweat running down my back in two lines either side of my spine, and I was glad for the second time that day that I hadn't brought a big pack. The others' packs kept getting caught in the branches, holding them up further.

I kept glancing at the clearing where the camp was. There were three buildings, all made of wood and thatch, all raised up on stilts from the ground like the buildings in our camp. It was set up like our camp, too, with a bigger cabin in the centre and two smaller ones either side. The buildings looked newer than the ones in our camp, less run down. There were no cars anywhere, though I could see lots of tyre tracks in the mud so there'd been a vehicle there recently. I couldn't see a generator, toilet, or shower, but they could be in the trees like ours are. And there was no movement anywhere. The camp was deserted. Unless of course there were soldiers, or *warring tribes,* lying in wait for us inside the buildings. It didn't seem likely. Why would soldiers do that? Why would there even be soldiers?

It didn't look like the kind of place where George and Lily would live. Even for them it looked basic. I'd thought they'd have flags flying, statues of Che Guevara or some shit. I'd thought they'd have a veggie patch, somewhere to grow all that weed they smoked.

I hadn't let myself think seriously about Pete's idea. He'd decided too quickly; soldiers had come and captured Lily and George. I'd laughed at first. But right then, pushing through the undergrowth, I wasn't so sure. From the glimpses I could see of the camp, it didn't look raided by soldiers or warring tribes. It just looked empty. But it didn't look right.

'This is about as far as we can go,' Pete said.

He turned back to us, tiny leaves stuck to the sweat on his face, twigs in his hair. There was a wall of thick green behind him, branches with small thorns and vines creeping everywhere, stopping him from investigating any further. We'd need a serious knife to get through it. Anyway, it looked like a snake pit.

'There's a bug on your cheek, Pete,' I said.

He flicked it off in my direction.

We got down on our knees and crawled closer to the buildings, until we were barely in the trees anymore. I could hear Sam behind me, almost feel his hot breath on my neck. There was still no movement in the camp.

'It's got to be deserted,' Nyall said.

I agreed. 'Let's just walk in.'

But Pete made us wait ages, watching.

'Should some of us stay in the trees?' Sam said. 'Just in case, you know, someone really is in there? Like, backup?'

'I told you,' I said again. 'They're just fucking with us. This is just one of their *tasks*.'

In the end we moved together, running quickly across the clearing to the buildings. As we left the shelter of the trees, I felt a sudden burst of nerves. What if there actually were soldiers or tribes here? What if, at any moment, gunfire ripped us apart?

But we all made it to the wall of the closest building. We were all breathing hard, our eyes wide. So, perhaps I was a little scared. So, maybe I was starting to believe Pete. *Maybe*.

We huddled at the side and looked at the wooden steps leading up to the entrance. We were all watching the windows of the other buildings in the camp, too, but nothing moved behind them.

'There's no one here,' I said, as much to reassure me as everyone else.

'Should we go up the steps?' said Sam. 'Check out what's inside?'

'Maybe we could shout as we do?' Nyall whispered. 'So we can scare them … y'know, have the advantage. Like they do in films.'

I rolled my eyes. 'If anyone's here they would have seen us by now. If they were going to kill us, they would have. I told you – it's just them fucking with us.'

I took the lead, bounding up the wooden steps to the door. It opened easily, swinging inwards. If it had been locked once, it wasn't now. My eyes wouldn't adjust to the gloom inside. Everything was shadowy. And there was a terrible smell like something rotten. I gagged immediately. Then I thought: what if there is something – *someone* – dead in here? What then?

I took a step away, stumbled back towards the stairs. I heard a gasp behind me as Annie joined me and looked inside too.

I don't want to write about what we found inside yet. It makes me feel odd. I haven't worked it out, what it means.

Instead, I'm touching the filleting knife, pressing its tip into my finger pads. The bubbles of blood it makes look like berries.

Here. I'll smudge some.

See it? The thing on the page that now just looks like dirt? Blood.

If I die out here, perhaps you can identify me by testing this smear.

I'll cut harder, I think.

There's a saying on a piece of card pinned up in the cabin just behind me – *a life lived in fear is a life half lived.*

And that makes me think.

Maybe I'm half-lived. Half-told. I'm half of two people who lived in 8 Edgemount Road.

I'm hunching away from what's behind me, not looking at what's in front either.

Trees. Heat. Trees.

Secrets.

Trees. Heat. Trees.

Darkness

       everywhere.

There's only one thing I want to write about, one thing I can work out.

The night that started it. The rest of that story.

I think I have to.

        So…

That night Sam pressed the accelerator, made it roar in the silence of our street.

'How old is this car anyway?' he said.

'Old as me.'

He took the handbrake off, and pressed the accelerator again. For the first time Sam looked nervous.

'Can you drive it?' I asked.

'Course.'

He didn't look certain. I wound down the window and checked the street both ways. 'You're clear.'

He stalled as he pulled it away from the kerb. There was a horrible moment when we were gliding in the middle of the road; when the houses on the bottom end of the street where it joined ours could have seen us; when Mum could have seen us if she'd been walking there. Then Sam turned the key again, and we were off. He checked the rear-view mirror as he pulled away.

'I told you I could do it,' he said.

He took a left into Cromwall Street, past the park, and headed on towards the ring road. No one was watching us, no one flagging us down. The night was clear and empty, the sky black as deep oceans. Suddenly, Sam was laughing. He thumped his hand against the steering wheel, and accelerated again. The lights from the strip of takeaways made a haze of orangey-red.

'You're going to get us in jail,' I said.

But I was laughing too. It felt amazing to be doing this: to be out in a stolen car with a boy without a licence, to be out there with Sam.

'Since when did you get so good?' I nodded at his hands on the wheel.

'Since I knew we were doing this. Anyway, Dad's always getting me to move cars around.' He smiled, happy I'd noticed. 'And Jake gives me lessons in the car park.'

I thought of Sam and his older, gangly brother bombing it round behind his dad's garage. I scrunched up the crisp packets on the seat and shoved them in the door.

'You're lucky to have a brother.'

And a Dad – but I bit back those words.

I watched the easy way he steered with only his right hand on the wheel, his quick constant checks in the mirror, and realised I trusted him completely.

'You're going to get me into trouble,' I said.

He looked at me, for as long as he dared keep his eyes away from the road. 'I think it's going to be the other way round.'

He reached his left hand across and pinched me above the knee. I slapped him away and the car wavered. He glanced at me, but I was still smiling. At that moment I didn't even care if the whole police force of Montford was after us.

'How long 'til the quarry?' I asked.

'Not far.'

Sam put both hands on the wheel after that. We weren't going fast, but it felt like it. The whole journey felt like a trip on a speedway. Sam flicked the full beams on. We wouldn't be on the ring road long, just enough to get us the other side of the woods below the mountain.

I watched Sam's profile in the moonlight; his sharpish nose and chin, his full lips, the way his hair bounced up and stuck to the roof of the car.

'You're too big for this car,' I said.

He reached out his arm and tried to pull me towards him. I shuffled across, but the gear stick was in the way again. In the end, I just leant over and rested my head down onto Sam's shoulder, my forehead against his neck. I could smell that perfect Sam smell: the car oil and the Lynx deodorant. It felt so comfortable, like I'd been doing this all my life, like my head was made to sit in the crook between Sam's neck and shoulder. It felt wrong we'd never kissed each other. It was weird, but it didn't feel wrong that I'd never kissed anyone, just wrong that it had never been him.

Sam moved his arm to change gear, then placed his warm hand back on my knee. It made the inside of me bubble and fizz. I didn't say anything when he did that and neither did he, but I was thinking: friends might steal cars together but they don't put their hands on each other's knees.

I kept my eyes on the dashboard clock. 9.45. There'd be enough time? I'd told Mum the film finished at eleven. And I could get through the woods below the mountain in twenty minutes, maybe fifteen if I ran. But perhaps we wouldn't be long out there, anyway. Perhaps we'd do exactly what we'd planned: we'd find the quarry, hide the car, and I'd traipse back one way and Sam another. Either way, I'd see Mum before midnight. I could stretch it 'til then; she'd be alright. And if she wasn't?

Sam was watching me, reading my mind again. 'Your mum OK with you going out, then?'

I shrugged, waiting to see if he'd say anything about Mum talking to him, warning him off. Surely he'd tell me if she had?

'You know what she's like,' I said when Sam kept quiet.

Sam was the only one who knew anything about how bad she'd got. But even he didn't know that lately Mum had been spending whole evenings on the mountain, or that she ate dinner there too sometimes, or that sometimes dinner was what she'd caught in traps she'd set to snare the Black Cat.

'What Mum doesn't know's not going to kill her,' I said.

A stupid phrase.

And I was stupid enough to believe it.

It got darker the further from town we got. I started noticing the stars through the windscreen. The curve of the Big Dipper, and the dim glint of the North Star above it. Mum had taught me them all once, lying in Gran and Gramps' garden, back when they were still alive, back when life with Dieter in the city almost felt normal.

I looked at Sam's skin, saw the freckle-constellations there too.

'Let's just keep going,' I said. 'See how far the petrol takes us. See where we end up.'

Sam smiled a small smile. 'We've got school in the morning. And there's your mum…'

'So?'

But Sam was already flicking the indicator for the turn-off to the quarry. I moved away from the window to wind it down and let the smells rush in. Car fumes. Manure. Pine trees. A part of me could leave our town behind and never ever miss it. A part of me could leave Mum too. Be like Dieter. I had all I needed right there in that car. I swallowed, guilt rushing in with the smells. Mum would hate this; if she saw me, she wouldn't speak to me for weeks. For the rest of my life, perhaps.

I thought about what she'd said, about boys only wanting one thing. About Sam wanting it too. I took off Sam's beanie, held it in my lap. The wind from outside picked up my hair and held it for a moment. I felt the ice of it on my neck. It pulled at Sam's jacket too. I could see the shape of Sam's chest through his shirt underneath. I wondered what it would be like to have my hand there, between the shirt and his skin, wondered about the warmth.

The car lurched as we hit the quarry track, the tyres spinning in the mud.

'Thank God for the frost,' Sam said, apparently oblivious to what I'd been thinking, 'otherwise we'd really get stuck. We picked the best night for this.'

He swerved around the old posts, driving over the wire fence that had come down in the last storm. It crunched beneath the tyres. The KEEP OUT sign was half-buried. He took a sharp left, driving cross-country until we reached the section Sam had cleared a few days ago; the place we were

66

going to store the car. The car clunked over a rock, then stalled. Sam flicked the key, the lights, then turned to me and said in his best sat-nav voice, 'You have reached your destination. Abandoned Quarry. Please hide your vehicle at the next available opportunity.'

Then he stared at me, mouth still open, not knowing what to say next. I don't think either of us did. We'd done it. We'd stolen Mum's car. Sam had driven it all the way there. There was so much illegal about the last half hour that it was better not thinking about it.

I thought about Sam instead. Watched him. In the near-darkness his skin looked silver, his eyes huge as a deer's. I didn't know what he was going to do next, but his eyes were full of thought. And something else.

'Thanks for coming with me,' he said. 'Thanks for not going with your mum.'

It was weird. I wanted Sam to look at me like that, I'd always wanted it, but his sudden intensity scared me, too. I looked away quickly. I couldn't help it.

'I guess we should start covering the car up,' I said.

Sam had already got the bracken and branches ready, and we only had to lay them across the car to make it look like a giant clump of vegetation. Sam had some crazy idea that he'd keep the car hidden until he was seventeen. Then he'd wheel it out, spray-paint it, and it would be his. It should be mine really, though. I was the one with the memories of it. And the car was technically still Mum's after all, wasn't it?

But I wondered: was Mum on the mountain, somewhere

not far above? Could she see down into the quarry? My stomach lurched. At least she'd have the moon for company, up there. The moon would make it easier for Sam and me, too. Through the windscreen and down the old quarry tracks, branches were swaying with the wind, and nothing else was moving.

'What's wrong?' Sam was glancing through the windscreen too.

I shook my head, tried to laugh. 'Mum always makes me feel so damn guilty.'

Sam half-smiled. 'But she's not here now. You don't have to worry about her for ages, do you?'

I couldn't answer. Glanced at the car clock instead. 10.09.

Sam watched me look. 'What time did you say you'd be back?'

'Said the film finished at eleven.'

He worked out the maths. ''bout an hour and a half?'

I nodded. 'I guess it will take a while to cover the car up, though?'

Sam's smile wavered, and I couldn't hold his gaze. I didn't know what I wanted, what I *should* want: to be there with Sam, or go back to Mum? Now that the car's heating had gone off, it was freezing, too. I crossed my arms over my chest.

'I'm not sure I'm ready to face the cold of the woods,' Sam said. 'Not yet.' His voice was so gentle. He pulled at a thread in the seat.

I watched his long fingers, traced my eyes up his arms to his face. He was chewing on his bottom lip, suddenly nervous as anything. He looked adorable. I didn't want to go anywhere else in the whole world, never wanted to go anywhere else again.

'Hug first, then?' I said.

And he reached out to me before I'd even finished speaking, just like that, and wrapped himself around me. I felt my whole body tense as he did. He must have felt it too. But he kept his arms there, around my shoulders. He buried his head against my neck. I heard his breath and the way his clothes rustled. I felt the cold of his nose on my skin. And he stayed there like that, for ages.

No other guy had been that close to me, ever. Not even Dieter. Only Mum had hugged me as intently, just after Dieter left and she was crying like a baby. It took me a while to breathe out, to hug Sam back. I placed my arms around his shoulders and sighed. Sam didn't speak. He just very slowly placed his lukewarm, soft lips against my neck, brushed them up towards my chin. Everything inside me was jumping, my skin and muscles tense to hold it in. He was breathing quickly, slipping a coolish hand between my jacket and jumper. I shivered.

'Sorry,' he murmured.

I almost laughed. 'No, you're not.'

I could feel him smiling against my neck. 'You're right. I'm not.'

I wondered how long he'd been waiting to do this, wondered what he'd do next. Is this what he did with all the girls he was friends with? He shuffled across the seat, getting closer to me. I think I stopped breathing altogether.

Then he was right there, in front of my face, his eyes a blur, his lips almost touching mine.

'Is this OK?' he whispered.

So, OK...

It's three hours later. I can't write any more of that other stuff now.

We're still here, at L and G's camp. I guess I should explain what we've found.

It's weirder than in our camp.

This camp is more open and the clearing in the middle is bigger; it's quieter than in our camp, too, but perhaps that's just because there's not so many trees so close. Or perhaps it's because we're not used to it. Our camp felt weird too, when we first got there. It felt horrible.

It didn't take us long to explore.

There's the first cabin we went into – the one with the steps I'm sitting on.

Then there's the biggest cabin in the centre of the clearing – like the big cabin in our camp, this one also has a long wooden table down the centre with benches either side. There are two faded, mothy couches at the back, and an old chest in between them being used as a coffee table. There's a lean-to kitchen tacked onto the side.

The third and final cabin on the other side of the clearing

is a bedroom. I didn't spend long in there exploring; it felt wrong somehow with all of us. Toilets and showers are hidden in the trees, too, like they are at ours, and there's a small hut containing a generator. All of these are empty of soldiers and warring tribes. No Lily and George, either.

But it's definitely their camp, there are signs of them everywhere. In the bedroom cabin, it's most obvious. Their stuff is scattered about, including clothes I remember them wearing: Lily's bangles, George's bandannas, flip-flops. Draped across one wall is a colourful square of cloth, and there are stacks of books beside the bed. Pete even found a whole stash of condoms in the bedside drawer. So, I guess L and G are a couple then.

Even in the main cabin it's obvious they were here recently. There were handwritten notes left on the table: Lily's writing. The pen beside them still had its lid off. Those notes were about us. Annie pinned them with a tack to the wall.

'We'll read those properly later,' she said. 'Once we know what's going on.'

There are half-used jars of spreads in the kitchen. A bowl of cooked, hard rice (with flies) near the stove.

So, where are they?

How can Lily and George just disappear?

It's weird. Creepy, actually. And yeah, maybe I don't think being left alone by them is a *task* to deal with anymore. If it were just my choice, I'd be out of here already, heading back to our camp, or maybe going further. But the others want to solve the mystery. So I guess I'm sticking here for now.

71

The cabin I'm sitting in front of is the weirdest bit of this whole camp.

I've been sitting here for a while, my back to what's inside. Instead I've been looking out, watching Nyall and Annie run around the camp, exploring and yelling to each other. Any soldiers or warring tribes within about fifty miles would have heard us, so I guess that means there aren't any. If I lean backwards a bit, I can see what's in there. That cabin's so strange, and it still smells bad too.

It was an old sandwich in the end, the smell, nothing dead like I first thought. Just tuna and mayonnaise on white bread. At least, I think that's what it was. The mayonnaise had congealed and there were flies and ants all over it, making the sandwich black and alive. It might as well have been a dead animal. Pete moved it because none of the rest of us would. He flung it far into the trees beyond the clearing. God help the poor animal that finds and eats that.

But the sandwich isn't the strangest thing in there.

I'm listening to Pete and Sam inside the cabin. They've been in there for ages, fascinated – I always thought George and Lily were filming stuff, but this? This is something else.

'Told you,' I said to Pete when I saw it all. 'Cameras have been watching us all the time.'

He didn't say anything.

We counted fifteen different views altogether, all flickering across four different screens in a timed pattern. They're small screens, placed on top of each other and making a kind of wall across the far end of the cabin. There's a desk in front of them with paper and pens strewn across it, and an ancient-looking computer in one corner that we can't log into. The whole room looks more like a shabby TV production room than something you'd find in a jungle hut. It doesn't take a genius to work out that if there are fifteen different images we can see, then there must be fifteen different cameras out there. Or more if not all the cameras are turned on, or some are broken.

'I was SO right about the red lights in the trees,' I said.

I recognised most of the images that flickered across the screens. We counted six views of areas around our camp: a couple of shots of the clearing in the middle, an image each of the two bedroom cabins, and a shot looking in on the main hut. There was a shot of the path leading to the showers too. Lily and George had been spying on us. I racked my brains, tried to remember if I'd done anything stupid in front of any of these cameras, but I think I'm safe. I don't do anything stupid anymore anyway; I skulk in the shadows.

There are images of this camp too. Five. Pete and Sam actually went outside and looked for the cameras. From inside the cabin, the rest of us watched them. Pete waved up at the camera pointing at the clearing in the middle. We waved back, even though we were on the other side of the screens and he couldn't see. Then Pete stuck his finger up at us. He cupped his hand and moved it up and down like he was wanking.

Wanker.

We all went looking for the other cameras then. The second camera we found was above the main cabin, looking out at the rest of the camp rather than pointed inside (like the cameras had to be at ours). When we found it in the rafters, I wanted to throw a stone and knock it down, but no one else said anything when I suggested it. Then there's a camera near the shower block, and another one looking at L and G's cabin. There must be a camera somewhere else on the edge of this camp too, as one of the screens is focused on images of the track we came in on.

That leaves four other cameras somewhere else. And that's the thing: these four other images we can see flickering across the screens – we've no idea where they are! Or what they are showing us. We looked at these pictures for ages, trying to work it out. These cameras are pointed at lots and lots of tall green plants. Thick, leafy undergrowth. Nothing else.

Crops for food? Maybe they are. They seem to be planted in an orderly enough way, and they all look like the same sort of plant. But four cameras pointed at it? That seems like a lot of surveillance for a bit of food.

Nyall's convinced it's Lily and George's personal drug stash. But these crops don't look like marijuana plants, I know that much.

Maybe we're staring at a new crop of drugs, something about to be unleashed on the world. But from here? I'm not sure I would've picked Lily and George for international drug smugglers. They look too much like pot-smokers for one thing – hippy-dippy and shambolic – and I thought serious drug smugglers were always the types you least expect. Kids. Elderly ladies. Accountants.

We've stared and stared, but none of us recognise the scenery around those crops, not from what we can see anyway. But then, we haven't been far into the trees, so how would we really know anything?

Sam and Pete are still in the cabin now, looking for clues.

I've just taken a moment to go back into that cabin.

I peered over Sam's shoulders for another look. In one screen, I watched Annie going through the drawers in Lily and George's bedroom cabin. Sam, Pete and me all stayed silent as she pulled out a pair of undies and held them against her.

'Oh, she's not going to try them on, is she?' Pete snickered. 'On live telly?'

'It's not live telly,' I snapped. 'It's just us watching.'

'Who knows who else is watching?'

That shut me up. Because I guess he's right. I actually had no idea what Lily and George were doing with all this footage, and no idea if they were *still* doing something with it right now. They said at the beginning they were filming us so they could study our group dynamics, so they could help us in the best way possible; we were part of a groundbreaking psychological project. We even had to sign a piece of paper that allowed them to do it. They'd make some amazing documentary and they'd make us all famous, they said. We'd get money.

I'm not so sure anymore. I mean, fifteen cameras, and four of them focused on tall green plants? Besides, they couldn't use this sort of footage for TV – in the images we saw, there's not even sound.

We've been idiots.

I'm beginning to wish we'd never found this cabin. Never left our camp. At least it felt safe in our camp, comparatively – like we were so hidden nobody could find us. But maybe I've been wrong about that, too.

After we gave up on Annie with the undies, we watched the rest of the screens. A small monkey skittered through one of the images of the crops and Pete started backwards, his head banging into my chest.

'Watch it,' I growled.

He turned around to look slowly at my tits. 'Nothing to bump into anyway!'

Sam whacked him across the head. 'Stop being an arse.'

I was glad Sam did that, though I didn't look at him to let him know. Pete went back to studying the rest of the screens, not saying anything else. It was so weird: these places we were spying on, the life going on outside this cabin that we saw so many glimpses of. It was like playing God.

Pete started fiddling around with the few buttons there were, trying to work out if he could do anything to the footage. He tried again to crack the computer's password.

'If we could rewind the recordings, we could see what happened before we got here,' he said. 'To Lily and George.'

'Well, duh!' I said.

Though there was no *rewind* button. Not that we could see. And the computer remained a dusty, useless brick.

'What if it's just a surveillance system?' I said. I was thinking about Dieter, how he used to tell me about working as a carpark attendant and watching screens of cars for hours; how he'd had to watch it all himself in real time as nothing was stored in the system for more than 24 hours.

I tried to explain this to Pete. 'Some surveillance systems don't store footage, not for long anyway. Sometimes it's just the live footage on the screen.'

'Why wouldn't they keep footage?' he said. 'We're part of some psychology programme, remember? They're making a TV show with us … they *need* the footage.'

I stared at him, and he stared back. We were both thinking it… *Are we? Are they? How much of any of it is real?*

Then Nyall walked into one of the images, and we all turned back to see. He was bare-chested, with a towel draped over his shoulder, and was heading towards the shower. We watched him look around. He must've been trying to work out where the camera was, trying to remember.

'Stop perving,' Pete said.

He lashed out at me, but I avoided him easily. I folded my arms in front of my chest. 'You're not looking away, either,' I said. 'Girl, boy, monkey … I reckon you'd go for anything that moved. Even now you're still watching him.'

He stood up to get me, but Sam held him back. 'Leave it, Kash.'

So I did. I came back out here instead. I don't know why I

bother provoking Pete. It's only cos I'm sick of him thinking he knows more than the rest of us.

BUT NONE OF US KNOW ANYTHING ABOUT ANYTHING!

That's the truth of it, and why doesn't anyone else realise?

Pete doesn't know what those crops are.

Pete doesn't know how we find them.

Pete doesn't know if we're still part of the psychological immersion programme. He doesn't know if this is just one more task.

He doesn't know what happened to Lily and George.

I'll get moving in a moment, stretch my legs. I'll check the other cabins again, look for clues. There must be something to tell us where Lily and George have gone. People just don't disappear without leaving something behind.

I can hear the boys laughing behind me. I hope it's because of whatever Nyall is doing on the screen rather than Annie. There's something so fragile about Annie. Sometimes I wonder where she came from, why she's here. She seems too delicate to be homeless, too much like a tiny bird. I bet she doesn't have a Dieter who could stump up the two-thousand-pound fee to get her onto this thing. How did Nyall get on this thing either, for that matter? Did they steal their way on? And Pete? I know Sam used his own money, saved up from his work at the garage.

They cackle like parrots behind me.

'Stop perving,' I yell back. 'You're like little kids.'

They don't say anything, but they shut up laughing. I want to call everyone together and ask the obvious question before it gets too dark: when are we going back to our camp? Or maybe the question should be: are we even going back to camp? Or are we going to walk out of here in the other direction instead?

Soon it'll be too dark for it to even be a question.

I can hear the creak of a chair being pushed back. It's Sam, walking towards me.

'Pete thinks we should stay,' he's just said. 'We'll go back in the morning.'

I guess I'll write more later.

***

It's *later*.

After we all got back together in the main hut, Pete gave his reasoning.

'There must be a rewind button,' he said. 'Or something on that computer. I want to play with it longer. See if I can get in, find out anything.'

I know enough about Pete to know he's a hacker. Perhaps that's how he got here – that was his *fuck up*. Perhaps him breaking into this computer is his special *Tribe* task, and Lily gave it to him on the sly. I get this flipping journal and he gets to play Mission Impossible.

Or perhaps his hacking is like my cutting.

Perhaps this challenge is irresistible for him.

'What about these soldiers or tribes you're so worried about?' I said. 'If we stay and they come back, we get popped off too.'

Pete smiled like a cream-got cat. 'We'll see them coming. Cameras now, remember? We're in the safest place.'

Annie tucked her head in against Nyall's shoulder, away from the rest of us. Nyall put his arm around her, and I felt a pang of something inside me. Jealousy? Not because I wanted Nyall to do that to me too. I don't even like Nyall like that; I don't like anyone. But the thought of an arm around me right now, any arm, wasn't a terrible one.

'You really think it's the safest place?' Nyall said. 'Lily and George disappeared from here, didn't they?'

Pete nodded at the cabin with the screens. 'From here, we'll be able to see who's coming for ages.'

Nyall shifted under Pete's gaze. 'Then why didn't Lily and George see…?'

'Maybe they were high,' Annie said.

Silence then. Were the others thinking of those crops, too? What they were … who might want them … what they had to do with us or *The Tribe* or L and G… We sat around the long table in the main cabin, staring at each other.

'Anyway, it's too late to trek back up now,' Pete finally finished. 'It's dark.'

'But we don't know where we are … we don't know anything!' Annie's voice came muffled from against Nyall's shoulder.

'We don't know anything about the other camp either,' Sam said quietly. 'Not really. Maybe whoever got Lily and George was going there next.'

That shut us up. And I was thinking…

It's become *whoever*.

It's become *got Lily and George*.

Eventually Annie undug her head from Nyall's shoulder, her face tiny with her eyes too big.

'At least the other camp was kind of familiar,' she said. 'At least we knew where the food was.'

'You don't eat anything anyway,' Pete snapped.

Nyall shot him a look, grabbed Annie's shoulder and almost seemed to push her straighter as he hugged her then looked back at us all in turn. 'I think we should explore everything here tomorrow,' he said. 'Thoroughly. Then we decide whether we stay or not. Then we decide what to do. We'll give Pete a chance to hack first.'

It was about the most I'd heard him say in one go the entire time we'd been here. He's a little like me in that, talking more each day, getting bolder. Perhaps it's Pete: the sheer dickishness of that guy makes the rest of us need to talk, even if it's just to hear another voice. Nyall's voice is quiet and gentle, nicer than mine, but there's iron to it too. He suits Annie, despite what I heard Lily telling them about being too co-dependent. But what does she know anyway?

Pete nodded. 'Fine, get some kip. I'll take the screens. I'll wake someone if I need a break.'

Nyall and Annie went back to the cabin that was Lily and

81

George's. I hoped they'd remembered the camera in there, and that Pete would be watching it. This left me and Sam alone in the main cabin. Secretly I was glad. It was dark enough out there; it would be darker without Sam.

'Night, lovebirds.' Pete laughed as he left. Not a nice laugh. He knows what's going on between us; he's seen it or Sam's told him. He knows Sam wants something I'm not giving. I watched him walk across the clearing to the cabin with the screens.

Then Sam and I sat facing each other across the long table. It was a while before my eyes flicked to the folded pages of notes Annie had pinned to the wall.

'We should know what they think of us,' I said.

I unpinned them and laid them out. Only a few pages. The text was faint and there weren't many words. Sam sat close to read. He smelt hot, like old sweat and dirt. I probably smelt the same. Neither of us had had a shower that day. I couldn't actually remember the last time I'd washed.

Lily's writing was spidery, like her, and the letters were faded from the sun. From what I could work out, she'd written a few sentences about each of us: brief words to sum us up.

Peter Samuels. Expelled from three schools. Bullying. Fighting. Alcoholic father. Has money. Posh. Then there were a couple of addresses, a couple of school names.

'Do you think he'd want us to know this?' Sam said.

When he went to move the papers away, I stopped him. There were more notes: about Pete's school grades and a description of Pete's house.

'Weird,' I said. 'Why do they want to know this sort of stuff?'

Next was Annie.

Annie Smith. Homeless? Ran away at thirteen. Drug dependence? Doesn't eat. Wants money. Won't want to go home. Then some notes about her next-of-kin.

I flicked over to Nyall.

Nyall Symder. Homeless. Boyfriend of Annie. Co-dependent. Desperate. Split these two up, they'd do anything to get back together.

I paused at that, looked up at Sam.

'What's Lily on about?' he said.

'What's any of this on about?'

Already my eyes were back on the page looking for what it said about Sam … about me.

Sam Wolton. Jacks cars, or so he says…?

Again, I looked at Sam. He didn't steal cars. Not that I knew about. There'd only been one, only once.

'You told her that?'

He kept his eyes on the paper. 'I had to tell her something,' he said quietly. 'I had to get on this thing.'

'Why would you say that though?' I'd thought that night – taking Mum's car – was private. I thought no one knew about it apart from me and Sam. I'd never told anyone and I didn't think Sam would either.

'I wasn't going to let you come here alone. We both know it was easier for you to get on this thing than me.'

The tops of his cheeks went red. I didn't know whether to

be mad at him, or let myself feel something else. I chose the mad.

'I thought you wanted to do this?' I said. 'That's what you told me.'

'I did.'

'It was your idea coming here.'

'I know,' he said, firm. 'I wouldn't use all my savings for nothing.' His eyes were still flicking across the page, still reading. 'It was meant to be our adventure, remember? You and me! Together we'd sort each other out, fix what happened. I thought it would … help!'

Abruptly, Sam scrunched the piece of paper into a ball and clasped it in his fist.

'What does any of that matter now anyway,' he said. 'Who we were? Maybe we're different out here. *Changing,* like they say.'

I lunged for the paper in his hand.

'Let me see that.'

'No.'

'There's stuff about me, isn't there? I'm the only one left.'

'It's not about you.'

I grabbed for it, pushing him to try and get to his hand. He tumbled backwards over the bench. I went over with him, still reaching for the paper. He huffed hard as he landed, but I leant across him.

'Just give it to me.'

His arms were too long to get anywhere near. Even if I could get to his hand, I couldn't unclench his fist.

84

'Fine,' I said. I'd get it later, when he was asleep. 'Just let me go.'

He wasn't making it easy. Every time I tried to untangle my feet from his, he moved his to tangle them more. He was trying to hold me there, trying to keep me. I went limp.

'What do you want?'

He stopped moving his feet. 'Nothing. It's just … you don't have to struggle all the time.'

His breath was suddenly on my cheek and his face so close. I looked down at him. His eyes were steady on mine.

'The note…?'

'Believe me, Kash, just once, you don't need to see. Anyway, it's about me.'

I could feel his ribs underneath my stomach, how his chest was breathing quickly, making me rise up a bit too. I wanted to believe him. Once I'd believed him without being asked to.

I felt his other arm curl up around my back, holding me. I was so close I could see the dirt stuck to the grooves around his nose. Once, I'd known everything about Sam. Once, I'd have liked his face this close. But now? Now, he could have a girlfriend waiting for him back home and he wouldn't tell me.

I wouldn't let myself relax. I was waiting for the moment his hand wasn't so firm against my back, then I'd be out of there, pushing him away.

He brought the hand with the crumpled piece of paper towards my face. I was too busy looking at the paper, trying to find its words, to see how close he was leaning. He uncurled his fist, touched the tip of his index finger against my cheek.

'What are you doing, Sam?' My eyes were on his now.

Still he leant forward, touched the tip of his nose to mine. His bottom lip quivered.

'Kiss me,' he said. 'Like before.'

'I can't,' I whispered. But I didn't move back. This wasn't real, this was a time long gone.

But did I want it again? Want him?

Kiss. Kiss. Kiss.

It might be so easy.

Cautiously – carefully – I brought my head forward. I fairy-touched my lips against his, as soft as leaf-tips feel when you brush past a tree.

But then I stopped.

I'd thought about Mum, hadn't I?

So quick, I'd got an image of her face – of how she'd look if she saw us doing this. And then I was thinking: had she seen us that night, had she been waiting in the shadows of the quarry? Is that why it happened?

I pulled away.

Kiss me – it was what Sam had said in Mum's car that night, when it had been darker outside than oceans. And I'd wanted to. I'd wanted to kiss him more than I'd wanted anything in my entire life, I think. *Sam Wolton.* I wanted him in the same way I wanted to hurt myself sometimes. I wanted all of him. Every single bit.

His lips on mine, so gentle.

I remember it.

So much warmer than the cold of the car. His tongue darted out and touched my teeth. I wanted to catch it, keep it. I felt the tiny bristles of the hair above his top lip against my skin. I smelt the car oil on him.

He pressed his hand into the small of my back, pulled me towards him. The gear stick and the handbrake were in the way, but I didn't care. I don't think I was breathing. I don't think I was thinking anything at all. His hand moved up my spine, tracing the ridges of my bones, stopping when it got to my bra. The tips of his fingers dug underneath it, fumbled with the catch. For one stupid second I wanted to tell him that I loved him; that I'd always loved him. Instead I leant further in towards him. Perhaps I could show him instead. I pressed my hands against his smooth, warm stomach.

His fingers worked out the bra catch, undid it. Then they were feeling their way around my body, across my ribs.

'We can't do this here,' I whispered.

'Why not?'

'It's Mum's car.'

'Not anymore it's not.'

I still wasn't breathing. At least, it didn't feel like it. All I could think about was his hand, moving up around me. I pulled back, tried to focus on his eyes, nose, mouth; everything was close together, jumbled. He stopped then, just looked back at me. His gaze was steady, his mouth slightly open. I thought he was going to say something. I wanted him to. I wanted him to tell me that he thought about me in the way I thought about him.

But my phone rang.

I jolted back from Sam immediately, hit my head against the car window. His hand slipped out from under my jumper. The phone was flashing through my jeans pocket; I could feel it vibrating on my leg. I didn't want to answer. It could only be Mum. Eventually it was Sam who moved away, who sat back in his seat with a thump.

He flicked his head towards it. 'Going to get it?'

But Mum had already gone. There were text messages from her though. Three. I took a breath before I read them.

I saw the cat, Kasha. It's here!

I flicked to the next, hoping Sam hadn't seen.

When are you coming? It's still here. I'll try to trap it for you.

Then, the last one made me put the phone down altogether:

I don't know what to do here without you. Hurry! The cat's angry.

I shoved them back into my pocket. I thought of Mum on the mountain summit alone. Was this the night she proved to everyone just how wrong they'd been not to believe her? I shook my head. A big black cat? Here? It was ridiculous. Just more proof of where her mind was really at.

Sam was already shuffling towards me again, getting ready to take up where we left off.

But I pushed him away. 'I've got to go.'

And I did. When Mum needed me, she'd stop at nothing. She might even go to the cinema to find me, might even look for her car. I swallowed quickly and opened the door.

'Hey, Kash ... wait!'

When I didn't, Sam came round the other side. He placed a hand on each shoulder and made me stop. 'What have I done?'

I shook my head, pushed him away again. 'I've just got to go.'

'I'll walk you.'

'No.'

Sam moved in front of me and made me stop. He crouched down to my eye level, made me look at him.

'Kiss me,' he said.

He was so close, centimetres away. It would have taken nothing to lean over and feel his lips on mine again. I could already feel his breath on my nose. And I wanted to.

I swallowed the desire.

I kept thinking of Mum. Alone on the mountain. How I hadn't checked her pills. How, recently, she'd been getting stranger and stranger.

I had to go. Shouldn't even be there. I'd spent too long already. So I turned away from Sam, ran through the trees. Sam could hide the car without me.

'See you tomorrow!' he called.

I turned onto the deer path that led through the quarry and onto the side of the mountain. I didn't need a torch. I knew my way from all the times I'd been there with Mum. I think if I was blind I'd know my way to the top of that mountain. Sam would be OK. He'd stick to the main track, find the road.

89

But … I'd so wanted to stay! I even paused for a moment, wondering if I could go back.

To Sam…

To being a normal teenager…

To making out in a car like normal girls did…

I was being stupid, hoping for that. I ran on. It had only ever been just Mum and me. Always.

Us against the world. We stick together, you and me. Us girls. Her words.

How could I think any different?

I leapt logs and clumps of bracken. Maybe I should've stopped and sent a message. I should've waited with Sam and called Mum first. But I just wanted to get there. If I could do that, I'd be able to calm her. I wouldn't feel so guilty.

I crossed the stream, balancing on the rocks, then went up the steep, quicker side of the mountain. I started shouting for Mum before I got to the summit. She'd hate that, the unnecessary noise, scaring her cat away; she wouldn't shout back.

I just wanted to let her know I was coming.

To wait.

It's the middle of the night again.

Seems I often write in this thing by torchlight.

Sam's snoring. The light is on in the cabin across the clearing. Has Pete found out how to rewind the footage yet? Or maybe he's just wanking in there.

I can see the scrunched-up paper Sam chucked across the room, the paper he wouldn't let me read. Did Sam forget about it?

I'm going to read it now.

OK, I have.
Not sure
    what
        to think.

It *was* about me. I guess I was right.
Sam just didn't want me to see it.
So.
So.

It says…

Kasha Fintry. Sixteen years. Killed her mother? She thinks so. No one will miss her.

There are other things too, but…

        No one will miss her?

Why would anyone write that? Even Lily?

91

Even spidery bitch-faced Lily?

I'm still staring at it. I want to wake Sam. I'm not even angry at him anymore for lying about it, or trying to hide it.

Maybe it's true anyway. No one would miss me. No one *does*. Not even Dieter. Definitely not Cynthia Sugartits. They're probably glad I'm not staying in their house anymore.

No one at school.

No. One. Would.

No. One. Does.

Perhaps I did do the right thing by coming out here. Perhaps the best thing to do now would be to stay out here forever, disappear into the dark. Never go back.

To go away now.

But why did Lily write it? What's it to her anyway, who misses me or not? What does she care?

Is this just another part of her strange psychology experiment?

It makes me feel weird.

Hollow.

Like nothing.

I've got a horrible shivery feeling down my spine.

I don't want to be here. A part of me would even rather be with Dieter and Cynthia, back in his plastic city apartment he keeps threatening to move me into permanently (as if the past ten months living there haven't been enough already).

No!

That part of me's stupid if it thinks that! Who'd want that? No mountain. No woods. No cubby. No ... Sam.

Perhaps Mum was right – *me and her against the world. Us girls.* Perhaps that's all there was.

The trees are moving out there, I'm sure. I've seen leaves part like there's something walking between them. Something that's not so tall as a human, unless that human is crawling.

Could it be a soldier like Pete says? Just one?

I keep looking to check that no one's crept up on us. It's creepy. As I look down and write this, I imagine someone is coming towards me ... and when I look up next, they'll be frozen mid-step across the clearing, like a statue. Isn't there a game like that? *Who's afraid, Mr Wolf?* Is that what it's called? Didn't I play it with Dieter when I was a kid?

I just did that: looked up quickly. But there was nothing in the clearing, nothing frozen or stalking close to us...

But in the trees behind ... still something...?

Something shadow-black. A cat? I'm not dreaming this time. I'm definitely awake. I'm writing this down, aren't I? Branches are definitely shifting. Waist height.

Is Pete watching it on the cameras too?

I have a thought which seems kind of crazy, but also kind of possible. What if it was a black cat that got Lily and George? Not soldiers, not warring tribes, not some stupid task that went wrong...

They have black cats in jungles, don't they?

Didn't I see one the other night?

93

And now I'm thinking something else … what if Mum's black cat was real? What if she wasn't lying about seeing it?

Or is this just the dark talking?

I'll go out and check.

Will I?

Even if I saw a cat out there in the trees, how could I convince the others? I can't even take a photo. It's Mum's paradox all over again. A cat, or not a cat … real or unreal. To look or not to look. How did I go halfway around the world and find myself in her dilemma? Maybe that's the whole point. Was always the whole point. It's almost funny.

And now I've just thought something else … perhaps there IS a camera here.

George's handheld. Of course. Where's that gone?

Sam's still snoring. No movement from either of the other cabins. Even the movement in the trees seems to have stopped.

I'll look for the camera while there's nothing much else going on.

Crap!

I need to write this properly – what I've found – there's so much.

Hang on ... Sam's up. I'll show him.

Hang on.

If anyone does find this notebook and reads it, you need to know this.

IT'S NOT OURS!

None of it.

That.

Is.

What's.

True.

We did not do this!

If anyone's reading this ... believe it!

We did not even know our bags were there!

So ... I'll explain.

I didn't find the camera, but I found the bags. *Our bags*. I found what they'd put inside them.

So, if this journal's found, and we're not...

Shit, there's no time to write properly. Do this justice. *Understand*. Sam thinks we should wake the others. Show them. He's right.

Hang on, there's a shout from Pete. Calling us to come.

Did he see what I just found?

He's still shouting.

'I've got in! I'm in!'

I'm going.

---

32 hours. That's how long it's been since I last wrote in here.
A lot has happened.

An understatement!

Under

Under

Under

And I'm stuck again,

in the understory I'm telling

and in the undergrowth I'm looking at.

So many unders.

At least it's dark and quiet when you're underneath.

I wish it were just Sam and me, curled up under a blanket,
somewhere far away, dark and quiet underneath ... and that's
all.

I was sort of joking before about writing down everything in
case something happened to us. I'm not joking about that
anymore.

I am alone here now.

It's hard to make jokes for one.

I should go out and look for them. Smash all the cameras on the way.

Or perhaps I should just start writing from where I left off, and WAIT.

It's not a bad thing, after all, to stay in one place. Wait for Sam ... the others ... *something...*

But until then?

I should write <u>All The Things That Happened</u>.

So, in order…

I saw the advert. Talked about it with Sam.

I went to the meeting.

Dieter paid the money after considerable persuasion.

So did Sam.

I got on The Tribe easily. Met the others.

Then there was all that information – the orientation, being told about the tasks, the TV documentary.

We took the plane.

It was night-time when we arrived on this island. Lily and George took our phones and bags (passports too).

Initiation dinner. We drank that harsh plant liquor shit.

The task of writing this journal. Therapy sessions. The talking to camera.

We learnt about bush foods with George.

More sessions with Lily. More plant liquor shit. Group bonding around the fire.

And then … the group task to put the flag on top of the hill behind camp.

Gunshots.

Coming down the hill.

Lily and George gone.

The quiet.

Finding the track.

Going to the other camp.

Finding the cameras.

Finding the bags.

Finding that footage.

I've stopped – just staring at the page now. I know writing keeps my hands busy. Keeps me good. Writing it like this, in a list, happens too quickly though.

In the 32 hours since I last wrote, my fingers have been busy in other ways. Making red tracks on my inner arms. Running through Sam's hair.

Cutting words into paper can be a good thing. Better than cutting into skin. The throbbing in my arms is testament to that.

So.

I'll write what I found, once again – document it here. I'll take as long as I want. If anyone is reading this, you'll just have to be patient…

I'll tell you about finding the bags. What was in them. What happened next.

I was opening up cupboards in the other camp, looking for George's camera, something to film that cat thing I thought I'd seen (still think I might've seen).

One cupboard under the sink seemed to go on forever – a gaping mouth of black.

I could hide in there, I thought, disappear from the others and from everything else in that place. We could all hide in there if soldiers actually did come. I leant into it to see how far back it went.

That's when I found the bags.

Our bags.

This was where they'd stashed them.

Lily and George had told us we'd only get them back once we'd completed all the tasks: only when we were ready to go home.

So I pulled them out, one by one, all five. There were some spider webs on them and that creeped me out a bit, but no big leggy guys scuttled out. When I got my backpack, it was heavier than it should've been. Something inside.

It'd seemed like ages since we'd unpacked. How many weeks though, was it? Two? Three? Not so long.

(Time moves weird here.)

They'd taken our bags and passports away so fast.

The zip was stuck, so I took out the filleting knife from my shorts to try and lever it free. I gave my fingertips little nicks while I was at it. I liked how it felt so I did it some more. Nothing bad. This wasn't proper cutting. Just a little taste, that's all. Just to see when I could stop.

I didn't mean to rip the material. Just got carried away with all the nicking and didn't want to tear strips off my own skin in the way that I'd really like (perhaps I've got better here after all. Maybe. A little.) Either way, the bag spewed open.

There were little packets inside. Hundreds of them. Filled with something that looked like tree bark – ripped-up strips of it. All zipped up in plastic snap-lock bags. I opened one and smelt it. Woody. Kind of sweet. It didn't look or smell like drugs, not ones I know anyway. But what do I know … it could've been anything. I checked the others' cases too, ripped them all open. Packets in all of them. All filled with the torn-up bark stuff.

That's when I called for Sam.

That's when he said we should call for the others.

I'm trying to be brief with this, not to get too emotional or jump to conclusions. But it doesn't look good, does it? Not for everything Lily and George said about the programme. Not for *The Tribe*.

Unless … could this discovery be part of it, another challenge; another task? Is that possible, even now? To go to such lengths? And if so, what exactly would the task be?

To decide what to do with hundreds of packets of bark that could be drugs? Were L and G watching even now to see if we'd freak out, or smoke them, or escape with the lot?

When I told Sam this, he thought about it too. 'That's kind of crazy,' he said. 'But … *maybe*?'

But this…

That…

A bridge too far?

We didn't have long to think about it because that's when Pete started calling for us to come.

We went.

We all went.

Nyall and Annie came into the camera cabin a few seconds after us. Somehow, Pete had got the ancient-looking computer on; he'd cracked the code and was scrolling through files.

'This is where they store the camera footage,' he said. 'You can see anything up to a week back. Not sure where the older footage goes though, if it goes anywhere … I mean, there's another folder on here called 'Tribe Members' which has files in it too, but I can't get into that one. That's proper locked.'

Annie rubbed her eyes, cat-like. 'How'd you get into the first bit?'

'Ah!' Pete tapped his nose. 'A man has to have his secrets.'

I rolled my eyes. Sam saw and frowned at me. Perhaps he

thought we had to be grateful to Pete for his wonder-work. Perhaps we did.

'You are going to freak when you see,' Pete said. 'Get ready. It's big.'

He had it queued. The footage he wanted was from the camera pointed on the clearing in the middle of that camp. Pete fast-forwarded through a whole lot of Lily and George moving around, doing nothing much – until he got to where he wanted. After a moment of Lily and George talking to each other in the clearing, a beaten-about van turned up. We all sat forward then. *This* was different. We hadn't seen a sign of anyone else since we got here.

'That's why there's tyre tracks coming in!' Nyall said.

Pete nodded. 'But wait till you see this bit.'

'Soldiers?' Annie asked. 'Tribes?'

'Don't think so,' said Pete.

The three men who got out of that van didn't look like soldiers, or even members of a tribe. They were in scruffy trousers and t-shirts; they were short and weedy. But they did carry guns. Two of them did anyway. AK-47s, like in the movies. They started talking with Lily and George. It was easy to see that the conversation got really heated really quick. None of us spoke as we watched.

After a while more, one of the two men carrying the guns started properly shouting at George. He waved his free arm about and then pushed George backwards. The other one got more animated too as he talked to Lily. She looked away from him, to the other side of the clearing … in the direction of our camp? Or, maybe, to where those crops were? It was hard to tell, but I think she was frowning. Was she thinking about us? Those crops? Or maybe she was just deciding what to say to the crazy gun guy. We must've been on the hill behind our camp by then, with that task of planting their stupid flag.

Can't help wondering – could Lily have known these men were coming and that was why she'd set that task? Or maybe I'm just jumping to conclusions. It was probably just a coincidence – those men being there when we were further away.

Either way, when the same guy started shouting at her some more, she just kept shaking her head. Really hard. Over and over.

'Wish we had sound,' Sam murmured.

'She's saying there's no one else here,' Annie said. 'Telling him to go away!'

Or…

There was another option.

Perhaps those men were just actors. It could all be an elaborate act to make us think … THINK WHAT?

Was this all some trick, some game?

Was there a chance that this stuff on the screen could be fake?

Nothing made sense.

Perhaps I'm going mad (like Mum) imagining these things. Thinking that strange men appearing in a van with guns could still be part of a psychological programme.

It's just another kind of Black Cat. Another kind of fantasy.

Either way, when this man – who may or may not be an actor – didn't get the answer he was after, he dragged Lily roughly towards the van. He grabbed her t-shirt tight with one hand and carried his gun in the other. Annie gasped when Lily fell.

And then, it didn't look so much like an act anymore.

George followed close behind, pushing and shouting. And unless he was super good at it, he didn't look like he was acting, either. None of them did.

We all sat up straighter, got closer to the screen. I felt the tension, holding us there.

We watched.

Lily was dragged to the other side of the van, and suddenly we couldn't see her properly – the camera angle wasn't right. We only saw the back of the man holding the gun, which he was still waving about.

'Is there another camera that shows it any better?' Sam asked.

Pete shook his head. 'Already tried. This is the only camera on that clearing.'

But we saw enough to know what was going on. That man who'd pushed Lily out of shot held his gun up. He pointed it out to where she might have been lying. Would he shoot? He was aiming at her, wasn't he?

Beside me, I heard Sam breathe in.

'The gunshots,' Annie whispered.

'We can't just watch this,' Nyall said.

Too late.

We saw shotgun man jerk backwards as he pulled the trigger.

Annie gasped hard, then. Sam did too. Nyall turned away.

But still, we couldn't see what'd happened. We didn't actually see her get shot.

So … did she?

And am I awful for thinking more about that rather than wondering if she was OK?

On the screen George ran, pulling the man with the AK-47 backwards when he got to him. The other two van men came over as well and started pulling at George. The screen was a blur of moving bodies. But where was Lily? Was that one of her trainers, on the ground, towards the corner of the screen? It was too blurred to be sure, there was too much else going on…

Annie leant forwards to pause the computer. Silence for a moment as we stared at that frozen image. Then everyone spoke at once.

'What just happened?'

'She got shot. *She got bloody shot!*'

'Who are these people?'

'Are they coming back?'

'We have to get out!'

'What do they want?'

'What just happened?'

There was an answer there lurking, but it was Sam who spoke it.

'Drugs,' he said quietly. 'That's what.'

When the others turned to look at him, I added, 'Lily and George hid drugs in our suitcases. Drugs, or something like it. I found the cases buried under the hut with the stuff inside them. I'll show you…'

And, really, what else could it be but drugs? It made sense, that strange bark with its odd sweet smell. The crops on the screens. We had what these men wanted, in our very own cases.

It was one theory.

But what did we have to do with it?

'Cocaine,' Pete said, nodding. 'That's totally green and bushy, like those crops. That's what they're growing here. And that's big money! But they'd need a decent kitchen…'

'It's not powder in the bags, it's bark,' I said. 'What about poppies? Opiates? Can't they be bushy?'

And something flicked across Pete's face like *well yeah, maybe, it could be that too.* And I felt smug then. Even though, what the hell did it matter? If this theory were right and there were illegal drugs here, we were part of something bad whichever way was up.

'We should get out of here,' Annie said.

Nyall shrugged. 'Or get the drugs first and get out? Make some money at least.'

Sam rolled his eyes. 'I'm not touching that.'

'But Lily and George as drug lords?' Nyall said. 'Seriously? They're just…'

'…hippies,' Annie finished.

'And therapists,' added Pete.

And then, my thoughts were like – why would someone

want to hide drugs in my suitcase anyway? Why would someone who's meant to be a *therapist* want to do that?

Unless…

'You know, it still could be part of the programme,' I said. '…seeing what we'll do, how we'll react to this…'

'You're truly crazy,' Pete said.

'I'm just saying it *could,* that's all!'

'Batshit! You're not thinking straight.'

And perhaps I wasn't thinking straight, hadn't been thinking straight since we got here. But maybe none of the others were, either.

And maybe that's exactly how Lily and George wanted us to be. We'd been drinking their plant liquor after all, smoking their stash, talking about our darknesses. Our minds were different now … weaker.

I just got up from the cabin to look for cameras in the trees around our camp.

Two red lights, still blinking. Still on, then. Still recording. Is anyone watching, though? I stuck my finger up in front of them both, just in case. I wished Pete were still there in the camera cabin in the other camp to see.

These cameras here are the real mystery. If it were just that L and G wanted surveillance cameras to protect a drug crop, why would they film us too? Why have cameras on our huts? On our shower? What kind of person needs to see that?

Maybe it is batshit, but I still can't shake the thought that we're part of some reality TV show, something else at least. There was that folder on the computer that Pete couldn't get into, after all – *Tribe Members*. What's in there?

And we've certainly had all the drama to make good telly – sex, crying, shouting, pleading, screaming. The group sessions.

But then, the footage has no sound, and it's not good enough quality for TV. So … what?

WHAT'S GOING ON?

Last night.

Only last night?

It feels longer ago than that.

Almost 34 hours since we saw Lily get shot on screen. Since it *looked* like Lily got shot.

We can't be sure, after all. It – *still* – could be a trick, couldn't it?

The others thought I was so mad to even think it.

'Why would someone play a trick like that?' Annie.

'It's sick.' Nyall.

'Why would anyone *believe* someone could play a trick like that?' Pete.

Batshit.

But anyone could do anything. And Lily and George are (*were?*) weird folk. I was wrong to ever trust them, to think they were like me or Mum.

There is something else that keeps niggling at me, too. That question is this – what happened to the two thousand pounds they took off me (or, rather, Dieter) to come here? And the money from the others too? They never mentioned it. Come to think of it, did they even take any money from the others? Perhaps it was a free ride for them.

The argument in the other camp started after we'd watched Lily get shot. Pete erupted when I questioned his theory about the soldiers taking L and G again. Annie started crying. When Nyall started rocking like he was a madman, Sam said he just wanted to go.

But Pete was determined that we should go look for Lily and George. 'We're the only ones who know what happened,' he kept saying. 'They may need our help.'

I wasn't sure I cared about whatever help Lily and George did or didn't need.

Annie didn't care either. 'They're bad people,' she said, jaw firm.

I nodded at that. 'Weird people.'

'Let's go find a town,' Annie said. 'We can't be the only ones on this island.'

'Yeah, there's the three guys with guns!' Pete said. 'Remember them?'

'Lily and George haven't told us something,' I said. 'There's something we don't know. More secrets.'

'*Obviously!*' Pete said again.

'There's a crop full of them,' muttered Sam.

I tried to explain. 'I'm serious – they said the immersion project would be unconventional … that we'd be tested to extremes psychologically, that we'd have to make difficult decisions…'

Pete crossed his arms. 'This isn't the programme anymore, Kasha. I'm going looking for them. With you guys or not.'

'And I'm getting out of here.' Nyall looked across to Annie for agreement.

She nodded, after a moment. 'You might be right, Kash,' she said. 'But I don't want to spend any longer here if there's a chance people with guns will turn up again.'

She had a point.

'I still think we should go back to our camp,' I said. 'Stick the flag up on the hill behind camp and fulfil any other tasks. Be sure we've done all we're meant to on the Programme first – eliminate that possibility. After that we go, we try to find a town. Once we're sure this isn't still a task.'

Sam moved his head, a little like a nod. 'I guess we've covered all bases like that.'

Pete made a scoffing noise. 'You really are batshit, Kasha. Maybe you're the only one of us who really believed in this Tribe thing in the first place. Who was really crazy enough to see it for something more than being famous, getting cash…'

'Enough, Pete,' Sam said.

'And you're just as cuckoo,' Pete added, '...believing her.'

I reached out and took Sam's hand, squeezed his fingers. Sam squeezed back. It didn't feel terrible, doing that. It felt nice.

Maybe I'm changing in that way, too. Letting Sam in.

Is that OK?

OK

OK

Sometimes I want to cut myself for thinking about what I did with Sam last night. Was that OK too? Was it OK what I told him – lying still in the dark – and OK what he said back? I don't know anymore.

Don't know much, it seems.

For instance – I don't know if it was the right thing, coming back to this camp only with Sam. Leaving the others to walk down that rutted track, away from us. Maybe we should have gone with them. Stuck together.

Maybe I wouldn't be alone right now if I had just swallowed my pride about the tasks. Maybe Sam wouldn't have left.

Last night, in the dark and quiet of our hut, I told Sam what'd happened with Mum. The truth. Finally. All of what I saw.

I'm going to write it here. I think I am. I'll try.

111

I'm going to keep writing so I don't use the knife. I can always cut the words out of here if I don't like them after. I'd enjoy that.

But if I start to write ... if I write...

Then, at least, I can say I've done all my tasks. No excuse on Lily and George's behalf for keeping me here. I'd have fulfilled my ... *what was it?* ... contract. The one that said that we'd get to go home after we'd done everything they asked.

Apart from the task about getting the flag to the top of the hill – that's not done yet.

So.

Here goes.

After leaving Sam in Mum's car in the quarry, I kept running, up the mountainside to the summit. I crawled through the ring of hawthorn that was around the edge of where she always made a fire. But Mum wasn't there. I spun around to make sure. Nothing. *No one.*

There was a fire in the middle, sure enough, but it was out. There was still a trace of warmth to it though, so Mum had been there recently. Rabbit bones were laid out neatly beside the embers. The lure she'd set for the black cat? Maybe she'd eaten that rabbit herself, picked the bones clean with fingers and teeth. I kicked the ash and sparks danced up. I went searching all around, even looking over the edge.

'Mum?' I called out. 'You there?'

I wondered if she was playing with me, whether she thought she was being funny and was about to leap out at any moment … even pretend she was the cat. She'd done it before. But nothing moved up there. I frowned as I traced my finger over the patterns in the dirt – animal prints, *cat prints*. Mum had drawn them, part of her art … her obsession. She had a tattoo just like these that led all the way down her spine.

But these prints, this time, led into the trees.

I blew hard to make them go away. I was angry right then, because Mum still kept on with this stupid pretence of a big black cat on that mountain, because Mum being crazy AGAIN had spoilt my one chance of properly getting with Sam. I mean, *as if* there was a big black cat, on that mountain, in our town? We're practically suburban, practically in the city. If a cat had ever escaped from a zoo it would've gone north, not here.

Right then, I would've blown and rubbed clean every single one of her black cat drawings and art works. I would've scrubbed raw the ones on her back! Perhaps it wouldn't have been the worst idea to move into the city and be near Dieter, like he'd suggested. Maybe that would stop Mum being so mad. Maybe in the city, she wouldn't be reminded of the cat all the time … if she could get some sort of friendship going with Dieter instead, like he said he wanted…

I followed the prints from the summit and into the darkness of the trees, rubbing them out as I went. The smell went sharp and pine-y. I checked my phone for any more messages –

113

nothing. Maybe Mum had gone home. If I was quick, maybe I'd catch her on the way down the mountain. I texted her to say I was almost back. I almost texted Sam to say sorry, too.

I went away from the summit, down the track towards our house at the bottom. I was listening for my phone, waiting for Mum to tell me she was home. I'd almost started to relax. Perhaps Mum had stopped to find patterns in the stars; she loved that. Perhaps she was already back, tucked up in bed and listening for me to get in; maybe she wasn't replying because she was still angry. Or maybe she was still out checking her traps, being quiet to prove some sort of point.

I swerved from the track, took a detour towards where she kept her masterpiece – the trap she'd modelled on a design from the Middle Ages. The one once used to catch wild boar and wolves when they'd roamed through these woods, stringing them up by the ankles to hang in the trees. It wouldn't take much longer to stop by and see if Mum was there. I jogged down the pathway, holding my arms out to bash back overhanging branches. It was darker there, spookier. I never went down that path by myself, usually. I tried not to go there at all.

Turns out I'd never liked those traps.

Long before I got there I could smell it. Blood. No other smell like it. Rusty and metallic and earthy.

She'd caught something.

For one crazy second, I thought it must've been the cat. She'd done it! Here was the proof that she'd been right all

114

along. I remembered the text message she'd sent when I'd been in the car with Sam – she hadn't been lying.

When I got closer, I slowed. I called out to her.

'It's Kash,' I said. 'You there, Mum?'

Then I saw it. The shape in the trees. Suspended above the ground. Hanging. Rope around its neck and legs, spread-eagled across the path, pointing like a star to the trees on either side. Here was the Masterpiece right enough, but it was too dark to see properly what it had caught. It looked big enough to be the black cat Mum spoke of, but surely it was a deer instead, *had to be*. But where was Mum? She'd gone home, leaving the trap still live? Hadn't realised what she'd done?

As I got closer, I saw the shape properly. Not deer shaped. Not cat shaped, either.

But there were two legs. Two arms. A head. There was long dark hair.

And when I got closer again, I saw the blood trickling in a stream from Mum's neck.

She'd caught herself. All trapped up.

Dead.

I told Sam that, last night, lying in the dark. Everything I saw and felt that night. Everything except about the paw prints in the dirt – I never told anyone about those.

'It's not your fault, Kash,' he'd said.

But it was my fault – all of it. If I hadn't gone with Sam that night. If I'd got to her sooner... I could have stopped her getting caught. Stopped her getting hurt.

I was the only one who could.

'You've got to stop thinking you're responsible,' Sam said. 'Something like that could've happened at any time. Your mum ... well, you know what she was like...'

I knew what he was thinking, what he was about to say. My mum was unhinged. Mad. It was only ever going to be a matter of time before she...

Snuffed it?

Popped off?

Killed herself?

Dieter had said something similar when he'd arrived to sort the house out after it'd all happened, and discovered just how strange and sick Mum had been over the last few months.

'Like tinder,' Dieter had said. 'Waiting to ignite.' Then he'd turned to me and said, 'I wish I'd known, Kash. Wish I'd got here sooner. Wish I'd helped. Wish I'd helped her too.'

And I'd thrown the closest thing to me – a vase, I think – right at his head, and said, 'Yeah? Well, you didn't!'

It missed, of course. Smashed against the wall on the other side of him. I left him to clean it up. I took one of Mum's secret bottles and went to the park. I hid in the concrete tunnel I used to smoke roll-ups in with Sam and drank it all until I threw it up on my shoes. When Dieter came to fetch me eventually, I hit him with it too. But the bottle didn't smash like the vase had. And it didn't stop Dieter from scooping me up and taking me back. Not even my foul tongue stopped that.

Sometimes – thinking about all this, writing it down – I think that maybe Dieter isn't so bad after all. Sometimes I think it would be OK to live permanently in the city with him. But then I think about his clean-smelling plastic box-house with Cynthia's nail-art equipment in my bedroom there, and I take that thought back.

Us against the world.

Us against men like Dieter.

Us against men who leave.

But you left too, Mum, didn't you?

And at least Dieter didn't make me clean up his mess.

And what a fucking mess you were, Mum. Beautiful at times, sure, and so so SO much fun – back when I was little you were amazing, back when you used to tell me stories and play games for days on end (why couldn't that Mum have stayed around?)

But maybe that was only another part of your madness.

And even if you were so ill … it wasn't my job to clean you up.

Sam said that too.

Maybe I'm starting to see.

Most days I think Mum's black cat wasn't real, was never real. It was just something she made up to mean something else. Maybe her own special metaphor for how it felt when she went into one of her episodes … her *mania.*

117

But then I remember those paw prints – so many that night, leading to the trap – and a part of me wants them to be real. Because if they're not real, if Mum drew them all out so carefully, leading to the trap, did she actually want me to find her like that? Spread out and bleeding and hanging, and…

No!

Mum would've known I'd follow her prints. And I don't think Mum would do that to me. I don't! Even if she was full sick.

That leaves the accident theory. Which goes like this – she set her trap to catch the cat and drew the prints just cos she always did and – *bang!* The Masterpiece went off with her in it. It was modelled on something hundreds of years old, after all – easy to make a mistake.

It's never been said officially – never proved – what really happened. Dieter thinks she meant to kill herself. I think Sam thinks that too.

Either way, whether she did or not, it's still my fault.

It's two more hours since I wrote all that. It's taken me ages to even pick up the pen again.

Nothing's happened in those hours. The cameras still blink. Sam still hasn't come back. I remember lying against him as I drifted to sleep. And then, this morning … gone.

The trees are still noisy. Still hot. There are no sounds of gunshots or trucks.

I could stay here, like this. Maybe no one would find me. I could hunt monkeys when I ran out of food. Could become like a black cat myself – stealthy and never quite seen. Stay here, waiting.

I just curled up for a while, hugging my knees.

Where are the others?

Maybe Sam's found someone – some help – and he's coming back for me.

Maybe they've all been shot.

Without Sam … no one knows where I am.

Without Sam … I don't know where I am.

Who I am.

What.

It's how he looks at me – as if he likes me, even after everything – even after all the shit I've done. As if none of that really matters. He looks at me like I'm here. I exist.

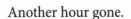

Another hour gone.

The flag is still where we left it in the corner of this hut, the flag we never planted on the top of the hill behind our camp: the final task. I can't stop staring at it.

I could do it. Then I've done everything. No one can say I didn't fulfil my contract. It wouldn't take long. Just to the top of that hill and back, we'd almost done it before.

If it hadn't been for those shots…

And at the top of the hill, I could see down. See where to go. Maybe I'll see where the others went.

See Sam?

I want to see Sam.

Maybe I'll fling this book into the trees if anyone tries to shoot.

This is Dieter's address if anyone finds this:

Dieter Fintry

Flat 33, Thomas Court, New Warehouse Lane, Porton Town, PW5 1GA

I'll write a note for Sam. Leave it on our bed. I'll tell him where I'm going.

If someone finds this book and not me with it, please try to find Sam too.

And look for my bones somewhere. Package them up and send them back to Dieter.

Dieter.

Would he care enough to call the cops? If I do disappear.

Does he suspect anything?

OK...

OK!

I don't believe this – what I'm looking at.

I've been staring at it for ages.

HERE!

I'm almost at the top of the hill with the flag, but I had to stop. Had to record this. Can I draw it? I'll try.

There.

See?

A paw print. Like the ones Mum drew in the dirt the night she died. The prints I followed to find her.

But this one's real.

Least I think it is. Unless Lily and George really are fucking with me.

But I didn't tell them about the prints that night. Told no one. Not even Sam.

I'm tracing my fingers over it, again and again, in between writing these words. It's SO like the prints Mum drew. How did she get it so right?

Four teardrop-shaped toes and then the firmer-indented pad beneath. It's almost as big as my own hand when I lay it flat on top. It's beautiful too. Art work in its own right. No wonder Mum drew them so many times, had them tattooed.

A real print.

There are other prints too, but away from the damper

ground they are so much fainter and harder to see – I think they are going into the trees, and anyway I don't want to follow them. I remember what happened when I followed prints into trees last time.

Where's its owner?

Mum would be so excited if she were here.

If I could write her a postcard:

Dear Mum,

I found the cat. Look, here's a picture I drew of its print. You don't need to keep looking anymore. You can relax, just be healthy. It exists.

I love you, Mum.

I'm sorry too.

Kasha

I've stopped to look around. Can't see any cat, but the undergrowth has gone quieter around me. That's a sign, isn't it, that there's a predator near?

Perhaps *this* is the real way I die, not by gunshot but by cat.

I think I'd rather that death.

I waited for ages and it didn't get me. Nothing came.

Nothing still comes.

All quiet.

Velvet-dark.

Cat-like-dark.

I'm going to keep going to plant the flag. And if this IS still some crazy psychology programme everything will stop then – bright lights will flash. Music will play. Sam will come running back. The others too. A million-dollar cheque handed over.

And it will all be done. I can go home.

But who am I kidding? It's not *The Hunger Games*. It's so much more real than that. But there's nothing else to try.

At the top I'll look down and see where Sam is, then I'll go join him.

These are the hopes I hold.

But first I have to get there.

I'm at the top.

I'm looking down at the view. Right from the top. There is so much green.

There is nothing else.

There is so much else.

Green. Green. Green.

Undergrowth for days.

Nothing but green, tangled trees.

It looks a bit like broccoli.

The programme didn't stop. Not after I planted the flag on the top. There was even a proper metal slot to slip the flag into, like there'd been a flag up there before, like L and G had planned it that way.

There were no flashing lights. Or theme music. No hosts leaping out of the trees to congratulate me.

No Sam.

But there was something.

Definitely something.

When I turned, I finally saw her. Properly this time.

I never heard her arrive. But, then, I guess I wouldn't. I'm not sure anyone would hear a black cat arrive unless she wanted you to.

A real black cat.

Following me, after all.

I don't know how I knew she was a *she*. But I did. I was certain.

And she was beautiful, too. So sleek. *Shining.* I wanted to touch my fingers to her fur, feel how soft she was. I forgot about everything else, even breathing. I just saw her. I breathed her.

She was so close, just the other side of the summit, staring right back with amber-gold eyes. Like tiny fires, those eyes. I could ignite them. I could burn inside them. It would take three, maybe four, strides for her to reach me … to stretch out one of her huge paws and cut me with her own knives. What would it feel like to die from claws? And what would it feel like to climb onto her back and ride her – away from this island and whatever fucked-up thing we'd got ourselves into, back home?

This *wonder-black-cat.*

Most of all, I just wanted to watch. See what she did. The power was hers, after all. What could I do if she did want to strike? I had no weapon, unless you counted the flagpole.

I don't know how long we stayed there – her and me – just watching each other. Was she waiting for me to run? Waiting for an excuse to chase?

My heart was catapulting in my chest the whole time. I'm not sure I'd ever felt so real. So completely *there.* Perhaps because any minute I might not be.

She could decide it.

She took one step towards me, just one. And my heart leapt about a metre inside, felt like it anyway.

I saw again – so clear – the paw print she left in the ground behind her. The same as the last one. The same as the paw prints on Mum's mountain. And again I was thinking – surely not even an artist could draw those prints so accurately, over and over. And, let's face it, Mum was never the world's best artist.

Maybe there *had* been a cat there that night with Mum, maybe it had always been there. Maybe Mum had followed the cat to the trap and was so desperate for me to see the cat too that she caught herself up instead.

It was one theory.

Or maybe … Mum just stepped back, too astonished by the cat's beauty when she finally saw her. Like I'd been just now.

Who knows. Accident, deliberate, caused by a cat… Maybe it doesn't matter why Mum died.

But that's what I was thinking as I was watching her – that black cat – that panther or jaguar or whatever else she might've been. Perhaps what that cat was didn't matter either. It only mattered that she was there, letting me watch her. That she was real. That I was too. That she'd seen me. She took one more step towards me – as if considering what it might be like to taste me – and then turned and merged into the trees.

After she left, I felt like I'd been in a whirlpool. Sweat-soaked. Shaking.

I stumbled back against the stone that had the flag wedged into it. I shut my eyes, then opened them again to see if she'd come back.

But of course not.

I was alone.

It took me a while – a long while – to move again.

And then, something else strange too.

Eventually I went to the edge of the summit and looked down on all the other sides, properly stared at everything below. I was expecting to find the sea, I suppose. The edge of the island. A town.

There was none of that. Only green. Treetops and treetops. An endless sea of those. Like countless heads of broccoli, stretching out. A blanket of vegetables … vegetation. Undergrowth for days. And so many different shades. Sea-green. Pea-green. Shoot-green. Grass-green. It was all there. It wouldn't be possible to describe it all. Couldn't even paint something so vivid as that.

And there were other things, underneath all that … in the undergrowth. Things I couldn't see, but there all the same. Things I could only hear or imagine. The monkeys we'd seen most days. The birds. The black cat, and probably more of her kind, too. Somewhere, out there, was our camp. Lily and George's camp. A rutted track. The others.

Perhaps there were other settlements too, other people.

Escape.

Sam.

Just what else did this undergrowth hide? It was so much bigger, out there, than I'd ever thought. It didn't look like an island. I couldn't see any ocean.

I walked around the entire summit, climbing up trees so that I could see out on all sides even further. There was no sea, not anywhere. No beaches. No cities. There was only the green, the trees.

But there was a different kind of green on one side. Leafy green. Vivid green. A whole big crop of it. I knew that green.

So, that's where the crops were hiding. Perhaps if we'd ever got to planting the flag that day as a group and looked out properly, we might've seen them then. Don't know if seeing them from here would have changed anything though; we probably would've just assumed they were another part of the jungle.

I looked at them for ages, still trying to work them out. After a while, I noticed … there seemed to be movement inside them. Another black cat? People? Just wind, or monkeys?

Where the hell are we?

I'm still watching out.

I should move, I guess. Go back down and wait for Sam. Get away from the black cat before the day gets any longer.

Alone again.

I'd even take Dieter to be up here with me right now.

I almost want him to be.

That's a shock, writing that.

But it's Sam I want here most, to see all this.

I'm going to write about him, to bring him up here with me. Going to put on paper the rest of what we did last night, too. Then I'll go down this hill, and I'll make a plan. I'll wait for him to return and tell him.

Now I know there's no programme end. Maybe no programme at all.

It's all one big fucking lie.

They've just been feeding us drugs and fantasy. God knows what they planned to do next. Somehow, I don't think it was good.

Last night, it didn't take Sam long to convince me to sleep in his bed. He only asked once. I went right in. And his arms folded around me straightaway. My head fitted onto his shoulder like there was a groove made specially.

He kissed my forehead. Squeezed my shoulders. Nothing else.

It didn't feel odd. Or even wrong. It didn't feel like he only wanted one thing, either.

If anything, he wanted me to talk. Just that. Just to be quiet in the dark with only my words.

So I did.

I told him things I'd been holding back for over a year … about that night, and about how strange Mum had got with her art and her illness … I said about the cat. And I talked about Dieter too, about the last few months living in the city with him and Cynthia. How Dieter wanted me to go to some posh school that could give me a better education. Then, quietly, I told Sam how I'd rather stay with him. He'd been surprised at that, hadn't believed me.

'I thought you hated me now,' he'd said. 'Thought you'd never forgive me for taking you away that night, for taking her car...'

And I shook my head and told him it was me I'd hated, not him.

But, still, he didn't believe.

So I leant up on my elbows and kissed him on the mouth. Just. Like. That.

Kissed him hard.

He was so surprised, I felt him breathe out right into me. I swallowed his breath. Then I kissed him again.

He tasted stale and sweet at exactly the same time. I liked it. I didn't want to stop, even when I imagined Mum in that hut with us, looking on.

I made myself think only of Sam. The sensation of being right there, with him, feeling his arms solid around me. Of how much I liked it. Sam didn't just want one thing. Everything we did last night was because of me.

Sam was always more than that one thing. He'd returned with me to our camp, when all the others had walked away.

Although, he did leave – this morning, when I woke, when he wasn't in our bed.

I'm thinking of the note I left him. Hoping he'll see.

I'd lain with Sam all night, talking and touching, getting close. I found all of him. He found me. We didn't do that one thing. And that was OK. With both of us. It was enough just to be

130

quiet and dark, to be under covers together. Enough just to feel him tangled with me, curled up so tight. Like two little mice. Like magnets.

KF 4 SW

Wound up in the undergrowth.

I can hear something. Steps. The cat again?

Coming closer, up the path I'm facing. Perhaps I should grab the flagpole. I've got nothing else to use if I need a weapon. Perhaps I could fling myself off the side, let the canopy of broccoli catch me. There's nowhere to hide up here.

But, no … I know those shoes. Those legs.

That smile.

Sam.

Come and found me, after all.

'Saw your note,' he says.

It's later now, when I'm writing this. But I think it's still important to do this … to say everything that happened next.

We walked down the mountain together, Sam and me. We looped around until we were walking down the other side from where we'd come up, not going back to our camp but heading towards those crops instead. Sam had found them too.

'And something else,' he said. 'Wait and see.'

There was a barbed-wire fence all around those waving plants, but Sam had already found a hole through part of it.

'How?' I asked.

'I followed paw prints,' he said. 'This morning when I couldn't sleep, there were prints in camp. I wondered where they'd lead. It wasn't long before I found the path here.'

'You could've been eaten up,' I said.

'Could've. Didn't see anything that might've made them though.'

He pulled back the barbed wire. Turns out he'd found a path right through the crops. And then, something else – he'd found a road the other side.

But … he'd found my paw prints, too. And that meant, I hadn't just made them up.

'Follow this track long enough and, after the crops, there's a dirt road. After that, it eventually gets you to a tarmac road,' he said. 'I didn't go down that though, because I wanted to get you first.'

He was taking me to see. Tarmac meant town. Or airport runway at least. I remembered it: sticky black melting tarmac, arriving in this place on that rickety old plane.

'Why didn't you leave a note for me?' I said. 'So I didn't think you'd died!'

'I thought you'd sleep for hours, after last night,' he said. 'And I didn't think I'd be gone so long.' He smiled, sheepish. 'And, anyway, I got kind of lost, coming back.' He pointed at the crop field. 'This place is like a maze.'

He was right. The plants were even taller and leafier than they'd looked from the screens, thick and healthy with growth. How had he found any way through?

'Bet there's snakes in there,' I said.

'Probably.' Sam stepped closer when he agreed, but then shrugged. 'It's crazy going through it, I know, but what hasn't been crazy these past few weeks?'

I half-laughed. And the sound felt so loud.

Sam pulled back the wire, made the hole big enough for me to crawl through. I stood up afterwards and held it open for him. The plants swished and whispered, letting us in. If someone made drugs from them, it was hard to believe it – they looked beautiful, bold-green and brimming with vitality.

'What do you think this is?' I said.

Sam shrugged. 'Maybe some sort of native plant. Made into a crop? Must be worth some money, with all the cameras, security… Who knows? Does it matter right now?'

I swallowed as I thought about my next words. 'I don't think we're on an island,' I said. 'Up from the top of the hill, I saw nothing but trees.'

'I've been thinking that too.'

I searched his face, he was serious. 'So … where?'

'God knows.' He hugged me close. 'But we've found our road out at least.'

The crops were taller than our heads as we weaved through. They brushed our arms, made me ticklish. I thought about the cat, maybe hiding there still, watching us. I thought again about snakes. About people waiting with guns. The cameras, watching. There was so much growth it was hard to see our way forward. It felt like the most stupid thing we'd ever done, walking through there, but also the most sensible. Either way, it would kill us or save us.

But we got there. To a dirt path the other side. We followed that until it eventually turned to tarmac. Just like Sam had said it would.

We followed that tarmac for ages. Until the day finally started to get dark. Until I was so thirsty and tired I thought I was hallucinating when we saw the first building.

***

And then…
And then…

It's hard to remember this part. I was pretty out of it. Seems Sam was too.

But…

Two people in that building – that house – sat beside us. They gave us some kind of tea; I remember that. And water, lots of it. There was an old lady with kind, crinkly eyes. She stared and stared at us, shaking her head. She spoke words to an old man that I didn't understand.

'Where are we?' I said. I tried to. My voice had dried up.

She told me to drink. The old man told me to rest. She looked at the bug bites on my legs and tutted. Then she pointed to where we'd come from, and I nodded. She spoke to the old man again. Sam talked to them more than I could right then, though I think he was babbling and I don't think they could understand. We were both half-delirious.

I thought about the others, wondered if they'd found a couple like this too. I hoped so. I tried to ask the old lady if she'd seen them.

And then, sometime after that – I don't know how long – that old couple walked with us to a town with more buildings. And there was food. And there was a phone. And there were so many other people staring and staring, too. Those people pointed to where we'd come from as well, they shook their heads.

'They know,' Sam said. 'They know about those crops. They know they're bad.'

And finally the police came. Not soldiers. Or warring tribes. Not Lily and George. Not the others. I'd thought I was so sick of police after the past year. I'd thought I'd never want to speak to them again.

But I did.

And I called Dieter.

He didn't sound surprised to hear from me. He sounded glad. Pleased, even!

135

'Kasha! I've been waiting for you to call! How's the programme going? You feel any better? We miss you so much! Next year you've got to come with us to...'

So, I guess he'd had no idea then, of everything that was going on. But he would've done soon enough, when we didn't come back, when he never saw me again.

Because later those two policemen sat with us in a small stone building with whitewashed walls and told us what could've happened to us. Gave us an idea of it, anyway.

Seemed that other kids had also disappeared in this country, they said, kids from overseas too. Recently, kids had been documented as arriving into the country and then, after that ... *nothing*. Disappeared. No one knew where they'd gone. They mentioned trafficking. And drug smuggling. They said they'd seen videos of children that were sent to rich men overseas to look at, to pick who they wanted.

But I could see total confusion in their faces as they told us: helplessness. They were glad we'd turned up, but not just because we were safe – we would help them.

'Who've you been with?' they said. 'Where were they going to send you? Which country? Which person?'

'We don't know,' I said. 'But I can tell you about Lily and George, a bit anyway.'

One of the police officers went off to look at the crops we'd told them about, speaking on his mobile phone as he went out the door and asking for other police officers to join him from somewhere. The one officer remaining took more notes

136

about what we said; he said there'd be English police on the phone to us soon, too.

'They've been preying on kids who have nothing else,' Sam said.

'Ones looking for an escape,' I added.

And that, at last, felt true.

'There's a ring we know of,' the policeman told Sam and me. 'We think someone has been grooming kids for this ring, making them carry drugs eventually, brainwashing … your Lily and George …'

It was their theory anyway. The only one they had. They wanted us to help them with it.

And I think it made sense, what they were saying … what I could understand of it.

I thought of the folder on the computer that Pete hadn't managed to get into. *Tribe Members*. What was on it? Addresses? Of where Lily and George were hoping we'd go next? Video clips of each of us? Just what exactly was this footage they were going to send out? I shivered when I thought about where some of those cameras had been positioned in our camp, then shut my eyes and leant my head down against Sam's shoulder.

The police didn't know who the three men were who had arrived in L and G's camp in the van, though they asked us for enough descriptions of them. They showed us tonnes of pictures of people we didn't recognise.

'Just look at the footage that's back in their camp. It's all there,' Sam said eventually, grumpily.

137

They didn't know whether Lily had been killed. Or even, really, who Lily or George were. Or what their exact motivations were, only that they were part of this ring.

They didn't know where Pete, Annie and Nyall had gone either. But they would search right away, they said, on all the major roads and towns: everywhere in the country. They'd send out alerts. They had leads now, they said. We'd have to be on TV, of course, do an interview: make our story known.

So.

Seems we'll be on television, after all.

And that was the other thing. We aren't on an island. Not even close.

We're in a country. Still on the west coast of Africa, but we've been mainland all this time. So Lily and George had lied about that, too. Seems nothing was ever what it'd seemed. No programme. No island.

I have to talk about these things in the police statements – I'm not even sure I'm meant to be writing this stuff here. And I'm not sure I want to write it down anymore, either – I mean, we're safe now. At least I don't have to keep writing this thing in the hope that someone will find it. Find me.

But the cops haven't told us everything yet. Sam thinks they're worried about scaring us. But I just think they haven't put it all together – they're as clueless as us.

And then there was Dieter, still waiting on the other end of the phone line. I remember the shock of feeling something – love? – when I heard him on the other end in that tiny, whitewashed town on the edge of the forest.

He was waiting for me to tell him how his two thousand pounds had been well spent and how I was feeling so much better, and much less guilty about everything, and how I loved him after all, and how – after this successful psychological programme – I now wanted to come and live with him in his box-house with Cynthia's nail art permanently. How I wouldn't be a teenage dirtbag anymore who binge drinks and swears … and maybe some of that was true, and maybe some of it wasn't. But, still…

'Kash?' he'd said down the phone, after it must've been an age since I'd said anything. 'Are you OK over there, really?'

And I'd reached out for Sam's hand and squeezed it before I'd said, 'No. I want to come home, Dad.'

'Why, honey?'

'Something bad's happened here, but I hope it's going to be OK now.'

I told him the truth: all the stuff I'd been hiding from him about the way we'd got on the programme. I even told him how I'd been thinking of escaping, just running away into the undergrowth and never coming back.

And, after a while of talking some more, I'd handed the

phone to the policeman, and I'd said, 'Can you tell my dad where we are? He's going to fly out.'

Sam had smiled. And I'd rested my head down onto his shoulder, and I'd traced paw prints across his skin as we waited for what was next.

And that's where we are now. Waiting.

They've moved us to a bigger town, where we can wait in a hotel, and where lots of police can ask us lots of questions. And those police might even want to read this journal at some point. I'm not sure about that part yet.

That's partly why I'm not writing so much anymore, actually – how much do I want them to know of my story? All that stuff with Sam? With Mum? Maybe some stuff's just for me.

Still, they've let Sam and me share a room. So that's something. It's got a ginormous double bed in it, and air conditioning, and a mini-bar filled with coke and orange juice and tiny bottles of whisky. (Least, it was filled with that!)

Oh, and they've found Annie and Nyall, on the side of one of the major roads trying to hitch out of there. So that's something too. We haven't seen them yet, but they're bringing them back to this hotel. I wonder if they've worked out we're on the mainland too.

If I look out of the window, I can see cameras and reporters gathering near the hotel's entrance below us. Waiting for us. So we're going to be famous after all. If I gave a couple of interviews to the right sort of people, perhaps I'd even get some money – pay Dieter back that way, at least. I'll tell Annie to do that too, when she arrives. She'd make great telly with that haunted baby bird look she's got.

They haven't found Pete yet, though they say they've got a lead on him. Even after him being such a dick, I hope he's not dead, or trafficked, or carrying drugs up his bum. I hope he's not with Lily and George, either.

One of the policemen actually told me where Pete lives, back in England – it's not all that far from where Dieter lives in the city.

'Were the two of you connected before the programme?' the policeman asked.

'You kidding?' I laughed at him. 'If I saw a guy like Pete on the street I'd run him over.'

The policeman had looked at me funny then, and I'd laughed again, but ... who knows, if it turns out he's not dead or trafficked, and we ever end up back there at the same time, I might look him up. I know Sam's said he wants to see him again anyway.

But, until then, Sam and me just get to curl up in this bed. For hours and hours. And there's not even one bedbug. And it's cool, cool, COOL... Literally. The first time I haven't sweated for weeks.

In a day or so Sam's mum, and my dad, will find us. And then, sometime after that, we'll go home.

All of us. Together.

And that doesn't seem so dark anymore.

Until the therapy begins again of course. The talking. The endless telling of everything that happened. But I'll do these things at home, in Dieter's house in the city: no more dream solutions of escape to tropical paradise. Now it's just hard work, I know that. And it will be hard, thinking of Mum, remembering her, trying to pick out what was true about her … what was good. I'm getting tense just thinking about it, and about all the decisions I'm going to have to make when I'm back, too – where to live, what to do next, who I'm going to be…

SHIT!

But until then…

Sam's looking at me from the side of his eyes and he's smiling in that way that makes his cheeks go red and gorgeous. He's just jumped onto our ginormous double bed, patted the space beside him for me. He's raising his eyebrows.

I'm going to join him. Course I am. Can't resist any longer. Sam is so flipping hot when he's acting like a dork (not that I'd ever tell him that).

And he's my hot.

I like that.

I like him.

So fucking much.

Did I really just write that in here? There's NO WAY the police are seeing this book now.

So, I'm signing off.

Laters…

The Twins of Blackfin

A Blackfin Sky novella

Kat Ellis

Chapter One

Lying on the grass next to a freshly covered grave, Margaret 'Bo' Peeps ignored the haunted weathervane that watched her from the school roof all the way across town. Ignoring it was for the best. Silas – whose spirit was supposed to inhabit the weathervane – was rumoured to have been an ill-tempered but harmless sort of fellow, and so his glaring presence was generally ignored.

Bo was not surprised by the existence of things like haunted weathervanes. She wasn't fazed by doors that would only open when they were in the right mood. Or birds that never landed, cats that seemed to read your thoughts, or the two-headed fish that occasionally washed up on the Blackfin shoreline. No, having grown up in Blackfin, Bo was used to weirdness. None of that weirdness had prepared her for the devastating reality of her best friend dying, though.

It had been a month since Skylar Rousseau had drowned. A month since Sky had fallen from Blackfin pier on the night of her sixteenth birthday. An accident, everyone said. A terrible shame, but just *one of those things.* But of all the inexplicable things Bo had seen happen in this town, Sky dying was something she simply could not wrap her head around.

Two weeks earlier Bo had stood in almost the exact same spot she now lay on as they lowered her best friend's coffin into the ground. Stood there, dry-eyed, trying to make herself believe that Sky was inside that box. It hadn't seemed possible. Hadn't seemed real that Bo would never see her friend again.

Perhaps that was why she had taken to passing through the cemetery's iron gates each night to lie on the grass next to Sky's mounded grave, talking to her dead friend as she would have had Sky still been alive.

Bo reached down and pulled a squashed packet of cigarettes from her pocket. She'd only started smoking the odd one to annoy her mother. Then, somehow, it had become a habit. She knew it was vile, and her friends hated it.

'Tell you what,' Bo said to Sky's headstone, 'if you're here, give me a sign and I'll quit right now. I swear, this'll be my last smoke. Ever.'

She waited. Nothing happened. The cemetery was quiet … *too* quiet.

'Fine. Give me the silent treatment. I'll quit, okay? I just need a bit of time to … to stop feeling like utter crap.' Bo pursed her lips to stop the quiver she could feel threatening to break loose. 'Honestly, if you really *had* to go and snuff it, you could've waited until after Cam's birthday.' Cam Vega had only moved to Blackfin two years earlier, but had quickly become close friends with both Bo and Sky. With Sky gone, their trio had been blown apart, leaving Bo and Cam to figure out their new Sky-less dynamic. 'Her birthday party was the most miserable one I've ever been to, and I was there when Bridget's pet rabbit choked to death on a bit of wrapping paper, so that's saying something.'

Bo yawned, feeling the late hour creeping up on her.

'Cam cried so much when she was blowing out the candles she made the cake taste salty. Honestly, it was disgusting. Though I suppose if we're ranking crappy birthdays, yours will always be the winner, won't it? Or maybe all birthdays are cursed now.'

Bo's cigarette smoke darkened briefly to match her mood, though only the keenest of eyes would have noticed. She ground the cigarette out until it was no more than a twisted stub, then stuffed it back into the packet. It really was vile.

In the distance, a clock began striking the hour – or striking *an* hour, at least, as it never chimed the correct time. Bo had no idea where the clock actually was. The chimes sounded like a church bell more than anything, though Bo couldn't see how that was possible when there was no church in Blackfin, nor had there ever been one as far as she knew. Whenever the unseen clock rang out across the town, its residents might exchange a glance and shrug, but as its chiming caused no particular inconvenience, it was left to continue without a lot of thought. Now though, its sound caused Bo to glance at her watch.

Midnight.

She scrambled to her feet. As understanding as Bo's mother had been lately when it came to her eldest child's need to visit the cemetery, she'd become very jumpy since

149

Sky's death. All the parents in Blackfin had. If one beloved teenage girl could be taken from the town without warning, then why not another?

'Bad things always come in threes,' Bo's mother often said. This was generally followed by three sneezes or some such that would allow her to narrow her eyes meaningfully in Bo's direction.

'Better shoot off,' Bo said, patting Sky's headstone. 'Do you want to pick tonight's song, or shall I?' She fished Sky's iPod from her pocket and wiped away the sticky fingerprints left on it by her twin younger brothers. Sky had left it at Bo's house only a few weeks ago, though it seemed like a lifetime had passed since then.

Bo knew she should return the iPod to Sky's parents, and she would ... just not yet. Gui and Lily Rousseau were both rather impressive people – Gui in stature, and Lily in temper – and grieving for their daughter hadn't exactly made them *more* approachable. Besides, Bo liked listening to her best friend's music. It made it easier to pretend Sky was still around, in a way.

'Fine, you can choose,' Bo said. 'But you'd better not pick something crap.' She put the earbuds in her ears and set it to play a random track. If Sky was there in any ghostly form, then surely she would steer the iPod to play something meaningful. Sky's favourite song, maybe, or something with a message for Bo hidden in the lyrics?

The theme song from *Ghostbusters* blared through the earbuds, startling Bo so badly she yelped.

Very funny. Still, she didn't kill the music, only turned the volume down a little. Bo made her way rather unhurriedly to the cemetery gate, stepping through it just as the clock chimes ended. Then she stopped.

Trees lined the road from the cemetery into town. It wound uphill like a silver-scaled snake, lit only by stars. Yet Bo could clearly make out the shapes of four shambling figures making their way down the hill toward her. None of the four carried a light of any kind, and their meandering steps made them look as though they were drunk, or sleepwalking.

Bo sighed. If the zombie apocalypse was starting now, *after* she'd finished all her maths homework, she was going to be thoroughly annoyed.

Keeping to the treeline so she could observe without being seen herself, Bo made her way up the road toward the figures. As she neared them, the starlight filled in their features enough for her to see who they were: Randy, Felix, Jordy, and Colby Swiveller. The sight of the brothers was enough to make Bo want to turn and walk in the opposite direction. The elder two – Randy and Felix, though Bo could never remember which one was the eldest – were also in Bo's year at school. They were the sort of boys who liked to burn ants under a magnifying glass, and would purposely swerve toward a cat crossing the road in front of their car. But as much as Bo couldn't stand the Swivellers, she was also not inclined to walk the longer way back to her house. So she waited, hidden in the dark cover of the trees, for them to pass.

Not one of the boys glanced her way as they shuffled by. They didn't even look at one another. Their dark eyes stared glassily into the distance, and none of them spoke. What were they doing out here on this road in the middle of the night? Where were they going? Had they been huffing aerosols or something? This was strange behaviour, even for the Swivellers.

Bo watched the brothers continue their silent, shambling journey along the road. They didn't stop at the cemetery gates, but continued until she lost sight of them among the shadows and trees.

Weirdos, Bo thought, and resumed her uphill trudge toward home.

The seat next to Bo in registration was empty. It had been empty since the start of the new term ten days earlier. Everybody seemed to feel the vacuum of Sky's absence, and their eyes were drawn to that empty chair. Bo caught Felix Swiveller eyeing the seat, his rubbery lips tilted up at the corners.

'You can sod right off if you think you're sitting there,' Bo said, not quietly enough to avoid Mr Hiatt's notice, though he said nothing.

Felix turned to his brother next to him rather than answering Bo directly. 'Do you think there's still tiny little bits of her on that chair? Bits of skin and hair and that?'

Randy's eyes gleamed. 'I bet there is.'

Bo sighed aggressively at them. 'Speaking of being absolute creeps, why were you lurking about near the cemetery last night?' It might have been a little hypocritical, she conceded, to accuse the brothers of lurking when she herself had been hanging around the cemetery, but she saw no reason to tell them that. The two stared at her blankly. 'I saw you, so don't even bother to deny it.'

'What's she on about, Ran?' Felix asked his brother. Randy shrugged.

'Maybe she's been dreaming about us.' He leered at Felix. 'Sex dreams.'

'Ha,' Bo intoned flatly. 'You're hilarious.'

Cam leant over to tug at her sleeve. 'Ignore them,' she whispered. 'They're fungus.'

Bo threw a final vicious glance in the boys' direction. 'They *are* fungus.'

The brothers had turned back around in their seats, heads together as they no doubt shared more unsavoury speculations about the state of the furniture. Bo couldn't hear them, but she also couldn't shake the needling feeling settling over her. It itched at her skin like a hair jumper.

Why had the Swivellers behaved like they had no idea what she was talking about? They had definitely been outside the cemetery last night; Bo had no doubt about that. But Randy and Felix were acting like she was speaking another language.

Bo shook it off. It was probably just Swiveller weirdness,

or one of those odd things that happened in Blackfin from time to time. No rhyme, no reason. And Bo had better things to do than wonder about the Swivellers' night-time habits. Like hurrying to maths before she got another detention.

Chapter Two

Had Mrs Brady's snoring gotten any louder, Bo would quite happily have taken a pillow to her face. It wasn't a nice thought, but a fairly reasonable one, Bo decided, as the elderly babysitter's snoring was loud enough for Bo to hear it all the way upstairs.

Mrs Brady babysat the twins whenever Bo's mother was at work. Mai Peeps worked three nights a week in a nightclub over an hour's drive away, and with Bo's father currently serving time at Her Majesty's leisure, that left looking after the howlers – as Bo's twin six-year-old brothers were affectionately known – either to Bo, or Mrs Brady from next door. And lately, since Sky's death … well, Mai hadn't wanted to add to her daughter's stresses.

So Mrs Brady generously stepped in, at least insofar as she came over to eat all the custard creams and fall asleep in front of the Peeps family TV. This would, in theory, allow Bo to do her homework and whatever else she liked in peace. In reality, Bo had spent the earlier part of the evening adjudicating an hour-long water fight between Levi and Scout in the family bathroom, and had then been called upon to tell them four (the bartered number) bedtime stories. Each story was an original work, all about the family of bogeys attached to the underside of Scout's bedframe.

Once the twins were asleep, along with Mrs Brady, Bo lay on her bed and tried to read the new graphic novel she'd picked up from the library. Mrs Brady's clogged sinuses were making it seriously hard to focus, though.

Bo turned up the volume on Sky's iPod, hoping to find a balance between drowning out the snoring and permanently damaging her eardrums. It didn't work. So she put on the pair of noise-cancelling ear defenders she usually reserved for when the howlers were at their most vocal. That helped, but she could still hear a faint rumbling gurgle underpinning the song she was listening to. At a loss for what else to do, she grabbed her dad's old fleece-lined deerstalker cap from the bedside table and shoved that on over the whole lot. That was better, admittedly, even if she was certain she must look like a right tool lying in bed wearing multiple layers of headgear.

Why didn't Mrs Brady just go home? Both the howlers had been in bed for hours, and Bo certainly didn't need babysitting herself. She flung back the bedcovers and stomped downstairs.

Bo found the old woman exactly as she had expected to find her: lying at full tilt on the recliner in front of the TV. Here the snoring was so loud, she could barely hear the music blasting directly into her ears.

Bo shook Mrs Brady gently. Despite any earlier smothering-related thoughts she might have had, Bo didn't actually want to give the woman a coronary by startling her. That wouldn't be very neighbourly, after all.

Mrs Brady didn't stir. Bo shook her again, just a tad more firmly. But the woman kept right on snoring like a clapped-out diesel engine.

Could she have had a stroke or something? Did people still snore if they'd had a stroke? Bo had no idea, but was debating the merits of calling an ambulance when she caught a flicker of movement in her peripheral vision.

Levi and Scout stood at the top of the staircase, wearing matching *Minions* onesies. Bo made a shooing gesture, hoping they would flee back to bed before noticing the unwakeable babysitter in the living room. No such luck.

The twins trailed downstairs, through the living room, and into the kitchen.

'Hey...' Bo went to pull out her earbuds, forgetting for a moment they were nestled beneath the ear defenders and hat, and almost snapped the cord.

FFS.

Giving up on her tangle of head accessories, Bo strode to the kitchen doorway with every intention of chasing the little buggers out of the biscuit tin, or wherever their sticky little fingers had taken them. But the howlers were nowhere to be seen. The back door stood wide open, though. Pausing only to slip on her trainers, Bo hurried out after them.

The garden was small but well-tended, and the starlight was enough to show that Bo's brothers weren't hiding among the rosebushes. Where had they gone? There wasn't a shed, or any other likely spot for two six-year-olds to conceal themselves. Bo ran along the path to the gate leading onto the road. It was open.

Levi and Scout knew they weren't allowed out at night, and never onto the street without an adult. What on earth were they playing at?

Bo shivered at the gate, wishing she'd grabbed her jacket from the hook by the door. It was only September, but winter liked Blackfin, and had a habit of calling early.

She hadn't gone more than a few steps when she caught sight of them on the road ahead of her. Bo jogged to catch up, expecting her brothers to turn at the sound of her footsteps, yet they kept walking without a glance in her direction.

What the hell is going on here?

Bo rounded in front of them, blocking the way. Still, the twins stared straight ahead. The only sign they gave that they'd noticed her at all was the slight swerve as they walked around her.

'Hey! Levi, Scout – wait!'

Bo fumbled with her iPod, trying to switch it off so she could give her brothers the thorough bollocking they deserved. But as she glanced up, she froze. There were other figures meandering along the street up ahead. At least a dozen of them, some small like the twins, and some as tall as Bo. Beyond them all a strange van idled at the side of the road.

Her fingers found the pause button on the iPod. The music

ended abruptly, and Bo yanked off her hat and ear defenders in one go.

'Levi! Scout! Come back...'

Someone was speaking. Another voice. It was so faint, she almost missed it at first.

'...find me...' the voice said. Bo couldn't see who had spoken, or even tell where the voice had come from.

'What...?' Bo began, but forgot what she had been about to ask. Her head was so woozy. What had she come outside for again? 'I...' Her voice trailed off. The bundle of hat and ear defenders fell from her hand. She blinked slowly: once, twice.

And then everything simply ... stopped.

———

Bo, never much of a morning person, was nevertheless awake before sunrise. She'd woken up wrapped in her duvet, with no memory of how she had come to be there, just some vague after-images of a dream about a girl with raven-dark hair, running through a forest ... all very strange and unsettling, Bo thought. The kind of thing it was best not to dwell on in this town.

She might have thought that chasing her brothers across town had been just another part of the dream, except for the fact that when she threw back her covers, she was still wearing her grubby trainers.

Bo clearly remembered running after the howlers in her

pyjamas, then turning off Sky's iPod to yell at them, and then
… nothing. Everything after that moment was a blank.

Oh God … the howlers!

Bo raced to Levi and Scout's room, flung open the door,
and stopped short. Both boys were tucked safely in their beds,
snoring softly. Bo took a deep breath, slumping against the
doorframe as she let it out. The twins were fine — they were
safe. That settled, Bo stomped across the room and shook
them both roughly awake.

'Oi! Don't come that with me,' Bo snapped as both twins
immediately played dead. 'Where did you two wander off to
last night?'

On cue, each twin peeled open his left eye just enough to
squint at her. 'What?' they said at the same time. Bo rolled
her eyes; she hated it when they pulled this twin stuff.

'I saw you sneak out after Mrs Brady went to sleep,' Bo
insisted, hands on her hips in a no-messing stance. 'Where
did you go?'

'We didn't go nowhere,' Scout said. 'Did we, Leev?'

'No,' the other confirmed, solemnly shaking his head.

Bo's little brothers could occasionally muster a convincing
lie, but under the pressure of silent scrutiny, one or the other
would inevitably spill the beans. She glared at them and
waited. And waited.

'We isn't lying,' Scout said at last. 'Did you have a bad
dream, Bobo?'

His worried tone chipped away at Bo's certainty. Was it
possible she had simply dreamed the whole thing after all?

160

Maybe *she* was the one who had sleepwalked downstairs, put on her trainers, and then wandered back to her bed in some peculiar trance state. That could happen, right? Sneaking out at night to visit Sky's grave had become a habit. Maybe her feet hadn't got the message that she was staying home last night.

'Maybe,' Bo murmured, then felt the twins staring at her. 'And stop calling me Bobo, you little rats. I'm not a bloody clown.'

'Bobo!' They both shouted in unison. 'Bobo! Bobo!'

'Right!'

Levi and Scout scattered like ants as Bo chased them around the room, walloping them with pillows while they squealed. At least, until their mother appeared in the doorway, looking distinctly unamused. The three siblings quietly slunk down to breakfast, pillow wars and night-time wanderings forgotten for the moment.

Bo tried speaking to her mother about the previous night's events over breakfast. But her mother was so exhausted after her late shift that she barely listened to what Bo was saying.

'You're not allowed out after nine on a school night,' her mother mumbled around a piece of toast.

'I'm not asking if I can go out. I was talking about the howlers...'

'*Margaret Peeps*. Don't make me ground you. And stop calling your little brothers that.'

Bo stewed all through her morning lessons. So much so that she hardly did more than grunt when her physics teacher praised Bo's assignment, and she didn't even notice when the lunch bell rang until Cam appeared in the classroom doorway looking baffled, her tangled halo of curls only adding to the effect.

'Did you get a detention or something?' Cam asked.

Bo shook her head. 'I was just thinking.'

Cam's naturally cheery expression dimmed a little, and she came to sit next to Bo. 'About Sky?'

'No,' Bo said, a little too sharply. 'Sorry. Didn't mean to snap.' Cam had lost her best friend, too. 'No, it's … something else.'

Cam reached out and took Bo's hand, threading their fingers together. If it had been anybody else, Bo would have shrugged them off; she categorically was *not* a hand-holder. But neither was Cam, and that made it okay, somehow.

'Anything I can help with?' Cam said.

Bo considered that. Maybe if she told Cam what she had seen, Cam would be able to make sense of it all – point out some glaringly obvious explanation that Bo had missed. But as she searched for the right words to sum up her encounter with the Swivellers outside the cemetery, and her twin brothers' zombie-like expedition, and the black spot where her memory shorted out, Bo realised the whole thing sounded laughable. If their roles were reversed, and Cam told Bo she'd seen people wandering around town late at night in some kind of trance, Bo would think Cam had popped

162

something a little stronger than her usual headache pills before going to bed. So instead she went for a soft approach.

'Cam, have you noticed kids wandering around town late at night?'

'No. Why?'

'You didn't see or hear anything weird outside last night, or the night before?'

'Nope. I was spark out by ten both nights after taking my meds. God, I can't wait to get rid of these braces.' Cam's braces were the bane of her existence, and the cause of her frequent headaches. 'Do you want me to ask Sean? I've heard him leaving Aunt Holly's pretty late some nights recently. I think he goes out walking. You know, to clear his head and stuff.'

Sean was Cam's older brother. There were barely eleven months between them though, which meant he, Cam, Bo, and Sky were all in the same school year. *Had* been in the same school year, Bo corrected herself, then felt irrationally guilty for it.

Sean had taken Sky's death particularly hard. Bo found it difficult to know what to say to him at school these days, even though she was probably the one person who truly understood how he felt. Bo stubbed that thought out, and shook her head.

'Or I can ask Aunt Holly?' Cam offered.

Cam's aunt was a police officer. In fact, she was the only police officer who lived in Blackfin, and as such was someone Bo tried to avoid as much as possible.

'Don't worry about it. I'll talk to Sean.'

163

While Sean had never been the prickling energy storm that Cam was, talking to him now was like trying to engage a door jamb. Bo spotted him as he sloped out of the school gates, not even bothering to swerve beyond the reach of the Penny Well, which everyone knew would take the coins from your pockets if you passed too close … yet another Blackfin phenomenon which nobody seemed overly inclined to question. Bo herself always swerved vigorously away from it; not only because she resented the theft of her loose change, but because she held a deep-rooted suspicion that the Penny Well might – due to some change of the wind, or simply a shift in its mood – start plucking entire *people* from the vicinity and spiriting them down into its dark interior.

Bo shuddered at that thought. She was not overly fond of narrow spaces, wet or otherwise. That un-fondness had increased to near phobic levels since the day Sky had been buried; imagining her stuck down there in a wooden box made Bo's chest tighten in quiet panic.

Scowling, she forced her thoughts back to what she had seen the previous night. Not coffins, or being buried under six feet of earth. Definitely not that.

'Sean, hang on a sec.'

Bo strode over to him, not quite stirred to run.

Sean was always somewhat dishevelled, and not entirely by accident in Bo's opinion. From his fitted faux-grandad cardigans to his artful bedhead, Sean was never quite convincingly rumpled. Today, though, Sean looked like landfill that had been picked over by a flock of angry seagulls.

'Hey, Bo,' Sean said. Bo might have been insulted by his bored tone if she didn't know what lay beneath it. It was Sky, of course. As far as Bo was concerned, Sean's feelings for Sky had always been obvious, though Sky herself had never seemed to notice.

Now she never would.

'Cam says you've been going out walking late at night,' Bo said, cutting to the chase. 'Have you seen anyone else wandering around town? Like groups of kids?'

'Uh … no. I mean, not that I've noticed. Why?'

'Or have you had any weird episodes, like where you're outside and then suddenly you're back at home, with no idea how you got there?'

Sean's gaze sharpened. 'I don't think so, but I haven't exactly been too clear-headed lately. What's going on?'

'I'm not sure,' Bo sighed. 'Maybe it's nothing.'

Why was she even bothering to try and solve this mystery? This was Blackfin. Weird was the norm in this freak show of a town.

'But … wait, I did see something strange when I was out last night, or maybe it was the night before. You know that new mechanic Gui has working for him?'

'Jared? I've met him, yeah.' Bo hadn't thought much about him except that he was excessively pierced. She had counted

165

five studs and hoops in his face alone, which surely had to be a hazard when working with machinery.

'Well, I saw him driving along Provencher Street, really late, and I thought at first he'd been to the garage, like maybe he'd left something there and had to go and pick it up... Anyway. I saw him a few times while I was out walking, like he was driving in circles or something. Is that the kind of weird you mean?'

Bo was about to say no, when something he'd said snagged on a fragment of memory. Last night, right before she'd heard that strange voice and spaced out, hadn't she seen a van parked down the street?

'What kind of van does he drive?'

'A Volkswagen camper,' Sean said. 'Why? What does that mean?'

It meant that Bo would be keeping an eye on the young mechanic, but she didn't say that to Sean. 'I wonder what he was doing.'

Sean shrugged. 'Just driving. It didn't seem like he was heading anywhere in particular. But I only saw him for a minute and then I realised it was getting late, so I...'

Sean's face scrunched up in confusion.

'You don't remember going home, do you?' Bo said.

'Hang on ... I heard the clock chiming, I thought I should go home, and then I ... then it was morning, and Aunt Holly was knocking on my door and saying it was time to get up. I guess I was kind of distracted.' Sean frowned down at his Converse like they might be able to fill in the blanks for him.

'Do you remember hearing a voice?' Bo asked. She thought she'd heard a voice right before her memory became a black hole. But it had seemed to come from nowhere, and had been so dreamlike Bo couldn't say whether she had really heard it, or if it was just some strange memory fragment that had gotten mixed up with her dreams.

Ugh. She hated this feeling of fuzzy-headedness.

'A voice? What...?'

'Forget it, it's nothing. Catch you later.' Bo turned to head toward her own house.

'Bo, hang on. What's going on? Bo?'

But Bo walked on, pretending she hadn't heard.

Chapter Three

Bo's efforts to track Jared down at the garage hit a gigantic, Gui-shaped brick wall. Heading over there on her way home, Bo tried to keep a brave face on when she saw Sky's father, but when he hugged her and invited her to stay for a cup of hot chocolate – which was always Sky's drink of choice – they'd both ended up in a mess of tears and snot. Only after they'd gone through the better part of a box of tissues did Bo get around to asking about Jared. She learned that he'd left work early that day, and Bo couldn't figure out how to ask where Jared lived without arousing Mr Rousseau's suspicion. The last thing she wanted was for him to think she was stalking his apprentice.

It was strange, though, that Bo had no idea whether Jared lived in Blackfin or drove all the way from the next town every day for work – no small thing, with the imposing Lychgate Mountains standing between Blackfin and neighbouring Camberley. Blackfin wasn't a big town, either, so it was even more odd that Bo hadn't already learned this about Jared through the grapevine.

As Bo sat in her room that night, peering out over the town through the telescope her father had *acquired* for her when she first expressed an interest in astronomy, she caught sight of him. Or of his van, at least.

It was parked just along the road from the Peeps' house, the lights off and dark within.

'Let's see what you're up to, then.'

Bo threw on a cardigan over her pyjamas and hurried out of her room. It was approaching midnight, and Bo's mum and little brothers had gone to bed long ago, so she tiptoed quietly downstairs and out through the back door without being seen. She was out of the gate and halfway to the van when she heard a sound that stopped her in her tracks: the never-seen Blackfin clock merrily chiming an hour.

She had heard the clock last night, hadn't she? Bo had no sooner finished the thought than the chimes fell silent, and an eerie voice took their place.

'Find me, Bruno ... find the east door ... I'm all alone in the dark...'

'Oh, balls,' Bo muttered, her head swimming. Then she remembered no more.

Bo sat doodling in the margins of her physics notes at lunch the next day and listening to a Harry Styles medley (Sean really had a lot to answer for when it came to Sky's playlists) as she went over what she remembered of the previous night. It had happened just like the night before: the sound of the clock, and a girl's plaintive voice, and then ... blackness. She'd woken up in her bed just before 2am with no sign that anything was amiss, other than that she was wearing a thick cardigan over her pyjamas and her mum's gardening shoes. That, and a stiffness in her muscles that told Bo she had, without her permission, performed some kind of … *exercise*.

But in that disorienting darkness, she had seen flashes of something else. Something between a dream and a memory. A teenage girl with black hair … a voice that was so unusual and compelling, Bo wanted to follow it into the woods … and a boy. A boy? Yes! There had been a black-haired boy, as well. The boy and the girl were so similar, they had to be siblings. Perhaps even twins. They were both fine-featured and slender, like a painting Bo had once seen of wood elves.

'You needn't be quiet on their account,' the girl had said to him, laughing as she gestured to all the children following them. She had a faint accent, though Bo couldn't place it. 'They *want* to hear you.'

'A trick!' One of the children shouted. 'Make him show us a trick!'

Bo, or dream-Bo, felt a rush of excitement at the prospect, even though she had no idea what kind of trick the child was asking to see.

The black-haired girl nodded. 'My brother's talents are even greater than mine. I can make all the little creatures dance, but he can move mountains. Go on, Bruno, show them.'

But the boy had simply smiled and shaken his head.

And then another figure – a man, dressed all in black and

shouting at the girl, 'Get out of here, you devil!' – and the girl laughing at him as he tried to swat away the flies she made buzz around his ears just by singing to them… And then darkness, and weeping, and a terrible, choking sadness that still lingered in Bo's chest even as the dream faded.

Bo sighed over her doodling. Then as she looked at the pencil marks she had made, she realised she'd been doodling the same thing, over and over: a clock face, the hands pointing to midnight.

It had been midnight when Bo first spotted the Swivellers outside the cemetery, hadn't it? And right before she'd zoned out while chasing her little brothers through the streets, hadn't she heard the clock chiming across town then, too? Although the clock itself wasn't much help in telling the hour, it was definitely after eleven because she'd had a text from her mum at quarter past. And last night… Sean, too, had said something about hearing a clock chiming right before he blanked out. But Bo had been back in her bed by 2am last night, feeling as clear-headed as one could be at that sort of hour.

If something really was going on in Blackfin, it only seemed to happen during a short window of time.

Hmm. Bo could work with that. It was something she could test. She turned to a clean sheet of her notebook and began listing all the details that seemed to overlap, or might be important.

– *Midnight – in at least 3 instances. Back to normal by 2am. Time important?*

– All kids – little ones & teens. Significant?

– The voice – part of the dream? Or somehow to blame
for blackouts?

Bo hesitated before writing her next point, chewing thoughtfully on her pen. When she'd seen the Swivellers outside the cemetery, *she* hadn't been affected by whatever was making them go spacey. She'd watched the Swivellers shambling around, and hadn't experienced any kind of blackout herself. The second and third times, she had. So, what had been different?

The track on the iPod changed, now playing a song called *Sign of the Times*.

'Helpful, Sky. Really helpful.'

Bo switched the iPod off, but as she did so she realised what she'd been missing: with the Swivellers outside the cemetery, she'd been listening to Sky's iPod. The second time, though, Bo had taken her headphones off to yell at her brothers. The third time she hadn't been wearing them at all. And those last two times were when she'd heard the voice.

So … if she couldn't hear the voice, then it wouldn't affect her?

'Well, that's another thing I can put to the test,' Bo muttered.

'What, we've got a test? Oh God, I haven't even studied!'

Cam's lunch tray clattered onto the table in front of Bo, sending her yoghurt pot rolling across the table. Bo watched her friend scrabbling to dig her physics notes out of her schoolbag.

172

'Not a physics test,' Bo said. 'I was talking about something else.'

Cam glanced up from flipping through her notebook. 'Are you sure?'

'Quite sure.'

'Quite as in very, or just a bit?'

'Very,' Bo said. Cam sagged back in her chair.

'Oh, thank *God*. What were you muttering about, anyway? Not more weird late-night shenanigans?'

Cam had started repacking her books into her bag, but stopped as something fell out of the back of a notepad. It landed on her lunch tray. Bo recognised the handwriting on the note immediately; it was Sky's.

Coming to the beach bonfire tonight? I've got marshmallows we can burn. xx

That beach bonfire had taken place a few weeks before Sky's birthday. All three girls had gotten a little drunk on a bottle of strawberry liqueur Bo had pilfered from her mum, and their hotdogs had ended up as cinders. It had been a fun night.

When Bo looked up, she saw Cam's eyes were welling with tears. Bo quietly slid the napkin from her lunch tray over to Cam, who took it with a watery smile.

'Nothing is the same without her, is it?' Bo said. Cam laughed and shook her head, still dabbing at her eyes.

'Sky would've hated to see us moping, wouldn't she?' she said, too brightly. 'So, tell me, did you figure out what was happening with all the kids wandering around the other night?'

Bo hesitated a moment, torn between wanting to share her worry with Cam, and not wanting to load any more onto her friend's plate. Finally, she waved her hand dismissively. 'Nah, it was probably just some random Blackfin weirdness, like always. And we know better than to pull on those threads, don't we?'

Jared was alone at the garage when Bo made her way over there after school. She hovered in the doorway, not quite sure how to get his attention when he was mostly obscured beneath a Ford Focus, with the radio blaring from the back office. In the end, she opted for nudging his leg with her boot. There followed a thud and a yelp as he whacked some part of himself against the car's undercarriage, then Jared slid out from beneath the car. His piercings glinted in the light, a smear of oil across his forehead giving him an unfortunate monobrow. It furrowed in confusion when he saw Bo standing over him.

'Uh … can I help you?' he said, and wiped his hands on the front of his overalls before clambering to his feet. He really was rather tall.

'You can,' Bo said, keeping her tone business-like. 'I saw your van near my house last night, and before that in the street a couple of nights ago. What were you doing there?'

Jared blinked. 'Aren't you… weren't you friends with Gui's daughter, Sky?'

He hadn't been living in Blackfin before Sky died, so he'd never seen her with Bo.

'Yes,' Bo said. 'But that doesn't answer my question.'

'Why are you asking about my van?' His tone was wary now, as though he was talking to the police instead of a sixteen-year-old schoolgirl. Bo rolled her eyes.

'Look, I'm not trying to get you in trouble or anything. I mean, do I look like a grass?' He narrowed his eyes in appraisal, but Bo didn't wait to hear his reply. 'Of course not. I just need to know why you were there.'

Jared laughed. 'Okay. Which street was I parked on?'

Bo gestured through the open door, pointing along the road to the exact spot where his camper van had stood idling right before the first time she experienced a blackout.

'A couple of nights ago, you say?' Jared looked to be considering the question, but Bo got the distinct impression he knew perfectly well where he had been, and what he had been doing there. No, he was considering *her*. Eventually, he sighed. 'Look, I haven't exactly got a place to stay right now, so I'm kind of living out of my van. And I know people around here won't want me parked outside their house or sleeping in their driveway or whatever, so I move the van late at night, park up, sleep, and move on at first light so nobody will see me while they're out walking their dogs early bells. Okay?'

Bo chewed this over. 'You were just … sleeping?'

Jared shrugged.

So you had nothing to do with the whole town sleepwalking?

175

You weren't sitting in your van and working them all like some freaky puppet master?

Ha. She couldn't exactly ask him *that,* could she? So instead she said, 'You haven't noticed people walking through town late at night, and acting all weird?'

Jared shook his head slowly. 'I can honestly say I have not. Is this one of those things that just *happens* around here?'

'Probably,' Bo admitted, grudgingly impressed that Jared had picked up on the town's quirkiness already. 'One other thing, though: when I saw your van, I'm sure the engine was running. You wouldn't leave it running while you were asleep, would you?'

Jared shook his head. 'I must've been awake then – probably reading or something. I sometimes leave the engine on for a bit if it's cold and I want to run the heaters.'

'And you didn't hear anything out of the ordinary? Like a strange voice, maybe?'

He smothered a grin. 'If you're hearing voices, you should be talking to a doctor, not a mechanic.'

'Ha,' Bo said, flatly.

So Jared had been awake, and unaffected by the peculiar voice she'd heard. Unless he'd gone into the same comatose state Mrs Brady had? And where had all the other adults in Blackfin been while their children were out wandering the streets?

Hmm.

Could it just be teens and younger kids who heard the command to go night-walking? Did everyone older just go

176

into a blank-stare state? But surely if anyone was out driving at that time of night and spaced out at the wheel, they'd have an accident? Even as Bo thought this, she mentally waved the thought aside; people in Blackfin generally stayed indoors after dark. It was just another of those things the adults expected Bo and others her age to accept without question. But Bo was finding it harder and harder lately not to ask questions.

Yeah, because Sky was always around to do the asking.

Bo took a shaky breath, trying to focus on Jared staring down at her instead of the hollow ache beneath her ribs.

'How old are you?' she asked. Jared looked startled. 'Look, I'm not sizing you up to be my boyfriend. I'm just trying to figure something out.'

'I'm nineteen,' he said.

Double *hmm*. Maybe he had been affected like Mrs Brady, and just sat in his van staring at his book while the sleepwalkers – Bo included – passed by outside. Well, it was another theory to test out, she supposed. She filed it away for later speculation.

'Does Gui know about you sleeping in the camper van?' Bo said.

'No.' Jared looked at her sharply. His eyes were the same gunmetal colour as his piercings. 'And I don't want him to hear about it, either.'

'He'd help you out if he…'

'I know,' Jared cut in. 'I'm sure he'd offer me a place to stay if he found out I'm roughing it in the van, but Gui's got enough on his plate at the moment, hasn't he?' Bo couldn't very well argue with that. 'I'll work something out soon.'

'You know, if you want somewhere to park where nobody'll bother you, I know the perfect place. Somewhere nobody in town ever goes.'

'You do? Where?'

Bo nodded toward a pair of bolt-cutters hanging on the wall. 'Grab those, and a padlock if you have one, and I'll show you.'

Chapter Four

Bo left Jared at the gate to Blackfin Woods. She had never ventured into the woods; neither had anyone else in town, as far as she was aware. It was off-limits, an enormous padlocked chain wound through the iron gates by Old Moley, Blackfin's resident handyman. Beyond the fence railings, the trees crowded together like some sinister clique, popping a hip and hissing at her to stay away. Bo didn't need the warning. She wasn't foolish enough to give in to curiosity.

But wasn't that what Bo was doing in trying to figure out what was going on every night in the town? Growing up in Blackfin, Bo had learned it was always best not to question the strange ways of the town, and now she was on some self-imposed mission to unearth one of its mysteries.

But I need the distraction, she admitted to herself. And wasn't this better than going to the cemetery every night like some music-loving ghoul?

She wasn't sure she was getting any closer to solving the mystery. Jared hadn't exactly been helpful, though Bo did feel a little pleased to have been able to help him out with his undesirable living situation. At least in the woods Jared wouldn't have some busybody knocking on his van windows at daybreak.

On her way home, Bo was walking past the library when it occurred to her she might have another thread she could follow up. The voice – what little Bo had heard it say – had mentioned something about an *east door*. Bo had never heard that phrase used in Blackfin, and certainly didn't know of anywhere in town with an 'east door'.

She walked past the ancient public computer, noting Ms Stacks' new sign to patrons: YOU CAN TRY THE INTERNET IF YOU LIKE, BUT REMEMBER THIS IS BLACKFIN. Bo understood exactly what that meant; internet searches here were more likely to send a person off on a total wild goose chase rather than divulging anything useful. But books were different. Even the weirdness of Blackfin couldn't touch books. At least, Bo hoped not.

She approached the librarian's desk. Ms Stacks looked up, smiling warmly when she saw it was Bo.

'Margaret! How are you? And how are your mother and those adorable brothers of yours?'

Bo hated it when people used her real name rather than her nickname (even though the nickname referred to the Little Bo Peep nursery rhyme, which Bo found ridiculous), but the librarian was so damned cheerful Bo had never quite managed to correct her.

'Mum's put the twins up for adoption,' she said, matter-of-factly. 'Fingers crossed they'll go to a family that breeds man-eating tigers.'

The librarian let loose a cackle which seemed far too sinister for someone wearing an angora cardigan with pearl snaps.

'Oh, you had me going there! Tigers, honestly.' She laughed again, then put on a more business-like face. 'But you aren't carrying your usual stack of books, so I wonder what I can help you with? Please don't tell me you've gone through our entire catalogue?'

'Actually, I'm not quite sure where to start,' Bo said, picking at the hem of her coat. 'I heard someone talking about an *east door* somewhere in Blackfin, but I didn't catch where exactly it was, and now I need to find it. Do you know anything about an east door?'

Ms Stacks pursed her lips thoughtfully, but eventually shook her head. 'Not that I can recall. East door ... It sounds like the kind of thing you'd find in an old building. A church, or town hall or something; buildings that were built more with the compass in mind, you know? Hmm ... there's no church here, of course, but maybe the school? It has a couple of centuries under its belt, and that ugly old weathervane on the roof.'

Bo consulted a mental map of the school. 'I don't think there's an east-facing door at Blackfin High.'

The librarian's eyes travelled over the shelves. 'Well, I would suggest looking at the local history section, if we had one. But Blackfin has never really caught someone's attention long enough for them to write about our history.' It was Ms Stacks' turn to sigh. 'A shame, really. Is there anything else I can help you with?'

Bo was about to say no when she remembered one tiny sliver from the dream she had had of the peculiar siblings: the girl had called her brother by his name. 'Would you happen to know someone named Bruno, Ms Stacks? I'm not sure how old he'd be now, but he was in Blackfin at some point when he was around my age … probably a long time ago.' She was thinking aloud, but it made sense. Bo would surely remember the two black-haired siblings if they'd been in town recently. 'He had black hair, and a sister. She might've been his twin. Does that ring any bells?'

Ms Stacks shook her head slowly. 'I'm sorry I can't help you.'

'Thanks anyway,' Bo said, and for the first time in her life, she left the library not carrying a single new book to read.

———

That night, Bo was determined to follow her brothers and whoever else she found wandering the streets. She would figure out what was going on once and for all – and ignore the part of her that just wanted to pretend that nothing was happening, just as she pretended every other day in this town.

But turning a blind eye had caught her out once before. Bo hadn't thought anything *really* bad would happen in Blackfin. Then Sky had died, and she couldn't pretend that hadn't happened. It hit her every day, as though Sky were dying over and over. Each time, the feeling of missing her best friend wrapped around Bo's ribs like a boa constrictor, squeezing the air out of her.

Bo turned up the music so it blasted through her earbuds. The random selector had chosen a classical piano piece (honestly, what had Sky been thinking with her playlist?) but Bo had changed it to a dubstep compilation that was just aggravating enough to keep her awake. When midnight rolled around, she was dressed and ready for action.

On cue, the twins crossed the hallway outside her room, padding along in their little slippers without a glance in her direction. Bo followed.

Their mother was at work again, so Mrs Brady had assumed her position on the lounger, an empty packet of bourbon creams in her lap. Her mouth hung open, bottom lip quivering on every outward snore like a leaf caught in a breeze. Bo gently closed the woman's mouth and continued her pursuit of the twins.

They headed for the coast road. It wound downhill toward the school, past the pier where Sky had fallen to her death in the icy water below. Bo watched Levi and Scout trot along, peering into nooks and crevices, prodding loose stones in the sea wall as though testing it. But they didn't pause for more than a few seconds in any one spot.

As they passed the school, the old swing hanging from the oak tree just inside the gate swung back in the breeze, letting out a loud creak. It was loud enough that Bo heard it even over her music, and she jumped.

When she turned to follow the twins, they were standing

near the Penny Well. Standing, and staring right back at her. She waved, but neither boy moved. There was something strange about the way they looked at her – looked *through* her.

A hiss of static stabbed at her eardrums. She fumbled for the iPod controls, trying to forward the track or turn down the volume, but nothing worked. The hissing grew agonisingly loud. Left with no other choice, Bo clawed back her scarf and yanked the earbuds out. She immediately realised her mistake.

'Find me, Bruno … I'm alone in the dark, and I can't stand it … can't rest… How could he do this to us? Twins should never be kept apart… Never… Never … the east door … find it, Bruno…'

The voice whispered beneath the echo of static still humming in her ears, so dreamlike and compelling it was almost a lullaby. Cold sweat prickled down Bo's spine.

'Who are you?' she muttered, her head starting to swim.

'…never be kept apart … find me, Bruno…'

Bo shook her head, fighting – *fighting* – not to succumb to the voice's pull. It felt like hours that she struggled against it, but in fact she held out merely seconds before the words snared her, and Bo fell deep into darkness.

There were lights ahead of her, beyond the trees. They moved like they were dancing to the discordant music that drifted to and fro with the breeze. But it wasn't the lights or the music drawing Bo forward. It was the sound of a girl's voice, singing. The song had no words, no rhythm or fixed melody, but Bo thought it might be the most beautiful thing she had ever heard. It made her want to move, to dance and to weep all at once. Very un-Bo-like.

The sound shifted with the scene, and now the girl was talking to her brother, giggling and whispering as he shook his head in mock sternness. There was a building in front of them, unlit except for the flickering of candles making the stained-glass windows glow.

The girl sang, a little trilling sequence of notes, and a big black bird – a raven, possibly? – flew down and landed at her feet for a moment before it turned and fluttered up to one of the windowsills. The building looked like a church, Bo thought, taking in the shepherd's image on the window.

As the black-haired girl continued her song, the raven began to peck at the glass. And peck. A crack appeared in it. As the raven continued to jab, the crack grew and spread, webbing out across the window. Then a door flew open, banging against the side of the building, and a tall man stood outlined in the doorway. He looked haggard, his greasy hair stuck down to his head and neck.

'Demons!' he bellowed, eyes searching the shadows where the twins now hid behind a large tree trunk. 'Devil children sent to plague this town! Well, I will not stand for it, do you hear me? *Do you hear me?*'

And the girl stepped from the shadows, calling out one final note to the bird still chipping away at the stained-glass

185

window. It cocked its head at the sound, then dropped from the windowsill and flew straight at the man in the doorway.

The image faded, sight and sound falling away as Bo felt herself drift out of the dream, but not before she heard the echo of the man screaming.

'My eye! My God, it's taken my eye!'

Chapter Five

Bo woke lying somewhere dark and ... rumbling? The ground beneath her seemed to shift and vibrate, and it took Bo a few seconds to shake off the eeriness of the dream and work out that she was in some kind of vehicle. A large vehicle, judging by the fact that she was lying at full stretch with her cheek pressed against a roughly carpeted floor. There was a peculiar smell, too, like dirty socks and burnt paper.

She tried to sit up, but couldn't. Her legs and arms wouldn't cooperate. Something held her ankles together and her wrists behind her, leaving Bo convulsing like a grounded fish. With an odd mix of weariness and panic, Bo came to the conclusion that she was currently being kidnapped.

Ignore the panic. Just think it through, one problem at a time.

Craning her neck, Bo could make out the back of a mussed head in the driver's seat. It was Jared.

Wait – *Jared* was kidnapping her? Though now that Bo thought about it, she should have worked that out from the fact that she was lying in a camper van. Such vehicles were not exactly common in Blackfin.

She still seemed to be wearing all her clothes, and couldn't feel any particular injury other than a mild cramp in her right calf, so maybe Jared would come out of this with his testicles intact.

Maybe.

Bo wiggled her fingers, testing the ropes. Doable, she decided. Something Bo had never been particularly keen to share, even with her closest friends, was that she and her siblings had inherited a rather unusual trait from their mother. They could all dislocate their joints at will, and bend their bones to degrees where others' would snap. This was something her mother found useful in her work as an exotic dancer, and which Bo had always thought was rather gross. Now, though, she saw the upside to it as she painlessly and silently slid her hands out of the bonds holding her. That done, she made short work of the ties at her ankles. Being unbound still left her with another problem, however.

Bo recognised the scenery whizzing past the van's windows; they were driving over the highest point of the Lychgate Mountains, and had just passed the town limits. The problem was how fast they were travelling. She couldn't simply jump out of the van's rear door – not without causing herself serious injury. No, road rash was not a good look.

She needed to stop the van somehow. Then she could make a run for it.

Ugh. Running.

But at least she would be running downhill, she consoled herself. First, though, she needed to make Jared stop the van.

She surveyed the junk scattered on the camper's floor. Clothes lay tangled at her feet, and amongst them all kinds of debris, including a plastic tub of hair gel (not heavy enough to whack someone over the head with), a tin of beans (better), and a small, near-empty bottle of tabasco sauce. She weighed the merits of spraying the hot sauce in his eyes, or perhaps breaking off the neck of the bottle and stabbing him with it. It only took her a moment to decide both options were ridiculous. She toyed with the discarded rope at her feet; perhaps she could use it to throttle him a bit? Bo let the rope drop, and was just reaching for the tin of beans when she spotted another item nestled in the litter of Jared's existence. It was a book bound in thick, cracked leather which was charred and browned over half its surface. Bo picked it up, testing its heft. It was heavy enough to deliver a decent blow, she gauged, but would probably be less effective than the tin of beans. She was about to toss it back among the debris when it creaked open in her hand.

Under ordinary circumstances, Bo would have been taken aback by a book autonomously exposing its innards in this way; however, she had come to expect the unexpected, so did no more than raise an eyebrow.

The book's pages were not printed. In fact, the book was not quite a book at all. At the head of each page was a date, though most of them were illegible thanks to the discolouration of the paper. It was a diary, written by someone some sixteen years earlier. Each page was lined with a scrawling cursive script, and though Bo could only read snatches of what was written between the grime, it seemed to have been written by someone with quite a temper. The pages were peppered with angry dashes and stops so full they practically punctured the paper. Parts had faded, as though damaged by water, which made it read as though the writer's thoughts had drifted in and out as they wrote. Bo was about to flip to the front to see whether the owner had left their name, but a line of text caught her eye.

Those wretched twins have returned to plague me.

Naturally, any mention of *wretched twins* brought to mind Bo's own brothers, though it only took her a second to work out that irritating though they were, it was unlikely someone had been complaining about them a decade before they'd been born. But the howlers weren't the only twins on Bo's radar. A finger of ice slid down her spine as she remembered the dream she had just woken from, with the giggling girl and her twin brother, and the raven sent to peck out a man's eye. Because Bo had no doubt that the girl's voice had made the bird attack him; its sound was so tantalising and insidious, she'd been half tempted to peck the man's eye out herself.

Bo closed the journal. Did it belong to the man from the dream? The one with the eye?

It seemed like a huge coincidence ... although perhaps not, given that the voice seemed to be drawing her and the other kids of Blackfin toward something. But what?

Scanning the pages, she saw Blackfin mentioned several times. That was a definite connection, wasn't it? And it probably meant the author was someone local. Who, though? And how had Jared come to have the journal?

Those questions would have to wait. She wanted very

much to keep reading, but there had to be a better time to focus on the old journal than when she was still very much mid-kidnapping, and getting further and further from Blackfin. Bo stuffed the book inside her coat and reached for the tin of beans. She probably wouldn't use it, she reasoned; knocking Jared out while he was driving might be a tad dangerous. Bo pictured the overturned van, glass flying everywhere, mushrooming flames and so on. But Jared didn't look like much of a fighter, so perhaps the threat of violence would be enough? She moved so she was right behind Jared's seat and tapped him on the shoulder with the beans.

'Oi, dickhead. Stop the van, yeah? Otherwise I'll have to brain you with this tin of beans.'

Jared jumped rather comically, and the van swerved while he looked from Bo back to the road.

'Oh, good, you're … well, *you* again,' he said. 'I hoped that would work.'

Bo was about to reiterate her threat when Jared clicked on the indicator (signalling to whom on this empty stretch of mountain road, she couldn't guess) and pulled over. The van idled there, waiting. Bo maintained her grip on the bean tin.

'What do you mean, I'm *me* again? And what the hell were you playing at, tying me up like that?'

Jared turned around, glancing only briefly at the makeshift weapon in her hand before meeting Bo's eyes.

'I saw you wandering near the woods, but when I tried to talk to you, you completely blanked me. I remembered what you said about kids sleepwalking, and I know it can be dangerous to wake someone when they're in that state, so I just started following you to make sure you didn't fall into a ditch and hurt yourself. But then you seemed to notice me following you, and you … well, you went for me.'

It was at this point, as Jared faced her fully, that Bo saw the red claw marks on his cheek. She looked down at her short nails dubiously. It was too dark to see properly, but she thought there might be a few bits of skin tucked under them.

'You're saying I attacked you? Scratched your face?' If that was true, then maybe – *maybe* – she could understand why he'd felt it was necessary to bundle her in the back of his camper.

Jared laughed. 'It surprised me, too. I had you down as more of a knee-to-the-balls kind of girl.'

Bo gave him her sternest, most narrowed eyes. Finally, he stopped laughing.

'So how did I go from scratching your eyes out to being hog-tied at the top of the Lychgate Mountains, then?'

'Ah. Yes. Well, I had a thought, you see. I reckoned that if people were wandering in trances all over the country, then we'd have heard about it in the news by now. So it must be something localised to Blackfin.'

'Well, obviously.' Despite her confident tone, it had never occurred to Bo to question whether the phenomenon might be more widespread. Everything weird she had ever seen had been tied to her hometown.

'So I put you in the back of the van and started driving out of Blackfin as fast as I could. I'm guessing you snapped out

192

of it right around the time we passed the signpost at the edge of town.'

He was right about that. 'But why weren't *you* all trance-y? Didn't you hear the voice?' Bo shuddered at the memory of that eerie, sing-song voice. A voice that could manipulate you to do whatever its owner wanted.

'I didn't hear any voice,' Jared said, frowning. 'Do you mean like a disembodied one?'

'Yeah. I suppose so. I couldn't hear it with my iPod on, and I'm guessing that's why I didn't go into the trance like the others at first. I think whoever's behind it all realised what I was doing, though, and made my iPod start blaring this awful noise so I'd pull my earbuds out. But that doesn't explain why you didn't hear it, and why you weren't affected.'

Jared shrugged. 'You said you've only seen kids out sleepwalking. Maybe I'm too old for the voice to affect me.'

'That could be a factor, I suppose. But from what I've seen, I think the adults might go into some kind of super-deep sleep while the kids sleepwalk. That's what happened to my neighbour when she was babysitting my brothers. *Twice.*'

'Okaaay,' Jared rolled his lip-piercing between his teeth. 'So if only kids get called out of bed by the voice, and adults go into a deeper sleep, maybe I'm just somewhere in between?'

He was nineteen: on that cusp between being a teen and a fully-fledged adult. That could be it, Bo supposed. But something in Jared's expression made her think there might be more to it.

'There's something else, isn't there?' she said. To his credit, Jared didn't try to lie.

'Yeah. I'm not really… Mind tricks don't tend to work on me. Family trait, you could say – like how some people can't roll their tongues.'

Bo thought of her own peculiar family trait, and how useless it had always proven to be. Well, except for extricating herself from the ropes Jared had tied her up with … she supposed that had been a little bit helpful. And, Bo grudgingly admitted, Mrs Peeps' flexibility had helped her earn her senior position among the club's dancers. But, generally speaking, being extremely bendy had little going for it.

'You say that like *mind tricks* are an everyday thing for you,' Bo said. Jared didn't answer, or meet her eye. 'Have you encountered something like this before, then?'

'Not exactly like this, no.' Jared shrugged, his shuttered expression telling Bo he didn't want to talk about it. 'If you've decided not to brain me with that tin, I'll take you back home,' he said.

Bo's natural instinct was to get out and make her own way home. Well, first to push him for answers, then make her own way home. But she hesitated. It really was a very long walk back into town.

She chewed the inside of her cheek as she glanced at the clock built into the dashboard. It was ten past one. Would the voice have gone quiet by now?

If she slid back into that strange, hypnotised state, she decided it would be better if it happened inside Jared's van

194

rather than wandering alone in the Lychgate Mountains. Setting aside the whole tying-her-up-and-abducting-her thing, Jared didn't appear to have nefarious intentions where Bo was concerned.

'Yeah, a lift would be good, thanks,' she said, finally. 'But I'm hanging onto the beans.'

She wasn't stupid, after all.

Bo took the seat next to him, watching silently as the signpost marking the town limits came into view at the side of the road. The van rumbled past it. Jared and Bo exchanged a glance, but she didn't hear the voice again, and didn't feel herself slipping from consciousness as she had done the other times. Whatever the voice was doing in Blackfin at night, it seemed to have passed.

The witching hour, Bo thought. She'd read about it in the library, though different texts gave different times for it. Some said it was as late as 3am. *Well, if anyone's looking for proof that the witching hour starts at midnight, they need only come to Blackfin and watch,* Bo thought.

She smiled to herself, imagining Sky's and Cam's faces when she told them about what she'd seen happening in town late at night, and then getting kidnapped by Gui's new employee and threatening him with a tin of beans. This was exactly the kind of random stuff Sky loved.

The smile slid from Bo's face. She wouldn't be telling Sky any of this, or at least not until she went back to the cemetery.

She rubbed her fist against her breastbone as though she might rub away the deep ache she felt there.

'Could you drop me off at the cemetery?' Bo said to Jared. 'There's something I need to do.'

An hour later, she crept through the back door of her house, her shoes clutched in one hand in case the sound of her footsteps woke her mother. But Bo needn't have worried; as she slipped through the back door and up the stairs, the whole house was silent. It was only when she reached her room and took off her coat that Bo remembered the book she had stuffed inside it, and which she had sort of accidentally pilfered from Jared's van.

Chapter Six

...rats everywhere, even in my ... woke in a bath of icy ... damn that girl! And damn that silent spectre of a brother! I see the evil in him just as plainly ... parents made of it, if such demon spawn even have parents? I should have drowned them at birth were they my... Curse them, as they have cursed me to a life with only half my sight ... swear it, if those evil twins come near my church again...

It felt as though Bo had only just drifted off to sleep when her mother knocked softly on her bedroom door. Bo blinked awake, the image of a wrinkled hand scratching words into a leather-bound volume lingering for a moment before her mum's face appeared in a crack in the door.

'Oh, Margaret! Are you seriously not awake yet? We have to leave in five minutes or we'll miss visiting...'

The use of her real name let her know that her mother was in no mood to be trifled with.

'I'm up, I'm up!'

Bo, who was blatantly *not* up, slithered out of bed and raked her hands back through her hair. Her black, Cleopatra-style bob fell neatly back into place, as always. She wasn't

197

entirely sure if that was another of the town's quirks, or a simple case of genetics; just as Mai Peeps was a wonder of orthopaedic dexterity, she too was blessed with always slinky hair.

Got to take the rough with the smooth, I suppose, Bo thought. Then she corrected herself: *The bendy with the smooth, anyway.*

'Wait, visiting? I didn't know we were going to see Dad today.'

Bo's father was currently serving an eight-month prison sentence for a little light theft – his latest stint of many behind bars – and Bo regularly managed to lose track of the visiting schedule.

Her mother sighed. 'I reminded you about it two days ago! And it's on the calendar in the kitchen.'

Bo winced guiltily. She really ought to make the effort to visit her father more often; but then *he* really ought to make more of an effort to not do things that would get him thrown in prison in the first place. Or at least not get caught.

'Well, you can come with me next time. It'll actually make it a bit easier for me. I've dropped the twins off at Ernie and Phil's; they're having a sleepover there tonight. If you're not coming to see your dad, I'll go straight into work afterwards. It's a late one tonight, so I won't get home 'til three-ish. Will you be all right to feed yourself today?'

'I'm sure I'll manage.'

Bo aimed for a warm smile, sensing she was still on thin ice for forgetting about visiting her dad. But warm smiles weren't exactly Bo's thing, and her mother only sighed again before disappearing from the doorway.

Nevertheless, Bo was quietly pleased about not having to accompany her mother. She would much rather be left alone to try and figure out what was happening in Blackfin, and what it had to do with the author of the journal she'd stolen from Jared's van.

Bo spent the better part of the day reading the journal. Among the fragments of a history she had never heard anyone in town refer to, she caught glimpses of Blackfin life: a sneering mention of Mrs Hemlock, then a teacher of chemistry rather than the formidable headteacher at Blackfin High; a reference to the two-headed fish commonly caught in Blackfin Lake, and which the diarist threw back in disgust at its 'deviant nature'; an entry about the lightning trees which edged Blackfin Woods, and the inconvenience of having to wear rubber-soled shoes to pass them safely.

All in all, the journal showed the author, who seemed to be some kind of vicar, to be a bad-tempered sort of chap. Quite stuffy and old-fashioned, judging by his writing style. It gave no name for him, though. What the journal did confirm were the names of the black-haired girl and boy: Bruno and Edita.

Unusual names, Bo thought. She wrote them down in her notebook.

There were a few more tantalising hints at who the mysterious Edita might be. She was around sixteen years old by the author's reckoning, and was indeed Bruno's twin sister. The pair had some peculiar talents which seemed to have brought them to Blackfin. The girl's voice, as Bo herself had experienced, could summon any child or animal to do her bidding, and put adults into a kind of mindless stupor. From the snatches Bo read, it seemed Edita rather enjoyed tormenting the journal's author with her particular gift.

The exact nature of the boy's talent was less clear, but something the writer speculated about. He wondered whether Bruno's voice held a similar controlling quality to his sister's, though the journal offered no examples of it being used as Edita's was. In fact, Bruno was invariably described as being silent, as though reluctant or unable to speak.

Bits and pieces of the puzzle were coming together, but there were lots of answers Bo didn't have. Not least of which was *why* Edita kept calling the children of Blackfin from their beds each night. But Bo would work her way through the puzzle piece by piece until she had all the answers, and could put a stop to the late night wandering.

And she would start by finding out who Edita and Bruno really were.

Ms Stacks looked up from the pile of returned books she was sorting and smiled when she saw Bo striding towards her.

'Back to research this mysterious east door of yours?' she said warmly. 'Or something else?'

Bo frowned, balancing the worn journal at the edge of the librarian's desk. 'Both, I suppose. You see, I've found this old journal, and it might be connected to the east door thing I was asking you about. Or it might not. The journal mentions twins who visited Blackfin about sixteen years ago, but I don't think they're here now...' Well, except for a disembodied and rather compelling voice. '...and I've never heard anyone mention them, so I was wondering if you have any records or old photos or anything like that where I might be able to find out more?'

The librarian made as though to take the book, but Bo found her fingers tightening around the leather cover to the point of becoming white-knuckled. Ms Stacks' smile twitched, and she withdrew her hand.

'Do you know the names of these twins? That would be a place for us to start our research.'

Bo nodded, relieved the librarian seemed on board to help her. 'Only first names, but they're quite unusual, so maybe there's something... They were called Edita and Bruno. I mentioned him last time I was here.'

She waited for the librarian to write the names down or tap them into her computer, but Ms Stacks didn't move. In fact, her smile appeared frozen in place, her eyes fixed on a spot slightly north of Bo's eyebrows.

Bo rubbed at the spot. 'Have I got something on my forehead?'

Ms Stacks blinked, and her features seemed to unfreeze. 'Bo! How nice to see you. Is there something I can help you with? Or are you just here to browse the shelves?'

Bo squinted at her, an uneasy feeling beginning to gnaw at her stomach. 'Uh … no. Just the twins thing I told you about.'

Ms Stacks' smile widened. 'Oh, lovely. That sounds like so much fun. Well, you let me know if you need anything, okay?'

With that, the librarian turned away from the counter and went back to sorting through the returned books.

'Ms Stacks? I really need your help with this, actually,' Bo said to the woman's back, but if Ms Stacks heard her, she gave no sign. 'Ms Stacks?'

She didn't so much as glance up. Bo was used to the way some adults avoided talking about certain subjects in Blackfin, but not Ms Stacks. She'd always been able to rely on the librarian before. Bo studied the mechanical way the woman sorted through the books in front of her, the glazed appearance of her eyes.

Ms Stacks was acting *weird*. No, not acting, there was no way the kind librarian was behaving like this on purpose, ignoring Bo and just changing the subject. This was supreme weirdness. Trance-y weirdness. *Blackfin* weirdness.

Bo took a step back. And another. And then she walked out of the library, the old journal held tight against her chest like it might absorb the thundering beats of her heart.

She couldn't ignore what was happening now, even if it was demanding an unreasonable amount of effort on her part to try to untangle it all. If it weren't for her and her little brothers being among the kids affected by the night-time wandering bug, she would quite happily ignore this phenomenon as she did all the others. But not this time.

'Oh, balls,' she muttered.

She could go back home and read some more of the journal, she supposed; but she'd been there all morning, and had honestly had enough of its bad-tempered ranting for one day.

Perhaps she should go to Cam's and see if her friend had any insights? Bo perked up as she always did at the prospect of hanging out with Cam. She glanced up the hill toward her friend's house, looking for a light on in Cam's bedroom window, but her eyes lingered instead on the police car sitting outside in the driveway. Cam and her brother had moved to Blackfin to live with their Aunt Holly while their parents went to work abroad. Holly Vega was Blackfin's lone police officer, and the reason Bo hesitated now. It wasn't that she disliked her, exactly, but it was difficult to bring herself to relax around the woman who had arrested her father no fewer than seven times to date.

No. Bo wouldn't be dropping in to ask for Cam's thoughts on the weirdness she'd witnessed. She'd just ask her at school.

Bo was about to turn and head back home when she caught sight of the small car-repair shop tucked away against the craggier ankle of the Lychgate Mountains. Her thoughts went straight to Sky, and how she would often head to her father's garage after school instead of going straight home.

Bo detested the phrase 'daddy's girl', but she couldn't deny that Sky and her dad had been close – much closer than Bo was to her own father. She had always envied them a little. Now Sky was gone, and Gui was … well, he was as you'd expect a man to be after losing his daughter.

The light coming from inside the garage blurred for a moment before Bo blinked her eyes, annoyed that the early wintry air had made them water. Jared's camper was outside. Maybe Jared had more answers than Bo had first thought. He'd had the journal, after all, and was somehow immune to the influence of Edita's voice. And if he didn't have answers, then he might at least be able to help Bo find some.

Having no intention of actually giving the diary back to Jared, Bo hid it inside her messenger bag, and stomped up the hill with renewed purpose. But when she reached the garage, Jared wasn't there. Seeing Bo's shadow in the doorway, Gui himself lumbered out of the office.

'Bo! What a surprise! Come in, come in … hot chocolate? Of course hot chocolate, what am I even saying?'

Bo allowed herself to be swept inside the cluttered office and took the steaming mug when he handed it to her a minute later. Gui was still waffling in his massive, deep voice, and kept at it while Bo blew on her drink, remembering how Sky would smile at her father at such moments, her blue eyes sparkling up at the enormous Frenchman. If Sky were here, Bo wouldn't be chasing some disembodied voice on her own. She wouldn't be feeling lost and confused and – though she would never admit it aloud – alone.

'I miss Sky,' Bo murmured. Gui paused, somehow hearing her over his own cacophony. 'Nothing feels right without her here.'

Gui's smile dimmed, and he sank a little lower in his seat.

'I know what you mean,' he said, and they fell silent, each hiding their misty eyes behind the steam pluming from their mugs.

Chapter Seven

The sky was beginning to darken when Bo arrived home, though it was just after four. It was only when the silence of the house hit her that Bo remembered her mother was out of town for the night.

Bo shook off her coat and kicked her shoes into the pile by the back door. She'd never imagined she would miss the near-constant bellowing of her little brothers marauding through the house, but at that moment she did. It was *too* quiet. There was too much space for her to dwell on things. And it had been a … a *trying* day.

'You've got it on you, haven't you?'

Bo almost leapt out of her skin at the sound of a man's voice coming from the darkened living room. In one swift motion, she grabbed a knife from the block on the kitchen counter, turned on the living-room lights, and slashed the knife in the likeliest direction.

'Watch out!' Jared squeaked. 'You almost got me!'

Bo took another step into the room and swung again, though her heart wasn't truly in it now that she saw who she was slashing at.

'Hey!'

'If you didn't want to be stabbed, you wouldn't be hiding in the dark in my house,' Bo said, reasonably. She stopped swiping at Jared, but held the knife pointed steadily in his direction.

'I wasn't hiding!' Jared spluttered, eyeing the blade. 'I came over to get the diary back, but you weren't in, so I decided to wait.'

'*Inside* the house?'

'No. Well, I mean, not at first, but it's bloody cold outside, and you were gone ages, so I just thought I'd try the back door. It was open, so I came in and made myself a cup of tea.'

'Because *that's* a completely normal thing to do? Jesus Christ, you don't let yourself into a stranger's house and help yourself to a cuppa, you idiot!'

Jared at least had the sense to grimace sheepishly. 'I didn't think you'd catch me in here, to be honest. I only meant to warm my hands for ten minutes, but I must've fallen asleep, because it wasn't dark when I got here.' Jared rubbed his eye with the heel of one hand. 'So, where's the journal, then? I couldn't find it anywhere.'

A hideous understanding dawned on Bo, and her hand tightened on the knife handle again. When she spoke, it was through gritted teeth. 'Have you been snooping in my room?'

Jared shrugged. 'Seemed only fair, after you stole it from me.'

'Only after you kidnapped me!' Bo snapped. 'Besides, the journal isn't yours, so technically I didn't steal it.'

Jared shrugged. 'Whatever. Where is it?'

Without meaning to, Bo had wrapped her free arm tight across her midriff, where the old book nestled somewhere between her many layers of knitwear. 'I'm not finished reading it yet.'

'Neither am I.'

'Well, I need it more,' Bo said.

Jared raised one pierced eyebrow. 'Need it for what?'

'None of your bloody business!' The words were out before Bo could remind herself that she had been looking for Jared only a few hours earlier to ask for his help. Shouting and waving a knife at him was probably not the best way to get his cooperation … at least, not unless she wanted to end up in the cell next to her father's. But then Jared could hardly complain after he'd let himself into her home and rifled through Bo's belongings.

He folded his arms and smirked at whatever he saw in her expression. 'Still chasing your midnight voices, then?'

'It's only one voice,' Bo muttered, and folded her own arms rather more peevishly. 'And yes, I am.'

Jared sighed. 'You think that old book I found in the woods is going to help you somehow?'

Bo paused in her sulking. 'You found it in the woods?'

'Yeah, in an old shell of a church. It was wedged under a rock…'

'There's never been a church in Blackfin,' Bo said.

Jared laughed. 'You might want to tell that to Reverend Silas Peale. That's whose journal you've got swaddled in your clothes.'

'Reverend... Wait, Silas? As in *Silas* Silas? The one who haunts the old weathervane on the school roof?'

'Yup, that's the one. His name was on a plaque above the church door – or what's left of it. And it's mentioned in one of the entries toward the back... Look, keep hold of the journal for a bit if you need to, but give it back when you're done, yeah? He talks about something that happened here sixteen years ago that I'm kind of looking into, and I haven't finished reading the whole thing.'

'What kind of something?' Bo asked.

'It's nothing to do with the voice you keep hearing.' Jared sniffed and looked away. It was the sort of sniff a liar would do, Bo thought.

'Fine, keep your secrets,' she sighed, then narrowed her eyes at him. 'It really has nothing to do with what's going on now...?'

Jared shook his head firmly. Less liar-ly.

'Okay. I'll give the book back when I'm finished. But you might want to bugger off now – Gui was about to lock up the garage when I left, and I'm pretty sure I saw your van keys still on the hook in his office.'

Jared's eyes widened. 'Damn it!'

Bo might have laughed as he tore out of the back door, but it seemed like rather a waste of energy when he was running too fast to hear it.

The girl's power is amplified by some talisman her father carries, it seems, but … theory that distance or other substances might mute her … Bruno's is more of a mystery, as he has yet to demonstrate it … perhaps weaker? Or perhaps even more powerful … both ungodly, and must be purged from this place … if it falls to me, then so be it … find a way. I swear.

The hour had grown late by the time Bo finished reading the diary. Not late enough for that eerie voice to come snaking in through whatever cracks it crept through to reach Bo's ears – and those of the other youths in Blackfin – but late enough that Bo helped herself to a double-strength cup of coffee to keep her eyelids from sliding shut.

The diary ended abruptly. Silas' tone in the final entry had been as irritated and unpleasant as all his others, but there had been a note of excitement there, too, at some plan to rid his precious town of the twins.

His plan hadn't worked, if Edita's nightly singing was anything to go by. But what exactly was Edita now? A girl, trapped somewhere for sixteen years and broadcasting her voice across town each night? Or was she something a little more … *ghostly*?

'For God's sake,' Bo murmured.

Why had Silas stopped writing his journal? And why had

Edita's spirit, if that's what it was, woken up now? It didn't seem likely the sleepwalking thing had been going on for the past sixteen years without anyone noticing, so it was probably a recent phenomenon. What had happened that might've woken a ghost? Surely ... surely it wasn't Sky's death?

Bo frowned, turning it over in her head, but she couldn't come up with any connection between Sky dying and Edita's ghost waking up, other than the timing.

Ugh. This whole thing was like a giant ball of spun sugar, with all the threads sticking together and getting messier the more Bo tried to pull them apart.

She shoved aside her notebook. If problem-solving and logic weren't going to help her, then she'd have to try something else. But what? Her gaze settled on the patterned cover of her notebook, the design a series of letters in different fonts and colours.

Perhaps the thing to do when dealing with a mystery involving a ghost was not so illogical after all: she should ask the ghost for help.

Chapter Eight

A good twist with two of her father's lock picks, and the padlock on the door of the fortune-teller's hut went spinning away across the boards of the pier.

The wind howled in Bo's ears, bitter and accusing. It whipped the sea against the struts of the pier below her and bellowed mournfully as it rattled the boardwalk. Had it sounded this way when Sky drowned? Had this been the last sound she heard? Bo couldn't remember if it had been windy that night. There were so many details she *could* remember: the way Sky's lips had turned a shade of blue that matched her dress; her one bare foot where the shoe had been stolen by the sea; the streaks of black mascara on Sky's face, as though she had been crying ... how could she not remember if it had been windy? Even now, she could feel the clammy chill of Sky's skin. It had shocked Bo when she touched her friend's hand. The water must have been painfully cold; it always was.

This wasn't the first time Bo had set foot on the pier since seeing her best friend's lifeless body being hauled onto it, but it still brought back that lead-weight feeling in her limbs she'd first felt watching Sean try to revive Sky. It was as though Bo had turned to stone right there on the promenade. Her heart had been the only part of her seemingly still awake, hammering away the seconds until Sky would open her eyes and heave in a breath... But that had not happened. Sky had remained stubbornly dead.

Bo knocked briskly on the door of the fortune-teller's hut and waited for a response. There was none. At just after 11pm, the hut was of course unoccupied, though now that Bo thought about it, she hadn't seen Madame Curio in weeks. But perhaps the fortune-teller felt the need to avoid the pier since Sky's drowning. Perhaps she, too, felt the deep sadness that had settled over the town these past weeks.

Bo narrowed her eyes. No, Madame Curio wasn't the sentimental sort. In fact, she was one of the few people in Blackfin who hadn't openly adored Sky. Remembering that lessened Bo's twinge of guilt at breaking into her place of work.

She reached for the door handle, turning her back to the seaward view, and stepped inside. The air in the hut was cold and tinged with incense, but not musty. It was a familiar smell to Bo; she visited Madame Curio whenever she had a spare couple of pounds to pay the old woman for a reading, though she would never admit that to anyone, not even her friends – and especially not her mother, who was extremely superstitious when it came to fortune-telling.

Bo wasn't entirely sure why she came to have her fortune told as often as she did. She didn't believe that what Madame Curio told her would help her in any way, and indeed it never had. But she couldn't deny the accuracy of the fortune-teller's predictions: an A in her next maths exam (not unexpected, but quite pleasant to hear); that Bo's misplaced sunglasses had not actually been misplaced, but instead broken by her little brothers and buried in the garden; a warning to steer clear of the Penny Well, to which Bo had lost more than a few coins over the years and not been granted a single wish. These titbits she found neither useful nor particularly surprising, yet Bo kept coming back in the hope that some important truth might slip out and make it all worthwhile. She had a feeling Madame Curio knew this, and would quite possibly withhold such a truth should it speak to her through her gnarled deck of cards. The woman had practically said as much on Bo's last visit.

'Not everything in Blackfin can be explained, my dear. Better to just take in what this town offers, and not poke and prod at its secrets too much.'

Isn't that exactly what I'm doing now? Poking and prodding at things that should be left well alone?

But Bo had good reason this time. Even setting aside the gut-churning thought of some outside force compelling her to act every night in ways she couldn't control, Bo was worried about her little brothers. Coming home covered in mud was bad enough; what if they got hurt? There were plenty of places where they could cut themselves or fall or...

Wait. *Wait.* Was it possible that Sky had been sleepwalking the night she fell from the pier? That leaden, heart-thumping feeling came over Bo again, but it only took a moment for her to see she was wrong. Sky had drowned well before midnight, and seeing as everyone else was looking for her at the time, they couldn't have been under Edita's control. No, Sky's death had been an accident. Just an accident.

Still, it wasn't safe for Levi and Scout to be out wandering at night. It really wasn't.

Knowing there was no electricity in the hut, Bo took out her lighter and used its flickering light to find one of the tealight lanterns Madame Curio generally left littered about the place. She lit the first one she found, but no others. Unlikely though it was, Bo didn't want anyone who happened to be out walking at this time of night to see the hut lit up like a beacon and wander over.

Candlelight dappled the small space. Though dusty and faded with time, the velvet wall hangings made the hut feel cosy. Tucked away in a corner sat a foldaway table laden with a gas camping stove, a kettle, and a mug, but that was as far as practicalities went. Madame Curio's little round reading table sat as always beneath the lone shuttered window, the crystal ball on it draped in a black cloth. The old lady's worn and well-used tarot cards had been put away somewhere, but Bo wasn't looking for the cards. There was something else here that she needed.

Bo's mother had always expressed a shuddering dislike for spirit boards, which was why Bo had never actually used one, despite being rather curious about the prospect of chatting to the dead. It didn't escape her now that *chatting to the dead* was exactly what she'd been doing at Sky's graveside for the past couple of weeks. But that had been rather one-sided, and not exactly useful to her now.

Bo was sure she had seen a spirit board laid out in Madame Curio's hut on one of her many visits. And she'd seen enough horror films to give her a pretty good idea how to use one. A pointer called a planchette was used to spell out words, delivering messages from beyond the grave. The board wasn't lying around anywhere obvious now, though. Feeling like a massive hypocrite after snapping at Jared for poking through her things, Bo started poking through Madame Curio's things.

Bo found the spirit board tucked behind one of the velvet hangings, its surface scuffed with use, but polished so its dark eye seemed to gleam up at her. For the first time since setting foot on the pier, she hesitated. Could what she was about to do actually be dangerous? From the safety of her kitchen with a strong cup of coffee in hand, the idea of talking to Edita's ghost – or spirit, or whatever Edita was – and finding a way to convince her to shut up had seemed both harmless and reasonable. Now, with the eye of the spirit board blinking up at her, Bo wasn't so sure.

'Oh, for God's sake,' she muttered aloud to herself, and pulled the board out from behind the velvet curtain. A red pouch hanging from one corner of the board held the planchette. She carefully took it out and placed both the board and the pointer on the table.

Sitting in Madame Curio's cushioned seat, Bo drew in a deep breath, then placed her fingertips on the planchette.

Now came the part she would have to ad lib; she knew there were always specific incantations and such in Hollywood representations of what she was doing, but Bo felt a more direct approach was probably best. Not only that, but she wanted to get this over with and be back home before midnight.

She had quite deliberately chosen the hour before the voice seemed to have an effect on the town: 11pm being close enough to it that Edita should be … well, stirring; but not so near that Bo would fall into a trance mid-summoning.

'Edita?' she said. 'Are you there? Please move the planchette to YES if you are.'

Bo closed her eyes, waiting to feel some tug at the pointer. And waited. None came.

'EDITA,' she said more loudly. 'The girl whose voice I've been hearing after midnight … you said something about being trapped. Does that have anything to do with why you're making everyone sleepwalk at night?'

Again she waited. Again there was no movement from the planchette.

Bo opened her eyes and peered around the hut, perhaps expecting to see a misty apparition hovering in front of the velvet drapery, but all was as it had been before. The only movement came from the candle flickering on the table.

Well. That had been a big waste of time.

Bo slumped back in the chair, letting her hands slide from the pointer. Then, as though propelled by a swift flick, the planchette whipped across the spirit board and hit the crystal

217

ball sitting at the edge of the table with a *ping*. On instinct, Bo bolted up and reached for it, worried it would fall and smash. But a split second before Bo's hand made contact with the ball, the black cloth slid away from it, and a light emanating from deep inside the crystal hit Bo squarely in the eyes.

The *ping* of the planchette's collision seemed to vibrate from within the crystal, making its smooth surface shiver beneath Bo's palm. Its sound undulated, twisting into a whisper that had become familiar to Bo. It was so faint she barely heard it: low and mournful.

'He trapped me…' Edita said. 'He left me here to die alone, without my brother, in the dark…'

Bo forced herself to swallow against the tightness in her throat before answering. 'Who did?'

The glow from the crystal swirled, light motes spiralling faster and faster at its core. Even as Bo fought against its intoxicating pull, she felt herself leaning closer. The voice whispered again.

'Can't get out … the air is so stale in here…'

'Where are you?' Bo tried again.

'Bruno? Bruno, can you hear me? I need you to get me out… The main entrance is blocked, you must find the east door…'

Bo took a shaking breath. She wasn't sure if Edita could actually hear her or was just stuck in some nightmarish bubble, but whatever was happening, Bo at least seemed to be hearing the spirit without falling under her control. Bo intended to keep it that way.

'Edita, look. I can help you or not, it's your choice. And I'll be honest, I'm not really the helping type, but seeing as I'm the only one who's noticed there's something weird going on, it looks like I'm the one you're stuck with. So, unless your big plan is to send little kids out wandering at night in their PJs for no reason, maybe you should talk to me, yeah? If there's something you want – preferably something easy – then I promise I'll try to help...'

'*Look*,' the ghostly voice breathed inside Bo's mind. 'Look what he did to me.'

Chapter Nine

Bo fought the urge to yank her hand away from the crystal ball, to sever the connection and run from Madame Curio's hut. But drawn as she was to the dancing light within the ball, her mind was still her own, unlike when Edita sang after midnight. That small nugget of comfort kept Bo in her seat, her eyes fixed on the crystal.

Edita's voice had become quiet, but Bo still sensed her there, as though the girl watched over her shoulder. Inside the globe, the light coalesced into vague shapes. No more than suggestions of outlines at first, then clearer and clearer until Bo saw a small stone church surrounded by trees. The building was unfamiliar, but Bo would recognise the trees of Blackfin Woods anywhere. Well, only in Blackfin Woods, but that was the point.

The sun could be seen setting beyond the sharp peaks of the trees, and a faint light shone from the high arches of the church windows. If it wasn't for the swaying of the trees in the breeze, Bo might have thought she was looking at a painting.

'What is this?' she whispered. Bo still felt Edita's presence, but the voice didn't answer. Instead she heard laughter. It wasn't inside her head this time; it was coming from the crystal ball. Edita's laughter. A moment later, the raven-haired girl came around the side of the church, practically skipping. Even in the fading light of sunset, Bo thought Edita was beautiful. She wore her hair long and tousled, and her dark eyes glinted with laughter. Her lips, previously pale, were painted such a vibrant red that she looked almost vampiric.

'Edita? What are you showing me?' Again, there was no answer. 'Come on, don't go quiet on me now.'

Rather than hearing a reply, Bo noticed the scene shifting inside the glass of the ball. She was seeing the church from a different angle, just outside its ornately carved oak door. This was the same door where Silas had been attacked by the raven. Or by Edita, depending on how you looked at it. And her *devilry*, as Silas had called it, had cost him his eye.

Edita stood outside that door now, grinning up at something on the roof. Then she began to hum, her voice sending shivers through Bo as she watched. There came a creak of metal, and now Bo saw what Edita was looking at: a weathervane sitting up on the church roof had begun to spin as though in a gale. But there was no gale, not even a stiff wind. The weathervane was spinning in a cloud of black insects.

It's her voice, Bo realised. Edita was using her voice to make the swarm of flies do what she wanted.

And now that Bo was watching the weathervane spin, she saw that it wasn't just *any* weathervane. She recognised the hollow, narrowed eye, the angry spikes of the cockerel's crest.

It was Silas – or rather, the weathervane everyone in Blackfin knew as Silas. Except Silas' spirit was presumably not yet inside it in this dream-memory, and the weathervane itself was not yet sitting on top of Blackfin High's roof.

The metallic screech rose in pitch and volume as Edita's swarm spun it faster, though her voice was still no more than a humming note. The girl grinned.

'DEVIL GIRL!'

The bellow sounded from inside the church, and it made Bo flinch. Edita only grinned wider. The bellow was followed by the appearance of Silas in the church doorway.

Silas, Bo thought to herself. How strange to put a human face to the name she had always known as a chunk of metal.

But that face was not as she had seen it in her dream. It was even more haggard, and a bandage covered his damaged eye. It made him look like an injured pirate.

His remaining eye flashed as he glared out into the darkness, searching the shadows until he spotted Edita standing only a few feet away. The second he set foot outside the door, Edita's insects swarmed down from the roof and buzzed around Silas' head. He batted them away, cursing loudly in a way pastors probably weren't supposed to. Within the crystal ball, Edita let out a squeal of laughter, turned on her heel, and set off towards the trees.

'Not this time, you demon!' Silas reached back behind the church door and then, with a grunt, threw something at the swiftly moving figure of the girl. It happened too quickly for Bo to see what he had thrown, but as it fell to lie next to the

222

suddenly motionless form of Edita, she realised it was a walking stick. From the limping way Silas now hurried over to the prone girl, Bo guessed it was his.

Edita had fallen when the stick caught the back of her head, but she was not entirely still. She groaned, trying to roll and get her feet under her. Silas reached Edita, pressing his knee into her back, shoving her down into the dirt. This seemed to energise rather than subdue Edita, who turned her head and took a deep breath as though to scream.

Silas clamped his hand over her mouth.

'Keep that devil tongue silent! I've seen how you use it for evil, how you turn your voice to tormenting a decent man of the cloth. I'll not have it! Not any…' Silas' rant turned into a scream of pain as Edita bit down on his hand. When he yanked it away, the girl's teeth were red with blood. She took a satisfied moment to grin at him before raking her nails over his face, tugging away the bandage to reveal a gaping wound where his eye should have been.

With a wild cry, Silas picked up the walking stick and brought it down once, twice, on the side of Edita's head.

Bo had never heard a gunshot in real life, but she couldn't imagine the sound could be any louder than the one the stick made as it connected with Edita's temple. Her eyes were closed, her body limp, as Silas dropped the walking stick and staggered back from her.

'Good God, what have I done?' Hand shaking, Silas raked it back through his hair. 'You made me do it! I said the devil is in you, girl, and I was right!'

223

There was no conviction in his voice, though. Only fear.

He's killed her, Bo thought, forgetting for the moment that what she had just witnessed had already happened, sixteen years earlier. *He's only gone and bloody killed her.*

The image inside the glass shifted. When Silas' drawn face reappeared, he was struggling under the weight of Edita's body as he dragged her down a set of stone stairs. It was difficult to tell where they were, or how much time had passed, but from the old, churchy look of the staircase, and the fact that Silas probably couldn't have moved the girl very far, Bo reckoned they were most likely inside the church.

Dots of blood marked each step behind them like gruesome confetti. Silas dropped Edita unceremoniously at the foot of the stairs, then limped away into a dark tunnel. A minute later the tunnel brightened, showing it to be a stone-walled and windowless corridor.

Silas hurried back to Edita. He muttered to himself as he heaved her back into his arms, then began dragging her along that dimly lit corridor.

'They won't find you down here, not once I've sealed you in properly...'

Silas was now piling up stones to fill a gap in a wall, slathering mortar between them to hold them in place. Bo couldn't see Edita, and she couldn't tell what Silas was doing until the flickering light of a torch landed on a pale hand inside the wall he was now frantically sealing off. Stone by stone, the hole grew smaller.

There were other uneven patches in the wall where it seemed as though other such holes might once have been. Was this some kind of crypt, then?

Sweat dripped from Silas' brow as he worked feverishly, muttering under his breath about 'devil twins' and the torment they had inflicted on him. Once the hole was completely filled, he plastered the rest of the mortar over it. It looked like a part of the wall, now, only a little rougher and darker.

Silas stood, mopping the sweat from his head and looking grimly satisfied.

'Can't let anyone know,' he mumbled. 'Mustn't have anyone poking around down here...'

Silas gathered up his tools and took off back along the tunnel and up the stone staircase, emerging into the church through a concealed door behind the font. Then his head snapped up at the sound of a door crashing open. The wind howled outside, but Bo couldn't look away from Silas to see who had appeared in the church doorway. Silas' eyes were wide, dark pits as he seemed to stare straight at Bo through the crystal ball.

'*You*,' he snarled.

Chapter Ten

Bo jerked away from the crystal ball, almost tipping over the table as she scrambled to her feet. She felt icy cold, and as she caught her breath she noticed that the door to the fortune-teller's hut had blown open. The heavy curtains billowed in the sea breeze, looking like a circle of cloaked figures surrounding her.

'Hello?' Bo called, popping her head outside. The pier was as deserted as it had been before.

Ducking back inside the hut, Bo rubbed her hand against her chest as if that might help to slow her racing heart. The wind had made the door swing open, that was all. She went to pull it shut, but hesitated.

'Was that what you wanted to show me, Edita? How you died?'

She waited for an answer, and for a moment thought that Edita had abandoned her. But then that musical voice spoke again.

'You must see … more…'

'But I saw him kill you! I know what happened now.'

'*More!*'

Bo hissed out a breath between clenched teeth. She didn't

want to watch any more. What she had already seen had been bad enough. What more could there possibly be, anyway? And why did *she* have to be the one to see it?

'You asked for this… For weeks now, you have been calling out to the dead.' Edita laughed, and Bo had the horrible feeling the spirit had been eavesdropping on her thoughts.

'I didn't, I…'

But Bo *had*, hadn't she? She had been talking to Sky, willing her to send some message from beyond the grave. Had that left her open to other spirits, too? Was that how she had made this strange connection to Edita?

Was *she* the reason Edita had woken up?

'You promised,' Edita whispered. 'Help me…'

Edita's voice sounded so close she might have been standing right at her side. Bo shivered again, and shut the door. The crystal ball sat on the small table just as it had before. Bo took a deep breath. Then another. And then she sat down.

'Right,' she said, and cracked her knuckles. 'Let's get this over with.'

A dull glow swirled inside the ball when she peered into it, but it quickly sharpened once more into an image. She saw Silas inside the church, just as he had been before. But he did not seem to be staring out at her through the glass now. He glared at a tall figure blocking the aisle before him.

Bruno's hair curled wildly, his eyes like black stars.

'You!' Silas snapped. 'What are you doing in my church?'

'Where is she?'

Bo gasped at the unearthly sound of Bruno's voice. It was not like Edita's, except for the faintly lilting accent. Edita's voice had seemed to twirl through the air like whispering smoke, but Bruno's might have been wrenched from some deep, dark part of the world: like a volcano roaring to life, or the metallic groan of a submarine's hull being crushed in the ocean's depths.

Bruno had been described in the journal as the silent twin, the one who never spoke. In the dreams Edita had shared with her in her trance state, Bo had never heard Bruno speak before. Now she saw why.

Bo braced herself as the scene in the glass continued to play out, and Bruno spoke again.

'I feel her … near. She is in pain. What did you do?'

The sneer wilted from Silas' face, and all the colour drained from it. The dirt smeared on his cheeks from his recent endeavours in the catacombs stood out in stark condemnation. He straightened, seeming to gather his nerve.

'To the best of my knowledge, she isn't hurt,' Silas said with only the faintest tremor, and Bo could tell he thought he was being clever with his half-truth. 'And she isn't in this church. Feel free to look around if you wish. Perhaps the Lord's light will reach you if you stay awhile.'

Bo couldn't believe how pompous Silas sounded. He'd just murdered a teenage girl and concealed her body in an underground chamber, and now he was goading her brother for looking for her.

Bruno didn't seem able to believe it either. Bo sensed some invisible charge building around the boy, like the build-up before a lightning strike. Or the stillness before a tsunami. He raised his hands, and for a moment she thought he might hit Silas, but he forced them to his sides and spoke through clenched teeth.

'Don't lie, preacher. I *feel* her pain.'

Was Bruno sensing Edita's death, and just unable to figure out what exactly he was feeling? Bo's little brothers did creepy twin things like that from time to time, so she couldn't dismiss the possibility. She heard a high-pitched screech, and a web of cracks spread through the stained-glass window nearest the pair.

'I know she has upset you with her games, but she meant you no real harm. Tell me where she is, and I will make sure you never see either of us again; our troupe leaves in just a few days.'

With each word, the cracks spread through the glass like broken veins, threading across one window, then the next. Then the pews began to tremble slightly, but then more, as though they sat upon an enormous bass speaker instead of a stone floor. Silas' gaze followed the movement instead of focusing on the boy. Sweat beaded his top lip.

'No real harm? She took my eye!' Silas' mask was slipping now, and he pointed unnecessarily at the bandage covering his wound. Bruno just stared. It took a moment for Silas to compose himself. 'I … I did see her, but it was earlier. Much earlier. In the morning. She said she was going into town.'

'Liar.'

'No, you must believe me, I…'

229

'*Liar.*'

That unearthly voice rose to a roar, a sound something no human or animal should have been capable of. The glass burst outward from the windows, leaving their arched frames empty. Through the trees outside, Bo thought she saw flickers of orange light, but her attention was pulled back to Bruno as he closed the distance between him and the Reverend.

'You are a hell-creature,' Silas whispered. 'Go back to the abyss you crawled out of.'

Silas backed up a step, but he was pressed against the curtain hiding the secret door, and he could go no further without Bruno seeing it. Instead he darted across the chancel to a narrow staircase leading up.

Bo followed his panting form as he struggled up the stairs, emerging into a circular stone space with open windows that had never contained glass, as far as she could tell. There was a great brass bell hanging in the middle of the space, and a rope dangling from it through a hole in the floor.

Silas slammed the trap door he had just come through and stood on it, searching about him for some way to hold it shut.

'He's coming,' he whispered. 'He's coming!'

Bo couldn't hear anyone running up the stone steps below, or Bruno's awful voice bellowing to be let through. For a moment she wondered if he had left, but then she saw him through one of the window-spaces. He stood outside the church, looking up from the treeline. Even from this distance, his voice carried as though he stood only feet away.

'Tell me where my sister is, old man, or you will die in your little tower. My sister's gift compels the small creatures, as you know, but mine … my power is far more terrible. I can make the sky *bleed fire*. I will bring you *death*.'

If Bruno had sounded angry before, his tone was now eerily calm. Too calm. It held the promise of absolute destruction.

'Go back to hell!' Silas roared, flecks of spittle arcing out over the sill. His knuckles were blanched white against the stone window frame.

'Edita!' Bruno boomed. The ground shook under the weight of his voice, and Bo saw Silas stumble as the vibrations reached him in the tower. Wind howled around the building. Biting shards of hail that hadn't been in the air moments ago now hammered the roof tiles. 'EDITA!'

There was a groan of splintering wood, and the tall oak nearest Bruno began to sway. Bo's heart stopped for a second when it seemed like it might land on the boy, but he stepped smartly out of the way and let its great trunk come crashing down onto the church. Silas screamed as the roof below the bell tower caved in around the tree, spitting out slate shingles like teeth in a bar fight.

'She's dead!' Silas shrieked. 'It was an accident!'

But Bruno shook his head angrily, jerking a finger at his temple. 'Not dead. I hear her. She is hurt and she is afraid, and cannot see where she is, but she remembers seeing your face last. Now *where … is … she*?'

One high wall of the church crashed inward, leaving it looking more like rubble than a building. A great, gaping crack threaded up the tower, right to the sill where Silas still clung. He leapt back with a screech.

'You're going to kill me, you damned idiot!'

In reply to this, Bruno drew in a deep breath and bellowed wordlessly, the tendons in his neck standing out taut under his skin. The crack in the church steeple widened, large chunks of stone falling away to crash onto the debris below. The sounds of destruction continued long after Bruno's roar ended.

The stone floor of the inner steeple began to crumble, and Silas practically danced in his efforts to avoid falling through the dark spaces appearing at his feet. Bo leaned in, willing him to find a way out of that tower. She might not like Silas, but she didn't really want to watch him die, either.

He scrambled up onto the empty sill of the tower then hauled himself up onto the roof, clawing at the tiles until he was able to grab the stem of the iron weathervane. His bandage had come away in his struggle, and he stood with his raw, empty eye socket glistening with rain. The weathervane had been spinning wildly in the wind but stopped now, its own vacant eyehole mirroring Silas'.

'All the while,' Edita's voice whispered in Bo's mind, 'I lay in my tomb, dreaming ... dreaming of escape, of finding Bruno ... but by the turn of the hour, I dreamed no more.'

Below, Bruno fell to his knees, and started pounding his fist against his chest.

'No!' he cried. It was almost unbearable to hear. 'Noooooo...'

Bruno looked up at Silas clinging to the very highest point of the steeple, his eyes as wild and inhuman as his voice.

'In the catacombs!' Silas called down, his own voice trembling now. 'She's down there, you can go down...' His eyes focused on the wreckage of what had been his church just minutes ago, and the tree lying directly over where the entrance to the secret staircase ought to have been. 'There's another way in!' Silas yelped. 'The east door...'

If Bruno heard these last words, he gave no sign. He was still, with one hand held over his heart, like he was about to give a rousing speech. But he didn't say a word. Instead he just stared at Silas.

'The east door!' Silas tried again. 'There's a tunnel, east of here. Another way into the catacombs. It's...'

Bruno roared. Light speared the sky, snaking over the town too quickly for Bo to follow. But she saw the exact moment the lightning struck Silas. One splinter of it glinted through the hollow eye socket of the cockerel as though bringing the weathervane to life at the same moment it took Silas' from him. The man fell limp, his body sliding down the roof tiles just as the bell struck one final, booming note. It was still echoing as Silas' corpse fell from the tower, and the scene faded to nothing.

Bo sat back, pulling her hand from the darkened crystal. Her fingertips felt numb. She rubbed her hands together, trying to stop them shaking. She took a deep breath and looked around her.

'Well, I suppose that explains how his spirit might've gotten attached to the weathervane,' she said, and laughed flatly. 'Doesn't help me find the bloody east door, though.'

Chapter Eleven

'I should be with Bruno… Twins should always be together…
Find the east door…'

Edita's voice whirled around Bo like mist inside the
fortune-teller's hut.

'Alright, I get it. You want to be back with your brother or
whatever. Any suggestions on how to go about it? So far all
you've achieved is pied-pipering all the kids in Blackfin
around town for an hour each night.'

An hour; that was how long it had been from the point Silas
knocked Edita unconscious with his walking stick to when she
presumably died, walled inside the underground crypt. Was
that why Edita's dream-voice or whatever it was only called to
the kids in town for that same hour? Bo's chest tightened at
that thought, remembering the dreams she'd had after Sky's
death, about being trapped underground, buried alive.

Wait, those hadn't been dreams about Sky… They'd been
Edita's memories, shared through whatever weird connection
her voice created. The connection that robbed Bo of her will
whenever she heard it. Even setting aside the fact that what
Edita could do was basically a gross violation of someone
else's mind, yes, even setting that aside, Bo couldn't exactly

234

help Edita if she couldn't think for herself, and midnight was looming.

'Look, here's the deal,' she addressed the disembodied voice in the tone she usually used to bargain with her little brothers. She just hoped Edita could actually hear her, and wasn't simply broadcasting her dreams to all the young people of Blackfin. 'I'll help you, and figure out where the heck you're buried and… well, find your brother and tell him, I suppose, so he can get you buried somewhere nicer. Somewhere that's closer to him, is that what you want?' Silas was dead, so revenge was hardly an option, and all of Edita's shared memories seemed to focus on being reunited with her twin. 'But if I do that, you need to keep quiet and not sing me into a coma again, okay?' She paused, then added, 'And leave everyone else to sleep normally, too. I don't want my brothers or any other kids wandering around town anymore. They'll just get in my way.' No need to say that she was worried her brothers might get hurt. She wouldn't have admitted that to the boys, so she would hardly tell a restless spirit.

Bo waited, unsure Edita had heard her until finally she answered.

'I will not sing my dreams tonight, or summon the little creatures from their beds. But only for tonight. I have woken and I am restless. If you haven't found my tomb before the clock strikes one, I may feel the need to spend my energies doing something … unpleasant.'

'What does that mean?' Bo snapped. Edita only laughed. It was a lovely, bell-like laugh, but Bo did not like it.

'Twins should never be kept apart,' Edita said. 'Tick-tock, Bo Peeps.'

'Yeah, yeah.' Bo checked her watch. It was half past eleven, which gave her just ninety minutes to locate Edita's tomb. That wasn't much time. 'Couldn't you give me a bit longer than that? I mean, I *am* helping you out here...'

There was no answer at all this time.

'Ninety minutes it is,' she sighed. She would just have to get cracking.

After replacing the black cloth over the crystal ball and quickly tidying away any signs of her visit, Bo left the fortune-teller's hut. She snapped the padlock back into place on the door, then set off for home, walking so briskly it was practically a jog.

In Year 8 geography, Bo's class had been tasked with drawing maps of Blackfin so that they could analyse how the ground had been sculpted by long-gone glaciers working their way down between the peaks of the Lychgate Mountains. Bo's map had been given the best mark of the entire class, as usual. And, as with all the other bits of Bo's work which were adorned with a red letter A or an 'Excellent!' Bo's mother had kept the map in one of several boxes in their cluttered garage.

It only took Bo a couple of minutes to find it, nestled between a folder of chemistry coursework and that year's school report which, she noted rather smugly, had been straight As... if you overlooked the D she had received in PE, which Bo utterly disregarded.

The map was carefully drawn on graph paper, each dip and rise of the coastline a perfect to-scale copy of the real thing, and every street, house, and footpath meticulously marked on it. The only problem with it was that the outline of Blackfin Woods held no interior detail. The teacher had specifically forbidden the class from entering the woods to map it more thoroughly, and as Bo knew it wouldn't earn her any extra marks, it really hadn't seemed worth the effort. But that meant that wherever the church was – or its ruin, now – Bo had no idea. And as the woods were broadly to the west side of Blackfin, it didn't really help her narrow her search area for the elusive 'east door'.

Why had nobody in town ever mentioned there being a church there? Even Ms Stacks at the library hadn't known about it ... or had she just neatly avoided the truth about that? Surely someone must have known about the church. Once again, Bo felt that surge of frustration that always tried to choke her when she tried to fathom the town's swathe of secrets.

If she only knew where the church had stood, the map would be very useful. So she would just have to ask the only person she knew who had definitely seen it recently.

That was, if she could find him.

———

Bo tossed items from her wardrobe, creating a moat of discarded totes and shoulder bags as she ransacked it for something suitable to carry what she needed to take with her. But she didn't own a backpack, a tote wouldn't work, and her school messenger bag would only get in the way. Cursing, she hurried down the hall to her little brothers' room and flung open their wardrobe. An avalanche of toys and games and more dinosaur onesies than two kids could possibly need spilled out onto the carpet. But then Bo hit the jackpot. Next to Scout's old Spider-Man lunchbox was a dark-blue backpack with a yellow skull and crossbones on the front. She grabbed it, then headed back to her own room.

Rolling the map and securing it with a hair bobble, Bo put it in the pilfered backpack, along with a torch, a hefty hammer (suitable for smashing into a tomb, she thought), and one of Scout's old school shoes which had a compass embedded in the heel. She paused, inspecting the items and considering what else she might need. Within two minutes she had added black leather gloves, a knife, and the old lock-picking set of her father's to the bag. She was about to leave the house again when the phone rang. Bo checked her watch; she only had an hour left before Edita's deadline. And as much as Bo hated toeing the line when threatened, she made an exception when the source of the threat was supernatural and capable of mind-control.

The phone kept ringing. At this hour, it could only be her mother checking up on her, or someone calling with Bad News. Stifling a frustrated curse, Bo answered.

'Bo! Oh, thank God you're there. I thought for a minute you might be missing too, but of course you're home because you're on the landline right now and I don't even know what I was thinking...'

It took Bo a moment to recognise the near-hysterical voice of Mrs Pearce, Ernie and Phil's mum. She'd always been a bit highly strung, but seeing as she let the howlers sleep over with her own boys every now and then, Bo suspected the woman was probably some kind of saint.

'Mrs Pearce, is everything okay?'

The woman stuttered at the interruption. 'Yes, well, no, but is your mother there? I know she was working tonight, but I thought maybe she would be home by now...'

'No, Mum won't be back until three-ish. What's up? The boys haven't driven you to throttling them, have they?' Bo laughed flatly, adjusting the backpack on her shoulder with one eye on the door.

'I haven't throttled them! Of course I haven't! Why would you say such a thing? Oh my goodness, that's what everyone will think: that I can't be trusted to take care of anyone's children...'

'Mrs Pearce,' Bo cut in again, far more calmly than she felt by this point. The woman's prattling was starting to unnerve her more than talking to Edita's spirit.

There was a gasping, snotty sound from the other end of the line and Bo was horrified to realise Mrs Pearce was crying.

'Mrs Pearce? What's going on?'

The sobbing ceased just long enough for the woman to choke out four words.

'It's Levi – he's vanished!'

All thoughts of Edita and her deadline flew from Bo's head at that moment.

'What do you mean, vanished? How?'

Mrs Pearce was sobbing in earnest now, but between the choking gurgles Bo just about managed to gather that all four boys had been asleep upstairs an hour ago, but when Mrs Pearce looked in on them again as she was heading to bed, Levi's sleeping bag was empty.

'None of the other boys had a clue he was missing or where he might've gone! He hasn't wandered home, has he?'

Bo had been in the twins' room just a few minutes ago, and there was no sign of her little brother there.

'No, he's not here. Can you put Scout on the phone?' Bo knew she shouldn't be snappy with Mrs Pearce, but it seemed to be the only thing that would stop her rambling. When Scout came on the line he sounded half asleep, and Bo could just picture him standing there in his onesie, knuckling sleep from his eyes.

'Scout, tell me what happened.'

'I dunno, Bobo. Levi wasn't here when Mrs Pearce woke everyone up.'

'And you've got no idea where he might've gone?' Of course, Bo was beginning to have an inkling about where he'd gone, or at least who was responsible. The echo of Edita's words: *I may feel the need to spend my energies doing something ... unpleasant* rang through her mind. And the *twins must never be kept apart* bit: Bo had thought Edita was

240

talking about herself and her brother, but had she been talking about the howlers? 'Levi didn't ... you don't know if that creepy voice spoke to him again?'

There was the sound of a long yawn before Scout answered. 'Maybe. He's sleeping somewhere really dark right now, so I can't ask him.'

'How do you know he's somewhere dark?'

Bo could practically hear Scout's shrug. 'I just know,' he said.

'Well, do you know if he's okay? Not hurt or anything?'

Scout sighed impatiently. 'He's just sleeping. Can I go back to sleep now, too?'

Bo hung up after quickly reassuring Mrs Pearce that she knew where Levi was probably hiding (which was a lie) and that she would let her know as soon as she found him (not a lie... she hoped).

As Bo at last stepped through her back door and out onto the streets of Blackfin, she knew three things for certain:

- She needed to find Jared so he could tell her where the ruined church was, and hopefully help her figure out where the east door was likely to be.
- She only had an hour left before Edita's *something ... unpleasant* deadline.
- Edita had apparently kept her word at least partly so far: it was after midnight, and both Scout and Mrs Pearce seemed in full control of their faculties.

Perhaps Levi really had just wandered off, and it wasn't anything to do with Edita. Bo rolled the idea around in her head, and decided she didn't like the taste of it; it smacked of wishful thinking. In any case, she would only know for sure when she found Levi, and she had a strong inkling that would happen more quickly if she located Edita's tomb.

'If you've got Levi, you'd better not hurt the little bugger,' Bo called out to the empty house. 'Even if he's really, *really* annoying. You hear me, Edita? Our deal is off if you do.' She wasn't sure how exactly she would get revenge on a girl who was already dead, but she would get creative if she needed to.

Chapter Twelve

Bo had picked the lock on the gates to Blackfin Woods easily enough. Then it had just been a matter of following the faint tyre tracks snaking between the trees until she found Jared's van parked beneath an enormous oak with branches like knotted tentacles.

Quite out of breath and hankering for a cigarette, Bo was about to knock on the door of the van when she spotted an arched shape silhouetted in the moonlight. As she drew closer, she saw it was a window. Or rather, a window frame; the glass had long since disappeared from it, and now the moonlight shone unhindered through the stone arch.

This was the church, right here. A wall of it, at least. The rough stones stood silent and grave, a forgotten monument. The rest lay mostly in rubble, the carcass of the huge tree she had watched fall on the building still lying diagonally amid the debris. It looked as though not a soul had been here since the night she had seen replayed inside the crystal ball. Someone must have visited, though, to have removed the weathervane from the slanted steeple and transplanted it to the roof of Blackfin High. And Jared had obviously been here when he found the journal.

At any other time, Bo might have explored the ruin, but that wasn't why she was here. Dropping her bag onto the forest floor, she rifled through it until she had her little brother's compass-shoe and the map she had painstakingly drawn of the town. She traced the path she had taken from the gate of Blackfin Woods to where she was now – in the middle of the green blob, according to her map – and drew an X on it. It wasn't as exact as it would've been had she been able to properly measure the distance she had walked in the indentations of Jared's tyres, but it would do. Next she checked the compass, and drew a neat line from the X pointing eastward over the map.

Hmm. It led directly back the way she had come, and she hadn't seen any likely candidates for 'east door' status on her trek through the woods. It was possible the door was nothing more than a hole in the ground, but thinking about that didn't help; there was no way she could conduct a thorough search for a *hole* in the forty-five minutes she had left before Edita maybe, possibly, did something nasty to Levi.

Forty-five minutes?!

What about beyond the woodland perimeter? Bo tried to regain her focus. The line passed over the roofs of a few houses, a pond, the park, Blackfin High, and then hit the sea roughly half a mile from where Bo now stood.

The school? Would an underground tunnel stretch that far? Perhaps, if it had been built to smuggle things brought into the bay by boat … or as a means for a clergyman to escape *to* a boat if he were being pursued, like when Catholic priests used to hide in priest holes back in the sixteenth century. She had initially dismissed the school because there was no east-facing door, but from what Silas had said, *east door* referred to its position to the church, not the way the door was facing.

Bo studied the map again, but nothing stood out as a more likely option for the location of the east door. And there must be some connection between the school and the church; after all, Silas had been moved from one to the other after the church was demolished. So maybe there was a more tangible connection, too? Like an underground tunnel. It made as much sense as anything in this town did, anyway. She tucked the map and the compass back into her bag, retraced her steps to Jared's van, and pounded on the metal siding with her fist.

A few seconds later, his bleary-eyed face appeared at the van window.

'Open up,' Bo called through the glass. 'I need a favour. Two, actually, seeing as you're awake.'

Jared dropped Bo at the end of the footpath leading to Blackfin High and the promenade.

'Are you sure you don't want me to come with you? I could at least keep lookout or something.'

Bo shook her head. 'You're more use to me running interference with my mum. Just go and sleep in my bed.

Then if she gets home before I do and she happens to look in on me, she won't know I'm not there.'

'You don't think she'll notice I'm not you?' Jared said, looking dubious.

Bo snorted. 'She's not going to run a DNA test. As long as there's a breathing body in my bed, that's all Mum will be bothered about. *I* can't be bothered with getting grounded again.'

'Oh, alright then.' Jared shifted the van into gear. 'But if she finds me and starts screaming that I'm some kind of creep, I will *not* be happy.'

Bo was about to leg it for the school when she remembered one final thing she needed him to do.

'And can you unplug the phone when you get there? I don't want Mrs Pearce calling Mum and freaking her out before I've found Levi.'

Jared gave a weary salute, and then the camper was chugging back down the road in the direction of the Peeps household.

The school was dark and silent ahead of her, the only light coming from the moon glinting off the high sash windows and the reflection of Bo's torch beam bouncing in her hand. It had only taken a couple of minutes to drive from the woods to the school path, but Bo didn't have any time to waste. She ran toward the school, yanking her bag when it snagged on the rough stone wall of the Penny Well, and through the school gates.

On the short journey back, Bo had decided that the most

likely spot in the school for an entrance to a tunnel would be via the basement, so she went around the back to where the building supervisor's office was. She paused at the back door. All quiet. Good.

Bo pulled out the lock-picking set for the second time that night.

The leather fold was empty. Not a single pick remained.

'Seriously? *Seriously?!*'

The leather became a screwed-up rag in Bo's fist. She glared back over her shoulder, remembering the tug on her bag strap as she passed by the Penny Well. It had stolen the picks straight out of her backpack.

Bo stomped over and shone her torch beam down over the stone wall of the well. The light disappeared after perhaps twenty feet, fading into complete and unfathomable blackness.

'Give them back!'

Her voice echoed back to her, thin and weak.

Now what was she supposed to do? Bo supposed she could break a window to get into the school, but she had a feeling that would set off an alarm, and she didn't *particularly* want to be arrested for vandalism. At least, not before she had found her brother.

She could go around all the windows checking for one that hadn't been locked properly, but that would take ages, and she probably wouldn't find a way in anyway. Then she'd be back to breaking a window with even less time.

With a growl of rage, Bo kicked the stony side of the well.

Pain shot through her foot, and she dropped to her knees to clutch it, a string of incoherent curses spilling from her mouth. She rubbed the tender toes through her shoe. Nothing felt broken, thank God.

Bo raised her head, about to resume her inevitable descent into breaking and entering (her dad would be so proud) when she noticed something odd about the curved stone wall in front of her. Under the dirt and moss covering the old well's wall in a patchwork of age and neglect, one of the stones had an odd shape. It was round where the others were all vaguely rectangular, and had two raised notches at the edge, as though to allow it to be turned.

Bo wrapped her hand around it. The stone was cold and strangely smooth against her skin. What was it for? It had to be a deliberate feature, but she couldn't imagine what purpose it served. Frowning, she tried turning the stone. It shifted a fraction. Bo twisted it harder. With an awful grating sound that made her jerk back her hand, the stone moved in a complete circle.

She waited. Nothing happened. Bo was starting to believe the turning stone was just some random quirk of the well's architecture when suddenly the ground rumbled underneath her. The rumbling grew into a clattering series of thumps, as though a giant was using rocks for a game of marbles. It only lasted a few seconds, and then all was quiet again. Bo stood up and peered over the side of the well.

At first she couldn't make out anything different, but as she passed her torchlight over the inner walls, she saw that there were now narrow, regular stairs emerging from them. The steps spiralled down into the darkness, disappearing beyond the reach of her light.

Bo smiled a small, satisfied smile. 'The east door,' she whispered, then threw back her head and yelled, '*The east door*!'

Because that was what it had to be. An entrance to an underground tunnel – what better place for it than inside an old well shaft? Feeling energised by the discovery, Bo climbed up onto the wall, swung her legs over the side, and started to climb down.

Chapter Thirteen

The steps were barely wider than her foot. Bo clung to the rough wall with her fingertips to keep her balance as she descended, one eye on the very deep, very black drop into the shaft. She did *not* want to end up falling down a bloody well.

Bo's torch beam bounced off the pale stones, making the shadows dance as she went deeper and deeper. She saw no sign of there ever having been water in the well; no tide mark, no discolouration. What kind of well had never had water in it? A pilfering one, Bo decided, thinking of all the loose change and other small items she had lost to it over the years … and very recently her father's lock picks. But it wasn't actually a well at all, was it? Not if its true purpose was to secretly connect the coast to the catacombs under the church, some half a mile inland.

Her feet touched dirt. The shift from the narrow stone steps to the gravelly base of the well shaft set Bo off-balance. As she reached out to steady herself, she instead stumbled into a dark recess that smelled damp and stagnant. But it was not actually a recess. A pass of her torch showed her the beginning of a stone-lined passageway. She checked around her in case there were any other tunnels leading from the base of the well but saw none. So, this was it. A musty, dank tunnel which would, she hoped, lead the way to her little brother. And a dead girl's tomb.

Yay.

Her torch pulled glints from the blackness. A coin, a dinner fork, and what might've been a tin whistle were all lodged in cracks in the tunnel walls, reflecting her light back to her.

There was no sound except the echo of her own footsteps, and yet Bo couldn't call it quiet. There was an odd kind of vibration in the stale air, as though something made a noise too low or too high-pitched to hear.

'Levi?' Bo called. The sound travelled away into the dark before fading. 'Levi? Are you down here?'

She waited for an answer, aware that she only had around half an hour left before Edita's deadline. Would the spirit really do something awful to Levi? Or would she simply go back to making all the kids in Blackfin sleepwalk? Surely neither would be of particular benefit to Edita if what she really wanted was to be reunited with her twin.

That means nothing, Bo thought. *There's no point expecting to find logic in Blackfin.*

Sky had always looked for logic in the town, and instead it had swallowed her in its icy waters. Nobody had seen that coming, least of all Bo. There was no logic in the death of a teenage girl.

Something cold touched Bo's neck, and she gave a yelp before realising it was only a drip of water from the ceiling.

251

As she hurried further along the tunnel, she saw how crudely it had been built. Parts were made from coarse slabs of rock, and others had been hacked straight through the ground with nothing but thick wooden struts keeping the earth from crashing down on her. If it fell, nobody would ever find her here, or even know where she'd gone. She would be trapped just as surely as Edita.

Bo swallowed, hard. What was she doing in some forgotten underground tunnel, chasing after a spiteful ghost?

Looking for Levi, duh.

She paused after a minute or so, peering into a dark nook that appeared to be an off-shoot of the main tunnel. There had been several of these smaller corridors branching off, and Bo began to doubt her decision to keep to a fixed path. She'd assumed it would be a straight line to the church, but that relied on her map being pinpoint accurate.

She peered into the deeper darkness. It was impossible to tell how far the off-shoot went without going further in, and Bo didn't have time to waste exploring. She pulled the shoe-compass out of her backpack and waited for the pointer to tell her which way was west and the church. But the pointer didn't settle; it just kept spinning.

'What the hell…?'

Then it struck her. *Magnetism.*

Magnets attracted metallic objects to them and affected compasses. All those coins and bits of metal stuck in the walls of the well shaft … something down here was magnetic, and Bo was getting closer to it.

She couldn't count on the compass to guide her now. 'Just stick to the straight path,' she muttered. 'The well was a straight line east from the church, so I should just keep going straight.'

It made sense, but it didn't stop an additional sheen of sweat prickling along her spine.

Those peculiar vibrations seemed to get stronger the further she went, too. It was almost a sound now, a deep sound, and Bo could feel the stone wall tremble when she laid her hand against it. She couldn't say for sure what was causing the magnetic effect of the tunnel, but it *had* to be something to do with Edita, didn't it? Was this what happened when she wasn't allowed to exercise her weird power? Was this why the Penny Well had been pick-pocketing the Blackfin locals for years? Had her power been building within the earth all this time, just waiting for Edita to wake up?

Again, Bo wished Sky were here to talk logic with her. Then she had a grim realisation: she was buried even deeper than Sky was now.

Her flat laugh echoed – but not like her footsteps had echoed earlier in the tunnel. She stamped her feet to check, and realised the echo was greatly diminished. Bo panned her torch around her and saw why: she was near the end of the tunnel. And in the wall, just to her right, she saw the same rough patch of mortar she had witnessed Silas hurriedly putting in place.

This was it. This was where Edita's corpse lay.

A rock pile had fallen from the ceiling in front of it at some point since Edita had been walled in. It sat almost as a marker: the burial she should have had. But it also blocked Bo's path, stacked as it was partly against the wall of the tomb.

She set down her torch so it shone toward the pile. The rocks weren't overly large, but she soon found herself sweating as she heaved them out of the way. They chafed at her hands, but Bo ignored it. She had no time to worry about blisters.

Minutes ticked away as she reduced the pile to around knee height – low enough, she thought, that she could start hacking away at the brickwork Silas had so hastily laid above it. Then Bo saw something glinting from within the remaining pile of rocks. She leaned in, peering closer. From this angle, it looked almost like a bony hand.

Bo picked up the torch. There was no way it was a hand. The wall of Edita's tomb was intact, so her skeleton had to be inside it. She shoved another stone from the pile. The hand-like thing seemed to be attached to a wrist-like thing. And on the wrist-like thing was what looked suspiciously like a watch.

She couldn't deny it now. She was looking at a dead body. Or a part of one, at least. But whose?

Ignoring the sensible voice in her head telling her to get the hell away from this place with its skeletal remains and weird, vibrating air, Bo held up the torch so she could see the watch better. It was quite big, probably the kind a man would wear, with a tattered leather strap. The face was shattered, probably smashed during the rockfall. The hands pointed to one o'clock.

The time Edita died, and when her voice now falls silent.

The time she promised to do something unpleasant if I haven't uncovered her tomb by then...

A time that was only minutes from now.

Swallowing her nausea, Bo reached out to turn the watch so she could get a better look at it. As her fingers came into contact with the bony wrist, she felt a vibration zing out of it, shooting up her arm until she felt it in her teeth. *This* was the cause of the magnetic anomaly. This skeleton was where the strange vibration in the air was emanating from, right along the tunnel.

Bo yelped as something moved in the rock pile, but she saw it was only the watch. The strap had given way, letting it fall face-down onto the nearest stone. Gingerly, Bo picked it up and examined it. There was something engraved into the back of it in bold, determined letters.

BRUNO.

Seeing his name etched into the metal casing felt inevitable, somehow. Edita's twin had found her. He had come down here and ... what? Been crushed in a freak rockfall?

Bo looked at his outstretched hand. It looked like he had died reaching for his twin, probably knowing they would always be held apart. But wait... This probably hadn't just been some random rockfall, had it? Why here, and nowhere else in the tunnels? Bo chewed her lip, picturing the young man she had seen in Edita's dreams, and inside the crystal ball.

He had avoided using his strange gift because it was too powerful, too volatile. But when pushed, he had used it against Silas. Had he used it to try to free his sister as she lay murdered in an unmarked tomb? It wasn't difficult to see how all that power might have brought the ceiling down right on top of him.

Even with Edita's threat hanging over her and Levi, Bo felt a pang of sympathy for the dead twins. They hadn't been good people, but they hadn't deserved to die like this. And they shouldn't be forever kept apart by Silas' wall.

'I'll make sure you at least get to spend the rest of your afterlife, or whatever this is, together,' Bo said. The tunnel hummed around her, the vibrations building as though stirring to life. Was this some remnant of Bruno's voice, or was he, too, being stirred awake? Bo didn't know, but she wasn't about to hang around and find out.

It only took a minute to uncover the rest of his bones from the rock pile. As tattered as they were, she recognised his clothes as the ones he'd been wearing during his fight with Silas.

Taking the hammer from her backpack, Bo started hacking at the wall of the tomb.

Bo knew she would find skeletal remains in the walled chamber, but it still surprised her a little not to see Edita's beautiful face when she shone her torch inside the tomb. The hair that had been lustrous and curly was now dusty and brittle, the lips and eyes that had captivated Bo now completely gone. Just a grinning skull was left in their place.

There wasn't a lot of space inside the tomb, but she carefully placed Bruno's remains next to Edita's, avoiding contact with his humming bones as much as possible. Her skin crawled. She was doing the right thing, though. The twins should be together. Bo would make sure they were.

Once both were laid out as neatly as she could manage, Bo stood back, noticing just how *loud* the tunnel had become. That hum in the air had changed, turning into a deep rumble she definitely didn't like. It reminded her of the sound Bruno had made at the moment he felt his twin die.

Bo checked her watch. *Balls.* It was almost one o'clock.

'Okay, I've done what you wanted – and I've got the blisters to prove it. Now hold up your end of the bargain and let Levi go!'

Bo flinched as laughter echoed through the walls.

'Bruno,' came Edita's sing-song voice. It still held such an appealing quality, even now. 'We are together again, and our powers can mingle…'

'Where is my brother?' Bo yelled, cringing at the reverberating sound surrounding her. It felt like it might bury her in this place. 'Levi!'

Edita's laugh rang out again before something in the air snapped. Bo's ears popped, and she heard cracking, crunching sounds digging their way through the rock walls. 'Twins should never be kept apart.'

'Where is my brother, you noisy cow?'

'Safe, now that the deal is done,' Edita said. 'Now leave us in peace. *Run.*'

And then the tunnel began to shake.

Bo fled. Her hatred of running be damned – she sprinted at a pace she hadn't known possible. Flying along the tunnel, she jumped as shards of rock and earth showered down on her head. It was like the tunnel itself was waking, straining its lungs and trying to cough her out of its system.

The light bounced, disorienting her as she ran, but Bo didn't veer from the straight path that would take her back to the well shaft, the east door, and back up to safety.

Stupid bloody ghosts and their unreasonable dying wishes!

She was going so fast she didn't see the newly fallen rock pile blocking her path until she ran headlong into it.

Bo took the brunt of the impact on her knees. Cursing Edita and her brother, she felt around for her dropped torch. Luckily it hadn't broken when she fell, but as she raised the light she saw that a large section of the ceiling had caved in, blocking the tunnel back to the well shaft.

'Oh God.'

She scrubbed one hand back through her hair, trying to force her brain to work. But all she could think was that she was buried alive, just like she'd feared. She was going to die down here, and nobody would find her, and she'd never know where Levi was or if he was okay…

'Shut up,' she snapped. Not to anyone in particular, but snapping made her feel calmer. Calm enough to assess the situation and try to find a way out of it.

Panning the torch beam over the pile of rocks, she saw there was no way she'd be able to smash her way through it with her hammer. Most of the debris looked too heavy for her to move, and she knew it wasn't a good idea to move it anyway: the rock pile was probably the only thing keeping the tunnel from collapsing completely.

But as she moved the light higher, Bo found that the way forward wasn't entirely blocked. There was a gap, up near the ceiling, perhaps wide enough for a cat to squeeze through.

Bo sighed, and dropped her backpack.

'This is going to be grim,' she said, and clambered up the side of the rock pile.

It took several minutes just to work up the nerve to begin bending and squeezing her body into the gap. The earth smelled damp and deathly all around her. Bo's heart pounded, thudding dully against the pressing soil, and she knew that on some level her nightmares had been warning her about this moment. Perhaps even Madame Curio had seen this coming, and that was why she had cautioned Bo to stay away from the Penny Well.

If I ever get out of here, I'm going to have a word with that fortune-teller about being a bit more bloody specific.

Bo pressed forward, wriggling her elbows and knees so she was propelled deeper into the gap between the rock pile and the tunnel ceiling. She paused to shift the torch, shining its beam ahead of her. *Thank God.* She could see where the space opened out, perhaps half a metre in front of her hand. She could do this, just as long as she didn't get stuck.

Don't even think it. Bo pushed on, more determined now, and with no time to think about the tons of earth bearing down above her head.

Two minutes later, she wriggled free and ran for the well shaft, only limping slightly. Her footsteps echoed loudly again, bouncing from the tunnel walls like laughter. Bo ignored them.

At last she burst from the tunnel. The pale moon cast a spotlight down on her, the silhouetted shapes of the narrow steps spiralling up the well shaft calling her back to solid ground. Clinging to the wall, Bo forced her burning muscles to carry her back up the winding staircase. She half expected the steps would disappear, sliding back into the wall and dropping her all the way back to the bottom of the well, but they held steady. Only as she hauled herself over the lip of the well and collapsed onto the gravel path next to it did Bo hear the tell-tale rasp of the stones withdrawing, the circular stone she had used to reveal them earlier now turning back to its former position.

She lay panting on the ground, looking up at the stars. Bo knew she needed to find Levi, to make sure Edita hadn't lied about him being safe, but that sense of panic she'd felt earlier was gone.

How strange. There was no echo of Edita's laughter now, no sound of falling rocks or air humming with power. Had she even heard that at all, or was it just some trick of Edita's?

Some last bit of puppetry before she rested, Bo hoped, in peace?

This was the last time Bo would get herself tangled in one of Blackfin's mysteries. This had all been far too much effort.

'There you are.'

Bo turned her head just enough to see Jared sliding from the driver's seat of his camper van. There was another figure in the passenger seat beside him, and Bo yelped out a laugh when she saw who it was.

'Oh my God, he's okay! Where did you find him?' she asked Jared, gesturing toward Levi, who was now making engine noises and pretending to drive the van.

'He was under your bed. I was just lying there, like you asked, dreading the moment your mum would walk in and start screaming, until a few minutes ago when this little voice tells me, *The girl says I can stop hiding now.* He scared me half to death.' Jared shook his head. 'You should probably change your sheets before you go to bed tonight.'

Bo laughed, then held out a hand for Jared to help her up.

'Thanks for looking after him. I take it Mum's not home yet?'

'No. At least, she wasn't there when I left.'

'Good. We can drop Levi back at Mrs Pearce's on the way home, and then Mum won't have a clue anything weird happened … that is, if you don't mind doing me one last favour?' Bo smiled, meaning it to be endearing but knowing it probably wasn't. Jared just shook his head wearily.

'I'll add it to the very long list of favours you already owe me.'

Epilogue

No voice summoned the children of Blackfin from their beds the following night, or any night after that. The weathervane still scowled down at the passing townspeople, and the Penny Well continued to steal coins from the pockets of anyone who wandered too near. But nobody questioned those things.

Bo certainly didn't. And although she often thought about the raven-haired twins lying in their underground tomb, she kept that secret to herself. She had meddled in the mysteries of Blackfin, despite her best and most slovenly intentions, and had suffered for it. She'd nursed blisters, bruised knees, and aching muscles for days after her misadventure in the tunnels, and had no intention of ever doing something like that again.

No, let Blackfin's secrets stay buried, she thought.

As for Silas … he remained as he had for so many years: watching over the town he had always loathed so very much; a part of it, yet apart from it. He didn't think much of Bo's pledge to avoid meddling in the ways of the town, either. Teenagers couldn't help meddling. And this town had so very many mysteries to unravel.

What really happened the night Sky died? What is Jared hiding? And what else is waiting to be discovered in Blackfin Woods? Uncover more of the town's secrets in BLACKFIN SKY, available now from Firefly Press.

Remember: nothing stays buried in Blackfin.

Matchgirl

Rhian Ivory

'Where words fail, music speaks.'
Hans Christian Andersen

Chapter One

'I thought you should know I've written a letter,' Nia's dad announced as he poured his first coffee.

'I didn't know people still sent those.' Nia offered him the milk jug. Her dad didn't smile; he'd probably forgotten how. She shrugged her shoulders – her wit was wasted on this audience. She waited for him to say more but he'd reverted to type and was now eating in silence.

'OK ... so are you going to tell me any more or shall I guess?' She coated her porridge thickly in brown sugar.

'I'm sorry.'

He anticipated the need to apologise. Nia put her spoon down and ran through the list of people her father could have sent a letter to. It was pretty short.

'The letter is to tell school that you won't be going on the Winter Festival Tour,' Jacob said. He drained his mug of coffee and stood up, bracing himself for her reaction.

Nia had known there'd be consequences; Sol had already been grounded for a week. After the phone call from school yesterday Nia had thought she'd be grounded too or that he'd take her phone away: something, anything, but not this.

Not this.

'*NO*! No, Dad! *Please*!' she begged. She didn't care how pathetic she sounded. She wouldn't let him do it.

'I warned you after the last detention. I can't trust you, Nia.'

He wasn't open to negotiation. This was it, her last connection and he was cutting it off, ripping it from her, tearing it away. How could he? *I hate you*, Nia wanted to scream at him, although it wasn't necessary, he could see it in her eyes.

'You have to understand why, Nia. The Winter Festival is too dangerous. You're too young to be away from home, to travel without me there to look after you. The rest of the choir are all a lot older than you. I'm sorry but there are too many unknowns, too many strangers, too many different towns and hostels. I can't let you go. *I can't let you go too*.' His words ran into one another, coming out too quickly for Nia to take in.

'Mum would have let me go,' Nia whispered, not sure if he'd heard her.

He wouldn't look at her.

'I'm never, ever speaking to you again,' Nia said, loudly this time, pushing her chair back from the table. She shoved on her coat, grabbed her bag from the hook near the door, forced her feet into her snow boots and charged out. She left the door wide open in the hope that all the heat would follow her out of the house and leave him in it, cold and alone.

She pounded through the woods, the cold air scratching her throat. She smashed into the outstretched arms of the trees that got in her way, the snow-covered branches clawing at her long hair. She stamped down hard on the frozen ground, trying to get rid of some of her anger before reaching Sol's house. This was where she went, where she always found herself running to now, running away from her father.

'*Uh oh*. What's happened?' Sol asked as he opened the front door.

'My dad,' Nia panted. He rolled his eyes; it was hardly a surprise. 'He's told school I'm not going on the Winter Festival Tour. He's written them a letter! As if he's never heard of email or the internet.'

Nia spat out the words as she searched for her gloves in her coat pocket. Then she turned away and started to make her way through the forest towards the bus stop. Sol had to jog to keep up with her.

'He says we broke the rules and now we have to pay for it. He says he warned me, *no more trouble*.'

She really hadn't been looking for trouble when they decided to leave the school grounds last week. She'd just wanted to do something different, instead of sitting in the canteen with all the others listening to the same jokes, the gossip as flavourless as the reheated food. She pulled Sol away from his half-eaten pancake and walked outside with him.

'We've got forty minutes of lunch left, that's just enough to get to the town square and back again before we're missed.

Fancy it?' she asked, expecting him to say no, as he always did.

'Go on then, but only if we can climb St Oswald's tower.' He surprised her and a smile broke across her face.

They walked through the town, school ties hidden under their coats. They tried to blend in with the lunchtime shoppers – parents pulling tired and hungry toddlers along and retired couples with all the time in the world to wander slowly along the cobbled streets. Nia and Sol ran around them, weaving and darting out of their way as they headed for the music shop first. The bell clanged, announcing their arrival to Carl, one of the new owners.

'Hello, is it that time already?' he looked at his watch for a moment, as if the afternoon had passed him by.

'Shouldn't you two be at school?' asked Harald, his partner. He didn't know them or their names, but the question was enough to put Nia on edge. She only dared enter the music shop because the owners were new and wouldn't know her dad, wouldn't mention the fact that she'd been in there to him. She mumbled something about lunch break and dodged any more questions by sitting down at the piano. As Nia stroked the keys, Sol wandered the aisles looking pointlessly at sheet music he couldn't read, let alone appreciate. His musical skills were all in his ears.

When Nia began playing Sol stopped what he was doing to listen, Carl sighed and settled down on his stool and Harald opened the shop door. Nia's playing was a great advertisement for the shop and might entice in some customers.

'No. Shut it!' Nia begged, jumping up from the piano. Harald looked bewildered. Nia gathered up her bag and coat and left the shop. Sol followed, hearing the bell clang again as the door shut behind them.

'He's at work,' Sol reasoned as they headed towards the church and the bell tower. 'Your dad's not going to suddenly appear in the music shop in the middle of the day, is he?'

'I know, but he could come into town for something.' She raised her arms to the air as if to say *don't ask me what*. Nia's father was a creature of habit, making his packed lunch every evening before he went to bed, placing it carefully in the fridge ready for the next day. He never came to town in the middle of a work day.

'You're paranoid!' Sol told her. Nia nodded but she didn't care. It just wasn't worth the risk. She'd promised her father. She'd given him her word that she wouldn't follow in her mother's footsteps, would leave music behind.

But she just couldn't do it.

She just couldn't stop.

Chapter Two

They'd climbed St Oswald's tower quickly, aware how little stolen time they had.

'Come on, I'll race you!' Sol challenged. They ran up the tight spiral steps, winding their way higher. This was Sol's favourite place and he never tired of the same view of Wildsee Lake. Nia held the heavy door at the top open for him as he caught her up. They walked out into a white sky like a sail billowing in front of them, holding the snow back, just. Sol reached into his pockets and put his gloves on. Nia did the same. They leaned against one another, watching the heavy sag of the clouds loaded with snow waiting to fall.

'So, why did you want to come into town? What couldn't wait until Saturday?' Sol was breathing heavily. The air was so thin and sharp up here, closer to the mountains.

'Hmm?' said Nia. She wasn't ready to answer. She wondered if he'd realise, hoped he'd work it out so she wouldn't have to say the words.

'Nia?' Sol was clearly unwilling to be put off. Perhaps because they never seemed to get a chance to talk about things properly these days. There was always something in the way; someone waiting to be dropped off or picked up, choir rehearsal, work, jobs around the house, homework, supper time, just always something. Now there was nothing, no one, just them.

'Why is this your favourite place, Sol?' Nia asked, switching the focus.

'You know why. Mum used to bring me up here. It would be the end to a trip into town, a way to keep me going as she got stuff done, I guess. A sort of reward, who knows? I'm seeing her this weekend, you know, she's finally moved into her new apartment.'

Sol smiled, running his hand over his hair before putting his hat back on.

'And you know I've always been a climber! This is the highest point in town, it has my name written all over it!' Sol raised his hands to the mountains and the sky as if the answer to everything was up there somewhere, if only he could get high enough to reach it.

'Come on, why aren't we in school, you know, where we're s'posed to be?' He nudged Nia's arm with his own, moving the focus back to her.

'It's almost been a year.' She knew she didn't have to tell him any more than this, didn't need to explain herself any further.

'Oh, right.' Sol felt flat, useless and too full of himself; his head filled with his parents' divorce. He'd actually forgotten about Nia's mother.

'I'm so sorry...' Sol began, but Nia shook her head and

talked over him, trying to make him feel better. She knew others had moved on; a year was a long time, but for her it felt like two minutes and just as fresh.

'I didn't want to be in school. It's too noisy today. Up here is good. I can hear myself think.' Nia's sentences were short, but he got what she meant. Sol put his arm around her shoulders and pulled her closer to him. Nia relaxed against his side.

'Nearly a whole year.'

'That's a long time.' Sol stated the obvious, searching for something more to offer her, something that wouldn't sound empty.

'Too long. And it'll just get longer from here. The time will go on and on and stretch out and away from me, getting bigger and bigger. And then I'll start counting. I'll say things like, "It's been five years," or I'll start talking about anniversaries or I'll just stop talking about Mum at all.' Nia rubbed her gloves hard over her eyes as she spoke.

Sol turned away from her, his eyes settling on the spires, the rooftops and the buildings coated in the first fall of snow. It looked so peaceful; they couldn't hear the noise of cars from up here, just the ticking clock and the wind moving softly around the large bells that hung above them.

'It'll be our first Christmas without her,' Nia whispered.

'It won't always be this bad. It won't always be like this, I promise,' Sol replied, guessing at the truth, trying to imagine how he'd feel if he was Nia. But it was impossible. Sol knew he couldn't imagine what it would be like because it hadn't happened to him – until something bad happened

274

to you how could you know when it would stop hurting?

Anything else was just a lie.

By the time they'd climbed back down, they were late. The bells clanged and clanked, ringing out their troubles. They held hands and ran through the town, nearly knocking a woman over. She shouted at them and they laughed nervously, embarrassed. Sol flung an apology over his shoulder as they ran on.

If it had been PE or art they'd have got away with it, Nia decided afterwards, as they sat in silence on the hard wooden chairs outside the Head's office trying not to look at one another. If only it hadn't been French and Madame Reinard. If only they hadn't been twenty-five minutes late; maybe if it had just been five they could have made something up about feeling ill or losing their school bags out on the field. But half an hour was too much. Madame Reinard had held her hand up as they entered the room ready with a tumble of excuses, and silenced them with the glare from all the gold rings on her fingers.

'*Sortir d'ici! Maintenant!*' she'd ordered, her long dangly earrings shaking as she gestured to the door with her head. The rest of the class sat up, anticipating a show but Nia had no fight in her and skulked out again, leaving Sol to try and appease Madame Reinard. It didn't work; he soon joined Nia on the world's uncomfiest chairs, presumably chosen to make the wait all the worse, until the red light above the Headmistress' door changed to green with a click and they were summoned.

Chapter Three

'But of all the things to take from me, Sol! *Of all the things...*'
They were climbing the spiral ladder to the tree house in
Sol's garden a few days later. When they'd been smaller, Nia
used to imagine she was a character from a fairy tale
climbing a spiral staircase, which weaved its way around
the tree trunk, leading to a treetop palace. Now it was worn
and weathered, nailed back into place too many times to be
a thing of beauty. Soon they'd be too big and too tall for this
place. But not just yet, not today.

'I know. Harsh, but I'm grounded too, which means no
snowboarding,' said Sol flatly.

Nia flung herself onto the floor next to Sol. He offered
her an earphone. Nia shoved it into her ear but could hardly
concentrate; for once the beat didn't appeal. The music was
wrong and for one cold second Nia understood how her
father felt and why he'd removed all music from his life after
her mother died. But it was only a second of empathy,
quickly replaced with a singeing hot anger that crackled
around her like fire.

'Has he said how long you're grounded for?' Sol asked, as
he offered her a sip of his drink. Nia shook her head; she

was too restless, wound too tightly to sit up here as if they were hanging out and nothing was wrong.

'No, forever probably. He's ruined my chances of ever singing in the choir again. They won't take me back when they finish the Winter Tour. Someone will have replaced me. I bet Isa asks to sing my solo; she's been practising it, hoping for something like this to happen. The only thing I am allowed to do is walk the dogs and go to work on Saturdays. Lucky me. He'll take my phone away next!' Even though she was furious with her father she didn't want to get in any more trouble – she wasn't sure what lengths he'd go to.

Nia and Sol had been coming up to the tree house since they were old enough to climb. Sol's dad, Caleb, had built it the summer Sol had scarlet fever, to cheer him up. Sol had watched it grow, drifting in and out of his fever, propped up on pillows, being fussed over by his mother, Hanna. His dad had climbed the ladder as if he was Jack in *Jack and the Beanstalk*, wearing his heavy tool belt, and created the best tree house Sol had ever seen. It had one main platform, a pitched roof, a window and a door. Over the years they'd added extra planks of wood that Nia's father had found lying around in his woodshed. So it now looked like a tree house with wings either side, casting wooden bird shadows on to the ground below. Nia's mother, Lorelei, had offered some cushions, rugs and blankets and the place had become *theirs*, their den, their sanctuary away from the adult world. But today it felt small, childish and confined.

277

'What's the point in all of this?' Nia gestured around the wooden square shed they were sitting in, elevated in the trees. Sol looked confused; she was asking some big questions today.

'I mean this, all these trees, forests, mountains, lakes, towns, cities? The world is full of wide open spaces and concert halls, museums, art galleries and theatres, but what's the point in any of them if I'm not allowed out to explore? What if I just stay here, in this little town, all my life? Like him.' Nia finished. Sol followed her gaze, taking in the tall pine forests that stretched above them like overbearing tree giants stolen from a child's drawing.

'I want to get out there and see it all, and go to new places, like Innsbruck or Salzburg, and travel, and he won't let me just because of all the things that might happen, all the things that could go wrong. I can't breathe.' She clutched at her chest with her hand.

Sol nodded his head; he knew how she felt but didn't share these feelings. Every time Nia talked about wanting to leave — wanting to travel away from Seefeld and escape her sense of small-town claustrophobia – Sol steeled himself, as if she might jump up that second, fly out of the tree house and away.

'You will, but not yet. You have to be patient. He cares about you … *he does, Nia.*' Sol repeated some of the things he'd said before many times, but they were wearing thin and he wasn't sure he believed them himself anymore.

'Look, why don't you sit down and carve something? Did

you bring your knife?' Sol gestured to the offcuts of wood lying around.

Nia shook her head, she didn't want to do anything associated with her dad. Carving wood was *their* thing and she knew if she touched a piece of wood today she'd split it or break her blade.

'Alright, how about you play instead? It'll make you feel better.' Sol passed her the guitar in its case, the one they kept hidden at his house. Nia wanted to push it away, but she knew he was right. Which was annoying.

Nia opened the case and sniffed, as she always did, bringing the guitar up to her nose to inhale deeply. She searched for something, just a tiny drop of her mother's perfume or her honeysuckle hand cream, but the guitar couldn't hold the smell, couldn't keep the essence of her beneath its layers of wood. The strings were stronger; they could store memories, holding on to the notes of her mother's voice and the music it made. If Nia tried hard, really hard, sometimes when she played she could just about hear her mum harmonising in the background as she washed up cups or joined in on the piano. *Sometimes.* But today was for *her* music, loud clashing notes and lyrics that had nothing to do with her mother and everything to do with her father.

She made it home with moments to spare, hearing his truck pull up on the drive as she let herself in through the back door. Nia sat down quickly at the table and tipped her books out of her bag. She opened the first one to hand, grabbed a pen and began to make notes. When her father came through the door, she was the picture of the perfect student.

He almost smiled at the scene but remembered the call from the school – the reason she was grounded.

'Dinner will be ready in an hour. When you've finished you can walk the dogs and then I want to see your homework diary.'

Nia narrowed her eyes at him. He paused to kiss her on the cheek but she bent her head low, pretending to write and so he dropped a kiss on her head, like a blessing instead.

Now that Jacob thought about it, he could see it wasn't so terrible, what she'd done. He'd been guilty of plenty worse when he was in school. It was the fact that he had thought she was safe when she wasn't. Jacob watched Nia pretending to do her homework and wished he could explain this to her. He'd been at work, confident that she was at school. Instead she'd been out in town, wandering around, where anything could have occurred and no one would have been able to help her. *He* wouldn't have been there to help her. It wouldn't happen again, Jacob decided. He wouldn't let it.

Images of endless possibilities, chains of *what-ifs* linked to *buts* and *maybes*, weighed down Jacob's dreams that night, until he relinquished sleep and sat on the edge of the bed, questioning his decision again and again. He considered taking it back, phoning school to say he'd overreacted and he wanted to change his mind. But he couldn't bring himself to make the call, even though he knew how much she hated him for not letting her be part of the Winter Festival. This was the only way to keep her safe from strangers, the only way to truly know she could come to no harm. Jacob was wise enough to realise this couldn't last forever: they couldn't keep on like this. But until a better idea came to him, *this* was all he had.

Chapter Four

'I can walk to Sol's by myself? I don't need a lift, Dad.' Nia tried to insist, but it came out like a question instead.

Jacob shook his head again, holding the door open to his truck. Her voice sounded sharp in the quiet of the early morning. She didn't want to be trapped in the cab of her dad's truck. She wanted to walk slowly to school through the forest with Sol and be the first to make tracks in the snow.

'You're not driving me to school, Dad. No way! It's too early, no one will even be there yet.' Nia protested, but Jacob just stood there in silence, waiting. Nia wanted to scream at him or punch him in the chest. She threw herself up into the truck and put her seatbelt on, angrily slamming it into the holder.

'Are you trying to ruin my life?' She kicked at her rucksack in the foot-well. 'Dad? Is that what you're trying to do, make my life as miserable as yours? Because it's working. This is so embarrassing, being driven to school like I'm a child!'

She had more, a lot more to say but wanted him to respond.

'For once will you just say something back, Dad?'

He turned the key in the ignition, head facing forwards watching the road, which was quiet and empty at this time of day.

'We're going to walk the dogs at Wildsee,' he responded, knowing this wasn't what she meant, that this wasn't what she wanted him to say, but he couldn't have that conversation with her, not while she was like this. The dogs were pacing up and down in the back of the truck, whistling and whining in excitement, oblivious to the tension. 'This is going to be our new routine, walking the dogs together before school. Like we used to, remember? Your mum loved the lake, didn't she?' He tried again, as if he wanted to remind her of how things were, a hint at how things could be again if they both tried. She ignored him, folding her arms, looking out of the window. He gave up and switched on the news, letting bulletins about the weather fill the chasm between them.

Nia knew he was trying to take up all her time, make it impossible for her to have a moment alone, no time to think between him and school. And with the Christmas holidays approaching, things would be even more intense – not that either of them had mentioned the fact that it would be their first Christmas without her mother.

'Sol's going to be waiting for me.' Nia tried another tack as they sped past the trees and the bus stop. It was empty, of course. Everyone else would be at home, getting ready for school, making breakfast, doing normal things instead of … *this*.

'No, he isn't.' Jacob shook his head.

'What?' Nia dropped her defences and turned to face him as he drove steadily along the road. 'What have you done? Did you tell him you're taking me to school? *Oh my god,*

Dad! Please tell me you didn't?' Nia looked at her father in disbelief.

He'd obviously decided that she wouldn't be calling for Sol, wouldn't be walking to the bus stop with him as they did every single day. What did it matter? Just another change being made without her permission, without anyone thinking to talk to her first, to ask her if this was OK? What was the point of this stupid conversation anymore? She'd give him silence back, that'd show him. She'd let him know what it felt like to be stuck with someone who didn't want to speak, who kept all their words locked away, buckled down, wrapped up beneath layers and layers and layers of nothing.

Sure, sure, it was completely normal to stumble through their lives in this way. Pretending would be a lot easier.

Jacob pulled up by the lakeshore. Nia climbed down from the truck and whistled to the dogs. Handel and Verdi jumped down out of the cab and ran past her, full of life, happiness and joy at the prospect of an early morning walk. Nia slammed the door shut and ran after them towards Wildsee, desperate to put some distance between herself and her father. If he was set on spending every second of the day with her then he'd have to do the talking. She wasn't going to fill any more of the silences with chatter about school, her day and her life while he sat there just listening but never joining in, never offering a story of his own to balance things out. She felt like she was on a conversational seesaw, with her stuck at the top, getting nowhere.

She caught Verdi up. He'd stopped at the edge of the water,

scenting something, probably a deer, and was snouting the ground excitedly. She looked over her shoulder, watching her father trailing behind her at a slower pace, then turned back to spot Handel further up ahead tracking something in the depths of the bracken. Nia sprinted towards him, leaving her father far behind, alone with his silence and his memories.

Chapter Five

Nia tried pulling the covers over her head so she wouldn't have to engage in another awkward conversation with her father. It was Saturday morning and she'd had more than enough of her father's company over Christmas; she couldn't stand another second of it. Nia would have been happy to pretend Christmas was cancelled this year, but her father couldn't quite bring himself to ignore it entirely. As if anyone cared what they did, which traditions they followed and which they could no longer face without her mother there to infuse them with life and love. Nia had blacked the days out on the calendar in the kitchen with a permanent marker, so she wouldn't have to see Christmas Eve and the blank space where her mother's neat writing should have been. Her father didn't mention this, if he'd even noticed. She was almost looking forward to going back to school next week after the New Year celebrations. But right now, the only remedy for this solitary confinement was a drastic one. And probably dangerous.

Nia tried to remember what it felt like to be on her own but all she could hear was her father's foot tapping on the wood floor. She could smell sap and wood smoke and his pine-scented aftershave. *Just go away,* she willed him. *Leave me alone.*

'I've got to work. And as it's Saturday, so have you. Come on, Nia, stop giving me grief and get up. I've made bacon sandwiches…' His voice took on a persuasive tone.

Nia groaned, threw the covers off and looked at her father. He looked back. Neither of them said anything for a moment, wondering which move to make next. She gave in first, swinging her legs out of the bed.

'OK. I'm up, you win. Again,' she said flatly. He nodded at her then left the room. She almost wished he'd say something, shout at her and demand she pull herself together, instead of this endless nodding and silence and acceptance of her anger. He was letting her punish him, which took the punch out of it somehow. Her mother would have laughed at her, would have pulled her out of bed and told her to grow up, but she wasn't here. Besides, her mother would have let her go on the tour, would have proudly bought tickets for the whole family for the opening performance in the Hofkirche in Innsbruck. The house was empty of her singing, her shouting, her laughing, her constant noise, chatter, music and life. It was a quiet place now, empty, waiting for something to come along and fill it back up.

Nia took as long as she could in the shower, unnecessarily washing her hair. She was even longer getting dressed, making an effort: plaiting small sections of her hair and matching her blood-red lipstick to her scarf. Her father had made it for her birthday and although she wanted to stay angry with him and not wear it, she couldn't: it was still her favourite scarf. She pulled on her thick red woolly tights and turned the waistband of her denim skirt over to make it just a bit shorter, flattening the pockets down with her hand. She looked at her face as she put on another coat of mascara. At least she could be herself at the craft market; she would sing and play her guitar and busk for the tourists. It wouldn't matter who saw her busking today as none of that would matter after tonight.

Nia put a third pair of studs in her right ear; these were just for her father. He'd refused to take her to get her ears pierced, so she'd done it herself with one of her mother's sewing needles, a lump of snow and an apple as Sol had looked on, laughingly covering his own ears to stop her doing the same to him.

'Nia, your breakfast is getting cold, come on or I'll give it to Handel!' he called up to her. She knew she was trying his patience. She sat down at the kitchen table and squeezed out a small *thank you* as she bit into her bacon sandwich. Verdi and Handel watched every mouthful, salivating. Her father looked surprised and then gave her a small wink, uncertain but pleased, as he sat down opposite her. She watched as he sipped his coffee and then she saw him notice her scarf. He looked like he was going to say something, but changed his mind at the last moment and bit into his sandwich instead.

They didn't speak over breakfast but maybe something had begun to melt. The air became less heavy, and when they got into his pick-up truck and he turned Talk Radio on, Nia for once didn't wish he'd let her switch to a station that played music. She sat back and listened to the news with him, boring as it was, more droning on about fuel prices and tax cuts. She rested her head against the window as her father drove carefully along the forest road to Seefeld and went through her plans for tonight one more time.

The colours blurred as they drove past the turning to Sol's house, the bus stop, the log-felling site where her father worked and then their school as they reached the outskirts of town. The colours changed from the green of the pines to creamy buildings topped with red-tiled roofs, which merged with a palette of pastel-painted town-centre hotels, broken up by the bell tower that crowned the skyline, Sol's favourite place.

Her father pulled into the car park and turned off the engine. Nia felt her stomach drop. This meant he wanted to talk, something neither of them did very well. He never turned the engine off; he usually left it running while she grabbed her boxes of spoons and matches to sell. She didn't want him being nice now; there was nothing he could say that would change her mind or make her feel guilty about what she was going to do.

They'd never properly spoken about it in detail – her mother's death. He'd never sat her down and explained exactly what had happened that night. The police had told her more than he had, answering all the questions that had staggered out of her mouth. Words spoken by a kind woman in uniform had merged together so that all she'd heard was accident, black ice, impact and then the small word at the end like a frightening full stop. She'd tried to black out her dreams, paint them over with the colour of the night so that she couldn't see the footage play, couldn't watch the words turn into pictures of a car going too fast, sliding on the blackest of ice, wrapping itself around a too-solid tree, before the tape stopped forever.

And when it was just the two of them, and when everyone else had gratefully crept back to the light of their normal lives, neither of them had had the right words. They tried them all, starting sentences, stopping, looking for directions, for signposts to show them the way back, to help them find the right path to one another, but they never quite made it. There'd always be another twist and turn, another fork in the road. And their compass was lost.

She hoped he didn't have any words now, because it was too late.

'I'll be back before it gets dark. Don't keep me waiting this week, please. And Nia, stay safe.' She should have known the only words he'd have were the same old ones. More words about safety and precautions, but they both knew the truth: no one was safe, not even here in their little town in the middle of the mountains. Nia wrapped her red scarf around her neck several times before jumping down from his pick-up truck. He said the same thing every Saturday as he dropped her off before heading to work, but today he really sounded like he meant it. His voice was clipped and clear, brooking no argument, which suited her just fine. The less said the better, as she didn't want to give anything away.

It had been like this for most of the holidays. What was the point in decorating the tree on Christmas Eve if her mother wasn't there to tease her about the decorations she'd made in Kindergarten? Lorelei had kept them all, wrapping them in gold tissue paper. But it was the singing Nia missed the most. Singing carols around the piano before bed was something that had still happened in their house. But not now. The house ached with silence and Nia was lost in the fog of it without her mother; looking for her North: her way home.

Sol's dad had invited them over for Christmas dinner, but her father had turned him down. Said he didn't want anyone's pity. If only he could tell the difference between friendship and pity, the two of them might not be quite so alone, Nia thought.

She walked around to the bed of the truck to get out her boxes, shaking her head at him in the rear-view mirror as he made to get out and help. He looked hurt. Nia didn't want his help, didn't need him; she could do this by herself. Even so, she gave him a quick smile before putting the boxes down on the floor, then slammed the door shut. Balancing the boxes in her arms, she watched as he reversed the truck and pulled away, heading back down the long straight road towards the mountains, pine forests and his shift at work. Nia waited until his navy-blue truck finally disappeared from sight.

Chapter Six

Sol was outside, next to his dad's truck, chopping more logs and adding them to the growing piles ready to take inside the market for sale. Tasteful fairy lights were wrapped around the enormous pine tree in the entrance hall beckoning passers-by. The smell of cinnamon and soda bread drifted enticingly into the car park, which was also strewn with white fairy lights. The weekend craft market was always popular; tourists travelled far to their tall and perfectly symmetrical Town Hall to sample Moosbeernocken – Seefeld's famous blueberry crêpes – or take home Tyrolean tapas or perhaps a small piece of local art which would remind them of their holiday. And that's why it was the perfect cover: she could sell her love spoons and matches; she could play her guitar, sing and, more importantly, earn some money. She was going to need it now. No one would really notice it was her busking, she was just background noise to the many strangers who came and went. Besides, she didn't care anymore.

'How long have you been here?' Nia asked Sol, dumping her boxes on the ground.

'About an hour or two, I think. Way too early whatever time it was, but Dad says New Year's Eve is always the busiest day of the year. Even busier than Christmas Eve. So, how was it, your Christmas?' Sol paused to swig from a large bottle of water.

'How do you think? Intense. Painful. And went on way too long. Never thought I'd be so desperate for school to start.' Nia forced out a fake laugh. Sol's father interrupted them.

'Morning, Nia. How are you, love? I've got some more matches for you inside. Come on, Sol, get a shift on, it's going to be a busy one today with the rehearsals at St Oswald's...' Caleb broke off as he saw Nia's face close in. 'Sorry sweetheart, *sorry.*'

He had nothing more to follow. What could he say anyway? It was already done. Too late to try and change her dad's mind now. She was stuck here at work whilst the rest of the choir practised in the candlelit church, their final event before they left to go on the Winter Festival Tour without her. Well, not if she had anything to do with it.

'It's a shame. You were born to sing, sweetheart, just like your mother. A true lark.'

'Nia, we'd better head inside before you freeze,' Sol said, noticing her teeth chattering. Nia, carrying her boxes, gratefully followed him inside the town hall.

The room was full, noisy and warm; stallholders were setting out their goods, placing price cards next to pieces of pottery, plump batches of baking and large canvases splashed with colour. Nia knew they would have all put their prices up this time of year – even Sol did, under Caleb's instruction – but she was keeping hers the same. Someone had found a CD of carols and cranked up the volume. She could smell mulled wine and other spices in the air. It all seemed a bit forced and fake, like they were desperately hanging on to Christmas, not yet ready to surrender to the new year.

'Bah humbug?' Sol asked, looking at her screwed-up face. Nia squeezed out a laugh. New Year's Eve wasn't something to look forward to any more than Christmas, but for Sol and for everyone else it still was.

'OK, OK. They could at least have tried to find some decent music though.' She cringed at the panpipes echoing around the hall.

'Check this out instead!' He offered her an earphone and turned up the volume to mask a painful piped version of '*Oh, Tannenbaum*'. They worked side by side, Nia handing Sol a packet of matches for him to place in each log bag which he then tied up with thick brown string. They bounced to the beat of the drum'n'bass, only stopping to join in with the growing chatter of the other stallholders. They weren't the only teenagers at the craft fair. There were others who had followed in their parents' footsteps, setting up stalls of their own to earn a bit of extra money for the New Year sales tomorrow. Nia waved to Clara, her friend from school, who had spotted a gap in the knitted-items market and made everything and anything a baby could wish for, in every colour under the sun.

'Here, Nia, I got you some more.' Caleb placed another long box on their table before leaving to check everyone had everything they needed before the doors opened.

Nia unpacked the box full of matches. They were made

from cypress tree offcuts which Caleb couldn't use for anything else. He dipped the ends of them in a chemical mix before giving them to Nia. They smelt funny, like the science lab at school. Whatever he put on them worked, each match had a slow-burn tip and they were very popular at this time of year. A company selling wood burners had set up a stall with leaflets and glossy-looking photos not too far from Sol's table. It had a queue of potential customers which was fine with her and Sol – guaranteed custom right on their doorstep. Nia looked at the pictures of the stoves; they seemed so warm and inviting with a model family gathered around them. They'd always had open fires and wood burners at home. It was one of her mother's favourite things to do, prepare a fire, sit back and watch the flames dance.

'Pass me one then, Nia? What you thinking about?' Sol interrupted, holding open a bag.

'Nothing much, just daydreaming,' Nia sighed.

'Well, wake up, customers approaching. Are you sure you don't want to up your prices? Everyone else does for New Year. It's almost expected, you know.' Sol pointed at her price cards.

'No. It's cheating. Just because everyone else does it, doesn't mean I have to. Don't you have any principles, Sol?' She had worked hard for the last few weeks carving more spoons than she would usually, for the Christmas and New Year market. She'd thought about putting her prices up because she didn't know how much money she was going to need. But it still felt wrong.

'Ha! I can't afford principles, not if I want that snowboard. Suit yourself and good luck. See you on the other side,' Sol murmured and turned to face the queue already forming in front of his table.

The great oak doors to the town hall were wide open, regulars and new customers already wandering in. Somewhere someone turned the CD up even louder as Nia's own first customer approached.

Chapter Seven

'I'll take one of these, please.' A young man pointed at one of her spoons.

It was a first-kiss love spoon, plain and simple without any twists and knots. Nia had made it out of a light lime wood which was easy to carve into simple lines and curves and didn't involve any cutting out or links. The rounded bit at the top looked like a man's head and the diagonal lines she'd made following this looked like a woman's arm around his neck with hair trailing behind her. Their legs ran down the handle, meeting at the bottom to curve into the bowl of the spoon.

'My wife will love this; her family are from Wales,' the man said as he handed over his money. 'That's where love spoons come from isn't it, Wales?'

Nia nodded, reassuring him. She smiled and wrapped the spoon in gold and silver tissue paper, tied it with a tiny red ribbon and placed one of her cards on top of the spoon as she passed it over.

'Do you make these then? Is this you, Nia Christian?' He pointed at the card.

She often got asked this question. People assumed she was selling someone else's products and that this was just a

Saturday job, and to start out with that's all it had been. But as she'd got more into carving, taking books out of the library as well as watching her dad for tips about sanding, staining and polishing, she'd found that she loved it and even more surprisingly that she was quite good at it. In addition to building up her stock for the Christmas market, Nia had also been working on one spoon for weeks now; it had twists, knots which meant a lot of cutting out. She'd messed it up several times and had to start again with a fresh piece of sycamore wood. It was a treble-clef love spoon, the trickiest she'd tried so far but it was worth it. The person she was making it for would have appreciated it, would have loved it this New Year's gift. Nia had modelled it on her necklace: a tiny silver treble clef hanging from a chain, the last present her mother had given her.

The man thanked her again and left.

'Have you got anything else?' two teenage girls asked, interrupting Nia's thoughts.

'Sorry, what do you mean?' Nia was confused.

'Well, anything that's not a *spoon* for a start!' They turned to each other and laughed, making the word *spoon* sound so simple and so stupid. Nia smiled as if she got the joke, as if it was really funny, and then snapped.

'No, this is a love-spoon stall! I only sell love spoons for people who, you know, have someone to love. Have either of you got a boyfriend or girlfriend to buy a spoon for?' She waited for them to say something else but they looked surprised instead, reeling at her sharpness.

Sol stepped in, leading the girls over to a jewellery stall further up the hall. He flirted harmlessly with them, pointing out a clothes stall and other crafts that would be more their kind of thing. Nia sighed, why couldn't she have done that? Why did she have to take everything personally? They were just messing around, just asking. Why couldn't she be more like Sol?

'Alright there, Nia? No need to bite their heads off. Love spoons aren't for everyone you know,' Sol told her as she rearranged her spoons with unnecessary care, as if they could think and feel and sense what people said about them. 'This might sound a bit out there to you, but to some people they're just spoons. Obviously you and I know better, but what can you do? *Customers*!' Sol made a joke of it before leaving Nia for the food section.

She knew he was right, they were just spoons. She knew that. Of course she knew that but still … they were *her* spoons.

'Nia, I got you a hot chocolate with a shot of espresso in it. Mocha something or other, Ana's gone all fancy today. She's even doing special soups. Don't know what half of them mean or what they've got in them: seriously weird combos like curried pumpkin and stuffed peppers and bacon with cream, lime and Russian green beans. Looked like cat sick if you ask me!' Sol ran on, stopping only to sip at the caffeine-fuelled drink he really didn't need.

'Sol, did you bring my stuff?' Nia interrupted.

'Yeah. So, are you going to fill me in then?'

'Isn't it obvious?' She grinned.

'Nope, not unless you're running away?'

Sol saw Nia's face and stopped joking.

'You're not are you … Nia?' He looked around, just in case his dad was able to hear.

'No, course not!' she snapped, the smile gone.

'That's a relief.' He waved a hand as if to bat away such a suggestion.

'I'm going to Innsbruck, Sol. I'm going on the Winter Tour!' she said, wanting Sol to get it, needing him to understand.

'What? How? I mean, when? *What*?' He looked like he almost wished his dad would turn up and overhear. Stop this in its tracks before it had a chance to start, like snow rolling down a hill. Except this wasn't a snowball. It was a Nia shaped avalanche.

Chapter Eight

'Sol, where's my stuff, please?' Nia got in there before he could try and talk her out of it. 'Did you bring my guitar?'

Sol nodded. He didn't know what to say.

She sighed with relief. It had been more than a week since she'd last held her mother's guitar in her hands; they itched and ached to reach out and touch the strings. She checked her watch one more time and nodded. Sol handed over the keys to his dad's truck silently; he'd left the guitar in the back with her bag of clothes.

He shouldn't have said yes, he thought, and it was too late now. He should have known better. He hadn't asked her why she wanted a bag of clothes hidden at his house because he was already hiding her guitar. He just presumed it was more drama about her dad. He'd been right about the drama part, he thought, as Nia ducked out of the hall and into the car park.

Nia opened Caleb's boot, reached in and touched her guitar case, instantly feeling calmer. She picked it up, slung it on her back, grabbed the carrier bag with her choir uniform in and shut the boot, locking it before walking over to her spot.

It was safer playing here in the town-hall entrance than in town. Her dad hadn't set foot in the town hall since her mother died. He could just about bring himself to drop Nia off there, speeding away down the road as if the mountain wolves were after him. The town hall was where her mother had sung as a teenager, where her father first heard her sing. And now it was another place he avoided, as if someone had put up a no-entry sign on the door or sealed off the area with police tape. There was still the chance someone would tell him, but today Nia didn't care, because none of it would matter after tonight.

The sheltered entrance was the only way in and out of the craft market, which meant plenty of passing customers. Nia opened the case, set it down on the ground and moved around the handful of coins she'd left in there from last week. She took care to leave lots of nice gaps for the crowd to fill with their coins. If today went well she'd have enough to pay for her train fare tonight. And hopefully a room in a hostel, if there wasn't room for her in the hotel with the rest of the choir.

Nia turned the volume off on her phone; she didn't want her dad ringing to check up on her right now. She tucked it away in her skirt pocket and cleared her throat. She took a quick sip from her water bottle and then began to play. She didn't play carols. She'd had more than enough of those. Instead she chose popular covers that usually worked well as crowd pleasers. Nia smiled gratefully at strangers as they dropped their copper, silver and gold coins into her case, happily surprised that people would think her music was worth something.

When she played she imagined a different version of herself standing there. She pictured another Nia, confident, knowing and peaceful. Playing the guitar made her feel as if she was making her own rules, imagining the future musician she hoped she'd have the opportunity to become.

Only a few more years of this, Nia told herself, as she tightened the strings on her mother's guitar. Only a few more years of being treated like a china doll and then she could go anywhere, sing whenever she wanted and travel to any city in the world, on her own legally, and there was nothing he could do to stop her. Not once she was an adult.

She really didn't get why walking into town with Sol had freaked her father out so much, but then there was a lot about him she didn't get anymore. If she wasn't safe with Sol, Nia didn't know who she was safe with. They'd known each other practically their whole lives.

A little boy wrapped up in a bobble hat, matching scarf and red gloves stopped to check out all the other coins before parting with the one his dad had given him. His eyes were wide, imagining what he would buy with all the shiny riches before him. He reminded Nia of Sol the day she'd first met him in the woods, playing on her turf, sitting in *her* tree…

Chapter Nine

'That's my climbing tree,' Nia told the strange boy who was halfway up it, standing on the weakest branch. He didn't jump when he heard her voice so Nia knew he'd seen her coming. The tree was a good lookout post. That's why it was hers.

'It can't be your tree. This is everyone's tree because it's in the woods. You can't own the woods,' he said, rubbing his face on the bottom of his t-shirt. It was hot, probably too hot to be out without a hat, but Nia's had fallen off somewhere along the way; she'd find it later on the way home. He had baseball boots on too which would be no good for climbing. Nia looked down at her trainers with grips on and nodded confidently.

'Well, everyone else knows it's my tree, 'xcept you, so you must be new. Which means you are Solomon,' Nia informed him, making the situation and the rules clear.

'Just Sol, actually.'

'Oh, OK. Sol.' She tried his name out again. The shortened version sounded more natural on her tongue. She didn't know anyone called Sol. 'I'm Nia. Don't put your foot on that branch; it won't hold your weight.' She pointed out the weak areas and shimmied up the tree to meet him, showing off happily. There was a breeze in the treetops at least. Nia twisted her hair up and off her neck and clamped it together with a hairclip from the front of her hair.

'Thanks,' Sol replied, watching her climb. When she was level with him she jumped up onto the branch opposite him and sat on it, swinging her legs with practised ease either side of the arm of the big thick wellington tree. His eyes widened as he watched her moving around the tree without a care. Sol took one of his hands off the tree and tried to copy her casual movements as she interrogated him.

'Where are you from? Why've you moved? Is that your house there? That's old Mr Hans' house. He died in there. Probably in your bedroom. Make sure you sleep with a torch tonight, just in case. Ghosts are with us everywhere.'

'How do you know which room he died in?' Sol asked, unconvinced.

'Because I used to go there. I dropped stuff off my mum made him: bread and that. Anyway, one day when I was leaving cakes and milk there was no answer at the door…' She paused to see if she had Sol's full attention. She did.

'I went round the back and put my hands up to the windows, like this.' Nia cupped her hands, wobbling slightly on the branch as she demonstrated to Sol. His eyes widened again.

'And then I saw him. Lying there in his bed. He was asleep though, not dead, cos when I tapped on the window he sat up in bed and shouted at me.'

'Was that the green back bedroom then?'

'Yes!'

'Ha! Well my bedroom is blue, so there. Can't be his and so I can't be haunted. Anyway, I don't believe in ghosts.'

'Well … if you're sure. I mean, if *you* don't believe in ghosts, it won't matter if your parents had the room painted, before you moved in.'

'That's my mum.' Sol pointed down at a woman in a headscarf and dungarees, her black hair coerced into braids that threatened to burst out at every opportunity.

'I know, I saw her at the post office; my mum was talking to her. They're going for coffee tomorrow.'

'Oh, OK. Well, I've got two cats.'

'I know. I can see them in their cages.' Nia pointed down at the cage a man was carrying into the house.

'But I haven't got any brothers or sisters.' Sol struggled to tell her something she didn't already know.

'Oh. Me neither. Snap!' said Nia, surprised. 'Everyone in my class has got a brother or a sister; some of them even have more than one. Clara, she's nice but she has three older sisters; they're not nice. Three! *Poor Clara.*'

'Do you want one, a brother or a sister?' Sol asked as they watched his parents traipsing back and forth emptying the truck full of boxes and cartons.

'Nope, don't need anyone following me about, taking my stuff, being a *pain*. No, thank you!' Nia visualised her carved animals being battered and broken by a little brother or having to hide her new hook knife from an inquisitive younger sister. No, thank you!

'Are you going to be at school on Monday?' Nia asked, eyeing Sol's watch.

'Yes, I think so. Why?' He wasn't sure what to make of this tree-climbing girl who seemed to know everything about everyone.

'Give me your watch and I'll borrow it from you 'til then.' Nia held her hand out. Sol's watch was small and shiny with a cream face and black hands. Nia didn't have a watch, just a few friendship bands covering her wrist.

'Why should I?' Sol's hand hovered over the catch on the watchstrap.

'I'll be your best friend and … I'll call for you on the way to school. You'll only get lost otherwise. I know all the best shortcuts.'

'OK.' Sol wasn't quite sure how this deal was going to benefit him but he slipped off the watch and held it out to Nia. She shuffled across the branch of the tree towards him, took the watch and put it on. Then she tipped backwards, swung her ankles over the branch and dropped, hanging upside down like a monkey.

'Don't! You'll fall! Please? Get back up, quick!' Sol searched for his parents below but they were inside the house now and the gardens and the edges of the wood were empty. It was just him and the upside-down girl.

'I won't fall. I've done this loads of times before. You should try it!' Her voice sounded odd coming from such a strange angle. She swung herself outwards and tilted her head, taking in his eyes and the fear in them. Nia swung once, twice, three times and then let go, jumping down.

'See, it's not as far as it looks.'

'OK.' Sol stayed where he was.

'Don't worry, we'll climb to the top next time! See you tomorrow!' she shouted over her shoulder as she ran past his new house and off into the trees, wearing his watch.

Sol wondered if he'd see her again. He hoped so, if only to get his watch back. He waited until she was out of sight and climbed back down the tree, taking his time with each step. He vowed the next time he saw her he'd be a better climber, even better than she was. Once on the ground, he took a deep breath, then turned and began the climb again, determination written all over his sweaty face.

Chapter Ten

'Can you play my tune, singing lady?' the little boy asked again, tapping Nia impatiently on her arm.

'Be patient, Anders. Give her a chance.' His father smiled apologetically at Nia.

'He's excited about New Year, we all are!' He placed both his hands on his son's shoulders, pulled him backwards and in towards his body.

'Sorry! What song would you like me to play?'

'Jingle bells please. I did put my coin in there for my tune. Look, there it is!' He shook his father off and came closer to point out a chunky golden coin in her case, as if she needed proof of his payment. Nia nodded, hiding her distaste at his song choice. She launched into her own version, trying to make the request less painful. The boy clapped his gloved hands enthusiastically.

By 12 noon, Nia's guitar case was filling. She'd have more than enough for a return train ticket and a hostel too, if she needed it. She had to be prepared, able to say, 'Don't worry about me, I can look after myself,' if there wasn't room for her. She packed her guitar away, picked up her bag of clothes and went inside to find Sol.

'I'm sold out. Oh, and I nearly sold that big spoon for you. I think she'll come back for it later. You've still got another box to sell. Should shift those easily this afternoon.' He handed over some folded notes and she tucked the money away in the secret lining of her guitar case.

'Thanks. Want to go into town for lunch?' Nia asked, shoving her bag and guitar under the table. 'Caleb, will you watch my stuff for me please?'

They bought pasties, iced buns and more hot chocolates from their favourite café, Nannis. Nia sat down on one of the benches in the market square outside St Oswald's church while Sol hovered in front of her.

'Are you sure you want to eat here?' he asked nervously.

'Why not?'

'Because … ah, well, you know why, Nia. *Come off it*, I can hear them rehearsing in the church already. I don't know why you'd want to make it harder on yourself?' He sat down reluctantly.

'I know, I know, but I can't help it. Anyway, I've told you, I'm not staying here. I'm going with them.'

'How are you going to go with them? There's no room for you, remember? They've given your place away. You can't just turn up. They'll call your dad. I'm telling you, this is a bad idea.'

'It's not a bad idea, it's simple. Look, if I turn up at the Hofkirche in my uniform ready to sing, they're not going to turn me away, are they? Where would I go? They can't just turf me out of the church into the night. And once it's over, they can call my dad all they like because it'll be too late.'

'I'm not saying anything, Nia, just ... don't do this.' Sol shooed a pigeon away with the toe of his boot.

'And all I'm saying, *Sol*, is that I'm catching that train. That's all. You make it sound like I'm going to the other side of the world.'

'Yeah, just a train to Innsbruck. On your own. At night. Without the rest of the choir. And then what, Nia? You'll just find your way to the church even though you've never been there before?'

'I have! I've been there to hear Mum, I know the way. I'm not six, Sol. I can work out a train timetable, and I've got Google maps on my phone.'

'You don't even have your phone on half the time! I bet it's flat and you've forgotten your charger!'

'Oh, just shut up, Sol. Eat your lunch.'

They carried on eating in a silence that Sol eventually broke with a rush of words. 'If you're really doing this, Nia, if you're really going to Innsbruck tonight, then you should know something first.'

'What?'

'Isa is singing your solo. I hate to tell you, but you've already been ... replaced. Sorry.' He shifted awkwardly, unsure whether to sit closer to her or move a safe distance away.

Nia tried to swallow the icing from her bun but it was stuck to the roof of her mouth. She forced it down with a sip

311

of her drink but it was still too hot. She coughed, choked, and almost spat the lot out.

'Are you OK? Sorry, sorry!'

'*Fine*,' she squeaked, brushing his hand away. She had tears in her eyes. She told herself it was because of all the coughing.

'Don't hate me, OK … but there's always next year. You don't have to do this? Just leave it for a while, let your dad settle down. He'll definitely let you go next year and you can avoid all this?'

Nia realised Sol wasn't going to understand. How could he ask her to wait until next year? The moment was now. It was *her* solo, not Isa's. She wasn't going to let her, or her dad, take it from her. Her mum would have understood, if she was here. If she still had her mum, she'd be going on the Winter Tour. Her mum would probably have come with her! Sol could say what he liked, she wasn't going to sit and wait and let it all pass her by. Life wasn't long enough for waiting.

Chapter Eleven

The church was a sacred place, somewhere Nia felt compelled to be on her best behaviour, which was often a struggle. The gothic building was a spindly web of spires, rainbow-glass windows and the watery-blue outline of the large bell tower. As she walked past the grey stone font, the music reached a crescendo, vocals flying up into the high ceilings, bouncing off the stained-glass windows, filling the cold place with beauty and sound. Then silence fell as the choristers paused before starting their next song.

Isa moved forwards and stood humbly, trying hard to look meek and mild centre stage as the organ played the opening chords of 'May it Be'. This was *her* solo. Nia made herself look up and take in the arc of singers gathering around Isa, standing where she should be. Nia sat down in a dark side pew, hidden from sight. Sol hadn't followed her in, sensing this was something she needed to do on her own. She was glad he was outside when Isa sang the first words, low, sweet and so soft.

Isa's pretty voice lifted up, replacing Nia so easily, so readily. As Isa sang, Nia knew it was over. She had been hoping for a last-minute reprieve, that someone would run forwards to her pew and take her by the arm and lead up her to the stage. She'd hoped her dad would magically appear or at least phone her and say how sorry he was, how wrong he'd been. But all this was nothing more than daydreams, wishful thinking.

As she sat on the hard pew, the warm tears fell without warning onto her cold hands. The desire to push Isa off the stage, dunk her in the font, and take back her place was horribly strong.

Nia walked determinedly up the aisle, leaving behind the haunting harmonising as her friends' beautiful voices came together. She didn't look back, telling herself it didn't matter that her father had taken this away from her because she still had her voice. And no one was taking away that power. That was all she needed really: her voice and her mother's guitar.

Nia didn't mention what had happened in the church and Sol didn't bring up her plans. But they hadn't spoken to each other for over an hour and Sol couldn't take the silence anymore. 'How many spoons you got left?' he asked.

'Only six. I've sold all the big ones now. Might as well take a break?' Nia tried to sound casual but she was desperate. She pulled out her guitar case and returned to her position back in the entrance hall.

She played 'May it Be' first, just to get it over with and out of her system. She played it to a different tempo, ensuring her voice was deeper than Isa's: pitched in a lower key. This made it more her own than she'd ever managed in rehearsals.

There was a good crowd; they didn't just drop a coin in and leave, they seemed to want to say and listen. Nia smiled as she played the chorus again.

Sol grinned as she played the opening chords of *his song* next. She'd been playing Green Day's 'Time of Your Life' since he'd bought her the sheet music. It was hardly seasonal but always popular and made them both feel good. It was the only way she knew to smooth things over. The song was her way of saying all the things she couldn't say to Sol.

Nia liked the clapping and even the whistling or cheering that sometimes followed her playing but this wasn't why she did it. This wasn't why she played. When the clapping died down, she picked a Beatles song, one her dad always asked her mum to play on the piano. As she sang about the blackbird she watched the parents in the crowd look more at ease with this than Green Day. But something kept putting her off beat. There was an extra sound, something out of place and discordant.

She looked up briefly, her eyes scanning the growing crowd, but couldn't pick anything unusual out. She didn't need to concentrate too much on the lyrics or the chords; it was like falling back into an old habit, playing music like this. She finished and thanked people for their coins as some of them left. Several small children moved towards the front as the crowd broke up, pushing their way forwards to get nearer. She smiled at them. It was time she decided, time to move away from all the easy numbers, covers and old favourites and take a risk.

'I'm going to play something original now. This was written for me. I hope you like it,' Nia announced nervously to the crowd, as an expectant silence fell. She bowed her head and touched her necklace for luck then hid her face in her long hair as she sang, accompanied by her mother's guitar.

Chapter Twelve

Nia's voice cracked open with feeling as she sang. Her mother had told her this All Hallows' Eve tradition late one October night: that family members would gather at the gravesides of their dearly departed to sing songs to them. If the spirits were pleased they would visit the singer that night in their dreams. All Hallows' Eve had long passed, but she knew her mother wouldn't mind the wait. Nia hadn't been ready then, but she was now. She closed her eyes and pictured herself sitting on the wooden floor watching her mother's fingers running over the black and white piano keys, pausing, pencil in mouth, to make a change to the notes. And now as Nia sang the words to her song – *Nia's Song* – she knew it had been worth the wait, worth practising in snatched moments, trying to recall the notes and the lyrics.

I watch your shining eyes light my way home.
And whatever is broken is mended by all of you.

The evening of her mother's funeral, after everyone had gone home – even Sol, Caleb and Hanna – her father had run upstairs. Nia followed him nervously, opening her parents' bedroom door to find her father ripping the clothes from the hangers in her mother's wardrobe. There was a multi-coloured heap on the floor which he gathered up and threw into the back of his truck. He ran out to the woodshed, returning seconds later with his axe. Nia begged him, pleaded with him, but he pushed her away before bringing the axe down on her mother's piano, over and over and over. Her father flipped open the piano stool, took her mother's music and shoved it into the log burner, watching it fold and crackle until all that was left were Nia's memories.

My soul will whisper secret notes for only you
To catch and cradle.

Later, when he disappeared into the night in his truck, Nia was left in the house alone. She seized the opportunity and grabbed her mother's guitar, running with it all the way through the woods to Sol's house.

My arms will push and pull you because
Mine oh mine
We two are one.

Nia felt she'd picked the right moment to sing this song to her mother. She hoped she'd see her mother tonight in her dreams, the last night of the old year.

The pieces of our sighs and smiles
are tied with heartstrings and harmonies
Which rise and fall like the air you breathe.
Because
Yours oh yours,
We two are one.

She searched for Sol, for his familiar listening eyes, but his phone was in front of his face, held up at a funny angle. And it was beeping. That was the sound that kept getting in the way, tinny and high pitched, interfering with the tune she needed to hold in her mind.

'*Damn it.* Sorry, sorry! Battery's about to die. Don't stop, carry on, Nia.'

He was *filming* her? She stopped singing. She couldn't really see the crowd, but she could sense their questions, imagine their confusion, mirrored by Sol's own.

'Stop!' she shouted at him. 'You were filming me? For how long? Why? You can't do that Sol, you *know* you can't.' Her voice strained.

He held his phone stupidly in his hands, taking in her face, her pain and her hurt. Parents reached for their children's hands, pulling them away from the front. A few people picked up their shopping and marched off muttering. A lady who had been standing close to Nia reached out, put her hand on Nia's arm and asked her if she was OK, but Nia ignored her. She couldn't speak. Sol didn't move, he stood at the back looking at her, searching for what to say to make

319

this better. Nia took her guitar off and placed it carefully in the case. It fell shut with a loud thud.

'Give me your phone,' she demanded, reaching out her hand to him. They were almost alone now, the crowd quickly departing. Sol crossed the space slowly, clutching his phone to his chest.

'What were you thinking? Were you going to upload it? What if my father heard it, what if he found out?' Nia forgot the remains of the wintery crowd gathered to hear her haunting voice, which was now a screech.

Understanding clouded Sol's face.

'I'm sorry. I wasn't going to upload it anywhere. *I swear!*'

His eyes stayed on the ground because he was embarrassed. He didn't want her to know how he'd felt, that first time he heard her sing a solo at school. Now all he heard was pain and sadness, but today she sang like she used to and he wanted to record it in case she never sang this way again. The song was perfect; exactly what they said they'd been looking for in the email they'd sent him. If only his battery hadn't been low she'd never have even noticed him filming her and then he could have just told her the good news once it was a definite yes. He'd wanted to surprise her. Instead he'd scared and exposed her.

'I said, give me your phone, Sol,' Nia demanded, holding out her hand.

Sol paused for a moment, wondering what the consequences would be if he said no. He handed over the phone.

Nia took it and began scrolling through. She'd promised her father, sworn across her heart to him that she'd take a different path from her mother. But she'd lied. She couldn't stop singing; it was her connection to her mother, that and the guitar. She found the video but she didn't want to watch it; she couldn't bear to. She clicked on the delete button.

Sol stood there, watching her looking at herself on his phone. He walked out of the entrance hall to the car park. He knew there were no words he could say to make this right. It would be better if he just walked away and let her calm down.

Nia ran after him, calling his name.

Sol stopped and turned as she threw the phone. It hit him sharply on the side of his forehead, cutting open his skin. Sol didn't make a sound, but others did, running towards him.

'Hey! What are you doing?' someone called.

'Stop! What's going on out here?' yelled one of the shiny-suited log-burner salesmen. Nia hung her guitar across her back and pushed past Sol, banging into the people gathering around him.

Chapter Thirteen

Nia ran around the back of the building. She leaned against the wall and told herself to breathe, to calm down. Why would Sol want to film her? Even though she didn't want to hear what he had to say, Nia knew she had to go back and find him. She'd hurt him in more ways than one. She'd only meant to throw his phone to him, hadn't she? Or maybe *at* him? She couldn't remember now. But she'd made him bleed, and she never meant to do that.

Nia picked up her guitar and forced herself around the corner, expecting to see an angry mob calling for her arrest or the police come to take her away or something else melodramatic, but Sol had gone and no one seemed interested in her anymore. She walked over to the large doors of the town hall and peered into the craft market. It was completely normal, as if none of it had ever happened, as if she'd just imagined the whole thing. But what if someone had called her dad? She needed to leave now, while she still could, and catch the train. She'd have to talk to Sol later, make things right with him somehow. She could message him once she was on the train. Nia turned around, ready to keep going, and then she saw him.

Sol was sitting in his dad's truck, in the driver's seat, holding a cloth to his head. He was watching her. Nia marched across, put her guitar in the back and jumped into the passenger seat. This couldn't wait until later or tomorrow.

'What's going on, Sol?' she asked, coming straight to the point.

'Get out!' he snapped.

'What?' she stammered, taken by surprise.

'Get out, Nia. Just *leave me alone*,' Sol hissed.

Nia moved away from him, pushing herself up against the window, but refused to get out.

'I'm sorry, OK?' she offered, holding her hands up. She was still angry with him but this wasn't the time.

'It was just a film, that's all.' He sounded pained.

'Yeah, but you should have told me. At least asked me.' She reached out her hand and pulled the reddening cloth away to see the damage. His skin was ripped open and raw.

'You're right.'

'So, why did you do it, Sol?' she asked, moving closer.

Silence.

'*Because.*'

'Because?' she pushed.

'YES! *Because*, Nia … because of you and me.'

Nia paused. 'You and me? Not just us, but *you and me* as in a thing? Like, an item?'

He couldn't mean *that*, could he? They weren't a 'you and me'. Were they?

Sol nodded.

'But, for how long?' Nia asked shakily.

'Forever.'

'You've felt like that all this time?'

'Yes. All this time.'

Sol took the bloodied cloth out of her hands, dropped it and moved across the bench seat. He reached out to put his arms around her, moved his face closer to hers as if he was going to kiss her. Nia moved backwards, banging her legs into the gear stick as the old leather seats creaked beneath them. There was a moment of silence which Sol quickly filled, his breath blowing out in front of them in the cold cabin of the truck.

'It wasn't just that film, OK, you're right. Look, I've done something for you. It's a good thing, I promise. Don't be mad, OK? I was filming you for a reason...'

'Tell me.' Nia braced herself.

'I've sent a demo of your singing to a music label; it's just a small one, an indie. They liked what they heard and wanted some pictures of you. Then they asked for something new, not a cover version, so when you started singing that song, *your song,* I got my phone out and thought I'd record it. But I swear I haven't uploaded your music anywhere. It's not online, or anything.' He stopped.

Nia sat in silence.

'You can't give up or forget your dreams just because you've promised your dad. He never should have asked you. That day, that day ... your mum's funeral wasn't the time. It wasn't the right time to make you make promises you can't keep.'

The truck windows were steaming up with their wintery breath and Nia couldn't see the car park anymore. All she could see and hear was Sol, his truth and his lies all tangled up.

'But I never asked you, I never asked you to do that for me. And it wasn't your promise to break. It was mine.'

Nia moved further away. Away from his hands now reaching out to her, away from his bloodied face and the marks it had left on her shoulder. She opened the truck door, jumped down and ran around to the back.

'Nia! Stop, come back, please?' Sol called to her, getting out of the truck to try and stop her. But she wouldn't let him, not this time. She pulled out her guitar and ran away from him, the falling snow covering her tracks.

Chapter Fourteen

Nia stopped running once she found the pathway that led from the car park to the train station. The heavy guitar case kept banging into her legs but she wanted the pain; she needed something to push her on as she stormed past trees spattered with more falling snow. She'd planned on leaving her guitar with Sol and hadn't imagined she'd be taking it on the train with her. She could see her breath puff out in front of her as she kept up a steady speed power walking, needing to put distance between her and what had just happened. She forced her body to keep going even though she had a sharp stitch in her stomach.

Nia told herself that people were chasing her, the legendary Wildsee wolves waiting for her to trip, stumble and fall. She'd never hit anyone in her life. She never meant to hurt Sol when she threw the phone; she just hadn't stopped to think. It was a second of rage and then … it was gone, flying through the air. Her music was supposed to be *their* secret, hers and Sol's. She'd trusted him, with everything. How had he thought this was a good idea? What had he been thinking leaning over like that? Had Sol *really* been going to kiss her?

If her dad found out that she'd been playing music, if he ever knew what she'd done, that she'd been busking for the last few months, it would break him. He hadn't ever asked her where the guitar was or if she'd seen it. He must have assumed her mother had left it at the theatre, in her dressing room. If he saw that clip of her singing the song her mother wrote for her, playing her mother's guitar, performing just like she had... Nia couldn't guess how he'd react. How could Sol put her at risk like that? How could he think that filming her busking, playing, singing and sending it off to someone, to some stranger in a record agency, was a good idea? Without talking to her first? He was just a kid, even if he wanted to kiss her. He was just a boy. Her dad was right. This wasn't what happened in the real world. Sol was just dreaming but it was a dangerous dream.

The path through the underpass led to the town centre and train station. Nia headed down into the wide tunnel busy with shoppers returning to the car park, keen to get home before darkness descended. She stopped in the middle of the underpass and put down her guitar case to look around. She wasn't the only busker, which made her feel uncomfortable. She didn't want any competition or trouble; she just wanted to make up the money that she would have earned selling the rest of the love spoons left behind. She didn't know how much she might need once she got to Innsbruck – she couldn't give up on going, despite seeing Isa singing – but she hadn't really thought about the next stage of the tour.

Nia stood and watched a couple busking together for a few minutes. They sat on upended wooden crates, singing Christmas carols. The boy was on a harmonica and the girl was singing and playing guitar. When they stopped for a break, Nia made herself approach them.

'Hi, would you mind if I pitch up down there and sing a bit?' she mumbled, expecting a negative response.

'No, the more the merrier, as long as you aren't better than us!' the girl joked.

'There's plenty of space,' said the boy. 'If you stick to that end and we stick to this end we should be OK. We won't get any clashing or worse, sing the same numbers. It's peak time, mind, and it'll get busy now. You'd better get set up.' He pointed to the far end of the underpass.

'Thanks,' Nia replied, relieved.

'See you later. Good luck.' The girl smiled and waved, then turned back to her guitar, strumming a few chords while she and her partner conferred which song to sing next.

Walking along, Nia thought how many questions she wanted to ask Sol, but she'd have to apologise first. There was nothing she could do about it now. She wasn't ready to go back and face up to what she'd done; she was still so angry, and unsure of him for the first time. She'd text him once she got to Innsbruck. He'd be worried about her and it would give her an excuse to try and fix this mess. But maybe she should ring Sol, not text him? She had to talk to him properly, not dodge the issue. Words like 'because' and 'forever' were too big for either of them to cope with right now. Nia guessed they'd have a lot to say once they'd both calmed down. They could meet up once she was back from the tour. If they let her go on the tour.

She pulled herself together and rubbed her eyes, making sure not to smudge any mascara she might have left. She combed her fingers through her damp hair and pushed it off her face. She needed to look normal, happy if she could manage it.

The underpass was full of people walking through, couples holding hands. Some small children noticed her open guitar case with delight and pulled their parents to an annoyed halt, waiting expectantly for her to play something. She began to sing, nothing adventurous, nothing emotional, listening with half an ear to hear what the others were playing.

Nia relied on the familiarity of covers to carry her through the end of the afternoon. She soon gathered an awkward crowd, blocking up the power walkers, the joggers and the anxious parents who didn't want to be in the darkening tunnel any more than she did at the tail end of the day. The case filled with more copper and silver coins than gold but she told herself buskers couldn't be choosers. She played on, stopping only to take requests.

'Can you play *'Stille Nacht'* plsss?' a little girl lisped, looking down at the floor rather than at Nia.

'Sure,' Nia replied, strumming the classic three-chord song as the little girl mouthed the words back at her, holding on tightly to her mother's hand.

Chapter Fifteen

Nia remembered the first time she'd ever listened to her mother busk — one of those surprise moments you can't organise or orchestrate, but which become extraordinary.

They were running late and her mother had forgotten to collect her from school: rehearsals had overrun or something. Nia stood next to Mr Grimm, reluctantly holding his hand as she watched the rest of the class leave through the glass doors. They stood there, just the two of them, both waiting and hoping, but her mother never came, and then the doors were shut and locked.

'Come and sit with me in my office while you wait,' Ms Andersen had told her, sending Mr Grimm away to telephone her mother, again. The teacher had passed Nia a box of crayons and some sheets of blank paper. It was cold and her itchy grey school tights were rubbing the backs of her legs.

'I'm sure she won't be long now. She's probably got caught out by the level crossing,' Ms Andersen tried to reassure Nia. Sol's mum had offered to take Nia home but apparently her mother was on her way. That felt like so long ago, and Nia's stomach rumbled, telling her it must be nearly teatime. Mr

Grimm came back with a carton of juice and an apple; he set them down in front of Nia and marched off again leaving her in the alien adult world of Ms Andersen's office.

When her mother finally ran into the reception area, she was red in the face, curls sticking to the side of her temples. She pushed her glasses onto the top of her head, which knocked some of her corkscrew curls back at funny angles. Nia laughed, losing the crossness she'd been brewing.

'Sorry! Sorry I'm late, rehearsals overran and then I got caught out. Two trains at the level crossing, can you believe it? Took ages! *Sorry, darling*, sorry!' She wrapped Nia in perfume and the fresh cold air.

'No trouble, she's been no bother,' Ms Andersen smiled and brushed off the apologies as she passed Nia her pile of drawings, gratefully ushering them both out through the door before locking it behind them.

They ran to the car, holding hands, laughing for no reason at all. Her mother switched on the radio and turned it up loud as she reversed out of the car park and swung out onto the road. They sang along to The Beatles as they headed away from school.

'Let's go round the long way and avoid the trains this time,' Lorelei suggested, clicking on the heating.

'Please can we have noodles?' Nia asked hopefully, trying to read the hands of the small clock on the dashboard.

'Yes, go on then, seeing as you asked so nicely.' Lorelei drove into town in search of a parking space near the takeaway. There was quite a queue. Nia inhaled the smell of

331

bacon dumplings, fresh egg noodles, vegetable broth and the yeasty aroma of freshly baked rye bread. She quietly rubbed the backs of her snow boots against her tights, hoping her mother wouldn't notice how dirty she'd got them playing tag on the field at lunchtime.

'What do you want, just noodles?' They were interrupted before Nia could answer.

'Lorelei Christian? Excuse me, but it is you, isn't it?' A group of young women had turned around when they came in but Nia hadn't noticed, the smell of the food overpowering all her other senses. Lorelei smiled and nodded. She cheerfully signed her autograph on the back of a diary, turning back to Nia, but more people had joined the queue behind them and had overheard her name. It was passed up and down the queue until the owner of the shop called out, brave enough to ask for what they all wanted.

'Give us a tune while we serve, Ms Christian? Keep the customers happy and your meal is on the house!' He winked at Lorelei, who looked around helplessly.

'Oh yes. Go on, love. How about "*Stille Nacht*", it's my favourite?' asked an older lady, waiting on a chair near the door. Nia smiled proudly and nodded at her mother, encouraging her.

Lorelei sang quietly to start with, but as the clapping got louder she relaxed and sang more freely, gathering a small crowd just outside the noodle bar, the queue now spilling out into the street. Lorelei kept it up until it was their turn to order and then a disappointed silence fell. Nia could feel it around her, a lull in the air. She looked across at the old woman on the chair; her shoulders sagged.

'Just one more while I parcel yours up?' the plump man suggested and Lorelei obliged. When he handed her the bag of food, he brushed away her offer of payment, leaning over the counter to whisper to Nia, 'That's made my day! Your mother is a star. Can't wait to tell my wife later, she'll be so sorry she missed this!'

The room had lifted. The old woman sat taller, prouder. Nia looked up and down the queue in amazement. People had put their phones away, stopped fiddling with handbags. Small children had stopped running around annoying their siblings and stood still and open-mouthed. Her mother had done this with just her voice. It was like listening to an enchantment.

Nia never forgot this moment: hearing her mother sing a spell.

Chapter Sixteen

A young couple holding hands were watching her, waiting for the next song, as the underpass began to thin out and clear. The other buskers had shouted goodbye, waving as they left. Nia had moved into the middle, hoping to catch more customers there. She found her eyes resting on one of the girls' bottles of water. She'd been steadily singing for over an hour and her throat was dry. She could stop playing, walk into town and buy a drink, but she didn't know if she had enough time before catching the train to Innsbruck. And when she looked in her guitar case Nia decided she needed to play on a bit more, just to make sure she had enough.

'This is going to sound weird, but could I buy that water off you? I've left mine somewhere.'

The girl smiled and handed it over. 'Sure. Must be thirsty work, all that singing. No, put your money away; how about you play me a song instead? You've got such a beautiful voice, it reminds me of someone famous. Can't think who but it'll come to me.'

She grinned up at her girlfriend, who rolled her eyes and pretended to pull her away.

'Oh, come on! Not our song *again*, Hayden?' To Nia, she said, 'She's obsessed with it. Keeps going on about having it at our wedding. We're not even engaged!' She threw a few coins into the case and stood back. Her girlfriend kissed her on the cheek.

'Well, I bet you're sick of playing Christmas music, right? At least my song is a decent one,' said Hayden, handing her the water. Nia took off her coat, flinging it in the guitar case, then twisted the lid off the bottle, drinking gratefully.

'Better?' Hayden asked.

'Much. Thanks for that. So, what's your song?' It was just the three of them in the underpass. Almost everyone else had left for home. It was getting dark and colder.

'"Make You Feel My Love", Adele. Know it?'

'Couldn't really call myself a busker without knowing a few Adele songs,' Nia said. It felt a bit funny singing to just two people when she'd had an anonymous mass of strangers in front of her the rest of the day, but they were nice. Intense, but nice. When she'd finished, Nia glanced at her watch nervously; she had half an hour left to get into town, catch the train and then decide how to convince the choir mistress that her dad had changed his mind. And somehow persuade Isa to stand down and let her have her song back.

'Hey! Don't suppose you've got a light, have you?' Hayden interrupted. Her girlfriend tutted disapprovingly.

'I chucked her lighter away to stop her smoking. Now she's buying matches. You're supposed to have given up, Hayden!'

'I did give up. Then I gave that up too. What can I say? I'm weak?' She was waiting for Nia's reply, but she'd given all the matches to Sol to put into the log bags. She was about to shake her head when she saw a packet in amongst the coins in her guitar case.

'Oh, yes I do. Look, here you go. Thought I'd sold them all.' She set her guitar against the wall, picked the matches out of the case and passed them to Hayden.

'Guess it's my lucky day. These are a bit long, aren't they?' Hayden said, a cigarette hanging out of her mouth ready. It was a new pack of matches; they must have fallen out of the box and into Nia's case. Nia watched as Hayden held the first long match in her hand then struck it against the wall of the underpass. They both jumped as a loud slam echoed up and down the dark underpass. Hayden dropped the box and match, which hit the damp ground sizzling. The other girl grabbed Nia's guitar case and ran for the exit.

'Hey! That's mine, come back!' Nia shouted after the girl. But she didn't stop. Nia turned back to Hayden to confront her, but Hayden was already reaching past Nia trying to grab the guitar, forcing her back against the cold, hard wall.

'Get off me! Get off!' Nia shouted, dropping the guitar to push Hayden away hard.

'Shut up! Just *shut up*!' Hayden spat, stumbling in surprise, then she sprung forward and punched Nia on the jaw. Nia's head snapped backwards, bouncing off the cold tiled wall, and she slid down onto the damp ground. Hayden took her chance and snatched the guitar, following in the direction her girlfriend had taken.

Nia shouted after her, but she kept on towards the exit until Nia could no longer see anyone or anything but the gaping mouth of the tunnel.

Chapter Seventeen

Nia touched the back of her head with her hand where it hurt. Her temples pulsed, her head in a vice. When she pulled her hand away, her fingers were coated in sticky blood. Nia looked up and down the underpass. They were both gone, with her money and her mother's guitar. The tunnel was empty of people, devoid of life and light. And outside it was dark.

Nia looked down at the ground, where her guitar and her case full of coins had sat moments earlier.

How had she not seen this coming? How? They'd stayed too long, they'd talked too much and she should have known, should have been suspicious of them, but they seemed so nice, so normal. They were in love, asking for their song, but it was all lies, a trick, and she had fallen for it. What was the *matter* with her? What kind of fool leaves a guitar case full of money unguarded like that?

Her father was right; you should never trust strangers. But if she'd been allowed to go on the tour she'd have spent the day in the church with the choir rather than arguing with Sol. It was all his fault – her father.

Nia felt sick. She knew she had to get up. She had to get back to the market before he turned up: if he found out about this he'd be furious with her for breaking her promise. And he'd never let her out again, ever. She could get back before he even realised what she'd been planning, where she was intending to go tonight. Sol would never tell. But first she needed to clean herself up and hope to hide her injury and everything else she'd been planning. She was still bleeding and the pain in her head was making her float. She could hear a flapping or a buzzing in her right ear as she untangled her father's scarf and looped it around her head like the world's strangest bandage, pulling it as tight as it would go.

'Pull yourself together Nia and get up!' she told herself and then laughed, the sound echoing strangely in the underpass. She tried to get to her feet, but slumped back against the wall as the tunnel spun in black-and-white spirals in front of her. She rubbed her eyes roughly and saw purple sparkles of light.

And then nothing. Not a sound.

She woke curled up on the ground, her body shaking involuntarily. She clenched herself tight, wrapping her arms around her knees. She tried to stop the shuddering but couldn't. The moisture from the ground had seeped into her clothes and settled on her skin, coating her in dampness. Nia felt around for her coat and remembered it was gone. She'd taken it off and thrown it in the guitar case. The girls had her money, her mother's guitar, and her coat too. At least they hadn't seen her necklace hidden underneath her scarf.

Nia unwound the sticky scarf from around her head, planning to wrap it around her shoulders, but it was clogged with dried blood. She knew she had to get somewhere warm fast or she'd pass out again, or worse. Bareheaded and trembling, Nia put her hands on the ground ready to push herself up, but felt something lumpy. Her fingers coiled around a packet. It was the matches, *her* matches that the girl had dropped. Nia ran her finger over them and counted: there were still three matches left in the packet. She smiled. Now she had a packet of matches she could find some wood, maybe those crates the other buskers had been sitting on, and start a fire! If she could only get warm she was sure she could work out what to do.

'It's going to be OK; I'm going to be fine,' she told herself, relieved to have what seemed to her then to be a sensible plan of action.

Chapter Eighteen

Nia found herself striking the first match before she'd really thought through what she was doing. She hadn't got up and found any wood; she couldn't see in the dark, let alone stand. Instead she'd struck the long red match against the grain of the packet but had nothing to set alight. She held the match in front of her, watching the pretty colours dance.

The sound of the strike quickly followed by light and heat made her smile and sigh with relief. It looked like a beautiful sunrise. She held the match up to the curved roof of the underpass and saw the burgundy and green tiles light up, red and bright, as if the fire from the match was reflecting back down on her, cocooning her. She felt her bones relax beneath her clammy skin. She kept her eyes on the roof as the slow-burning match lit up the underpass. Nia relaxed into the heat of the moment and the memory that followed.

———————

The TV went off at the exact moment the kitchen lights popped out, leaving them in soundless darkness. Her mother tutted from across the room and put something down on the table. Nia froze. She wasn't comfortable in the dark. The outlines of objects familiar to her in the light took on a different shape, menacing, threatening and full of the unknown. She waited for her parents to sort things out, to get up, to find the light and make things right.

'Power's out again, I'll get some candles. Where are they, Lor?' Jacob muttered, putting down his carving knife and the boat he was working on. Lorelei's voice came from beside the fireplace, followed by the rustling of the newspaper she had been reading.

'In the top of the larder, I think.'

'Big larder or small one?' Jacob asked, moving carefully towards the kitchen.

'Small one, top shelf, matches next to them,' said Lorelei, lit only by the glow from the stove.

Her father rummaged in the larder for matches and candles and then set them down in front of the fire, which gave out the only light in the room. Nia sighed with relief and let go of the remote control which she'd been clutching to her side, poised, ready for anything. Jacob passed the packet of matches to Nia but not before examining them, screwing his eyes up to try and see which brand they were.

'These ones look new. Where did you get them, Lor? They're really long,' he asked, lighting the larger candles first. Nia copied him, striking matches, lighting the biggest candles first and then the old gas lamp her granddad had passed down to her father.

'Caleb left them here. He's been experimenting again, making longer matches with a slowburn tip,' he said. 'They smell funny though, don't they? He's dipped them in a new mixture, reminds me of something chemical like that toilet cleaner I bought last week!' Lorelei added more logs to the stove and put two of the bigger candles down on the kitchen table.

Jacob sat back down, took up his carving knife and continued shaping the bow of the boat. After a few minutes of silence he paused and stopped to look up at Nia who had been watching him, staring, transfixed as the knife moved back and forth, shaving and shaping the wood.

'Why don't you have a go at this instead? Much better for you than watching TV.' Jacob held out a shapeless lump of wood towards her and a small carving knife. Nia took the wood from him reluctantly; she didn't really understand the fascination her father had with making his own things and cleaning his tools, locking them away carefully in his wood shed each night. Woodcarving seemed like an old man's thing to do, something Caleb or even maybe Sol would be more interested in rather than her, but the TV wasn't back on yet and she had nothing else to do.

'Try something simple, like a spoon, maybe a love spoon? That was the first thing I ever carved and I'm sure you can do a better job than I did!' said her mother, settling back down to her newspaper. Reading that looked as appealing as trying to carve shapes out of lumps of wood. Nia didn't even know what a love spoon was.

'Oh! Do you remember that first one I made, Jake?' Lorelei scrunched up her face. Jacob laughed at the memory.

'Yes, it was awful. You should have seen it, Nia, all lumpy, nothing like a spoon, didn't even have a proper bowl at the bottom, it just sort of stopped. Where did you put it, Lorelei, let's show her!'

'I probably threw it on the fire but there's that lovely one your mother gave us, where's that?' She headed upstairs with a lantern and after a bit of banging and crashing she came back triumphant.

'Here it is. Bit dusty. I really should have put it up on the wall, but like all those pictures in the attic, it's another thing I've never quite got round to doing.'

Lorelei passed over a long wooden spoon to Nia, who held it up to the light to examine it. It was long and pretty with hearts cut out of it and other small symbols. There was no way she could make something like this.

'Why don't you just try to copy the outline, the shape? It isn't as difficult as it looks,' said her father.

'Go on, have a go, Nia, your father will help you. Maybe he'll even make a love spoon too, for his lovely wife?'

Jacob laughed. He held the boat up to Lorelei to show how busy he was, but put it down again when he heard Nia sigh. He passed a small knife to her; it fitted neatly in her hand. Nia held the lump of wood in the other hand and looked up at her father for further instruction. He tucked the boat he had been working on under his chair, selected another block of wood and picked up his own carving knife, considerably larger than the one he'd given her. Jacob struck the first blow and Nia watched the curve of wood-shaving fall onto the rug at their feet. She looked at her father, who smiled, nodding encouragingly as she did the same to her lump of wood, trying to copy him. Step by step they began to carve the shape of the wooden bowl, Nia following her father. She mirrored his every move until something began to take form, a shape appearing underneath all the flakes of wood.

'That's it, that's my girl. Only seven and you're already doing better than your mother. Clearly you get your carving skills from my side of the family!'

'Hey! I heard that. Well then, she definitely gets her singing skills from my side!' Lorelei called over, her head still bent over her crossword.

'It might even make a decent mother's day gift if you keep going like that. Reckon you're a natural, Nia. *I knew you took after me,*' he leaned in to whisper. Nia could smell his aftershave. He smelt of pine needles, of the forest and of wood carvings. It was a nice smell, the smell of home, she thought, as she inched closer to her father to watch him more carefully.

And then the match went out.

Chapter Nineteen

Nia lit another match. It reminded her of the candlelit church she'd sat in earlier, enveloped by music and lights, safe and warm. She could almost hear the singing now. Nia relaxed into the heat of the colours and the memory that followed.

Her mother placed a *Sachertorte* down on the kitchen table. She'd iced Nia's name in loopy writing across the shiny chocolate ganache. Nia counted the candles silently, pretending to be embarrassed but secretly pleased. A birthday wasn't right without a cake, but this was the first year she hadn't asked for one, she'd just quietly hoped they'd know to make one.

Her mother strummed the opening chords to *Happy Birthday*, singing it in all the languages she knew, perched on the edge of a chair. Her curls fell over her face as she leant over the instrument and switched into a jazzier version of the song, adding in her own lyrics, extra notes, chords and riffs, making it sound like a different song.

'Happy Birthday to you,

Tillykke med fødselsdagen
Buon compleanno, cara Nia
Alles Gute zum Geburstag!'

They sang to her together, her father trying to join in, slightly off-key but smiling. She watched the candles flickering brightly in the darkness of the room, even though she was far too old for such things. Her mother always made up a different version of the song each year, something silly and fun, and for once Nia was glad Sol wasn't here; glad it was just the three of them and no friends, no party, no family arriving, no fuss. She needed an early night before her big day tomorrow, birthday or not.

She'd been practising her solo everywhere and anywhere: singing in the shower, walking through the woods to Sol's house, playing the piano next to her mother; even as she fell asleep at night there would be a phrase or a harmony on her lips or in her ears. She was sure her dreams had a soundtrack to them now.

Her mother leaned her guitar carefully against the wall before returning to the kitchen table. She scooped up Nia's tangled hair and twisted it into a neatish ponytail, before taking a hairband off her own wrist and tying it up. 'Don't want your hair getting covered in chocolate icing and apricot jam, do we? Not a good look for tomorrow.'

Nia nodded. Tomorrow, it was going to happen tomorrow, she was going to sing in front of the rest of the school choir and after that she'd know, they'd tell her straight away if she'd

346

got in, if she'd be part of the Winter Festival Tour next year. Or not.

Her dad cleared away the remains of the roasted goose, then passed her a plate ready for the cake. Her mother poured tea from the steaming pot and they all fell silent, waiting for her to blow out the candles and make her birthday wish. She didn't have to think: she'd been making the same wish for months now. Nia scrunched up her eyes, leaned forwards and gently blew out the candles, wishing hard, so hard.

Please let me pass, please let me get into the choir and go on the Winter Festival Tour, she mouthed, silently crossing her fingers and her ankles and her arms across her chest.

She looked across the cake through the smoke-filled haze of candles fizzling out and her father winked at her, nearly laughing at the serious look on her face.

'Going to tell us what you wished for?' Jacob asked as he cut a big wedge of cake and put it in front of her. Nia shook her head. If she said it out loud it would never come true, she'd jinx it for sure. It was safe to wish in silence in her head, but she couldn't speak it. Any time the subject came up at home or at school she changed it, just in case.

'She doesn't need to tell us.' Lorelei answered for her, taking her own plate from Jacob's hand. Jacob reached behind Lorelei and grabbed a present. It looked squishy and soft. Maybe clothes?

'That one is from me!' her father announced as he handed over the beautifully wrapped gift.

He'd used silver and gold paper and wrapped it all up with a tiny red ribbon. Nia undid the ribbon carefully, not wanting to tear it or the paper. It was a very long, bright-red scarf, so long that it went around Nia's neck three times.

'Perfect. Thanks, Dad.' Nia kept the scarf on as she leaned over and kissed her father.

'And here's mine.' Lorelei pulled a box out of the bottom drawer in the kitchen, where they kept the pans.

'What's it doing in there?' Nia asked.

'I only finished wrapping it earlier and you came into the kitchen, so I had to think fast.' Lorelei tapped the box, impatient to see her reaction. They nearly always made her presents, separate ones, which was fine by Nia as it meant more than one present to open. This was perhaps the only downside to not having a brother or a sister; surely a sibling would have to buy a present too? Nia peeled off the tape and opened the lid of the box. Inside was another box, a smaller one. She took it out and set it on the table wondering if her father knew what it was.

'I hope this isn't going to be a Russian doll kind of present, Mum, with smaller and smaller boxes.'

'Keep going,' Lorelei instructed, giving nothing away. Nia opened the box and sure enough inside was another box. She kept opening boxes and peeling off tape until she came to the last box. It was bright red and small and covered in velvet. Lorelei grinned as if to signal the end. Nia lifted the lid of the box and inside sat a silver necklace. Hanging on it was a treble clef, a tiny sparkling symbol of music. Nia held it tentatively in her hands, as if she might break it. Her mother stood up and took it from her and placed it around Nia's neck, securing the catch.

'I had it made just for you. Happy birthday, my darling.' She kissed Nia as Jacob cut one last slice of cake.

Lorelei pulled away to look at the necklace. 'It fits. Do you like it?' she asked.

'I like it. *I love it!* It can be my good luck charm for tomorrow.' Nia ran over to the hallway mirror to see what the necklace looked like on her. Lorelei followed her over and wrapped her arms around her tightly, studying their joint reflections in the mirror. She tucked away the strands of hair that were already escaping her ponytail before whispering warmly in her ear, 'Sometimes wishes do come true.'

And then the match went out.

Chapter Twenty

Nia took out the last match. She tried to remember what she was going to do with it; there'd been a plan, hadn't there? She was going to do something with the match, wasn't she? As she struck it the colours curled up into the air and then down again, a flaming sunset.

Nia relaxed into the heat of the moment and the memory that followed.

Tonight was the finale before her mother's choir went off on tour, and the last evening of the year. It would be their last night together for a few weeks. Nia had mixed feelings: she was excited for her mother but selfishly knew she'd miss her.

Nia and her father were going to collect a takeaway on the way home and wait for Lorelei to catch them up after she'd packed up her dressing room. They'd see midnight in together, but after that Lorelei was setting off. Nia wanted the night to last as long as possible before the new year started and brought with it change. She knew they could talk on the phone and Skype, but it wouldn't be the same as having her mother in the house. It would be strange and new with just the two of them at home, Nia and her father.

Nia leaned forwards on her plush red seat, peering over the mahogany edge of the grand box to look down at the audience. She held her opera glasses to her eyes, watching the crowd below. People were still arriving; the house lights were on and hadn't flashed yet. Women in dresses and heels were walking carefully down the aisles, clutching *The Immortal Hour* programmes with her mother's photograph on the front. Men in bow ties stood up to let people past into their seats. The air was crisp and crackling.

Nia never came on the first night. That's when the cast were nervous and tense and waiting for the first reviews, and she didn't want to see her mother's face strained when the curtain came up. Tonight would be different. This was no matinee, this was like the last night at the Proms, and after the final curtain call the cast were going to go out onto the balcony with a skeleton orchestra so that when the audience left the theatre they would be met with a surprise encore. They'd never done this before, but it was the hundreth anniversary of the theatre being opened, the first tour of *The Immortal Hour* and of course New Year's Eve, and these occasions needed marking. Even better, it was a big surprise for the audience, and for anyone walking past at the time.

Nia had kept her mother's secret – apart from telling Sol. But at least she'd waited until the last moment; she'd managed to hold out until she saw him in the foyer earlier. They stood together under the magnificent Christmas tree, admiring its height and splendour.

'Don't go straight home after the performance. Make sure you stand outside the balcony, *something's going to happen!*' Nia whispered quickly in his ear. 'Promise me you'll wait?' She pulled on his arm until he agreed.

When the red curtains opened, Nia saw her mother's face lit up by the footlights. Lorelei was dressed as Etain, the faery princess. She was wearing a purple headdress and a wig that tumbled down her back. Her face was painted with symmetrical markings of a butterfly on her cheeks, which looked like wide-open eyes watching everyone. Her gown fell past her feet like a waterfall so that when she moved she looked like she was floating across the Wildsee.

Lorelei looked up at Nia and sang the first long high note as if there were no one else in the theatre. Every face in the auditorium was on hers, every pair of eyes was fixed on the faery in the spotlight. Lorelei sang as if it were just the two of them, at home practising at the piano together with Jacob listening in the background. She sang a solo accompanied by a golden harp, in front of a full house on a stage flooded with light. But in her heart, she sang to her daughter and her husband.

The match flickered dangerously and nearly went out, but flared up again, highlighting her mother's silhouette in the exit of the underpass. She was coming closer, now walking towards her, now floating: her purple outline fluttering in and out of focus. Despite her best efforts, Nia's eyes began to flutter too, opening and closing like the wings of a butterfly.

Chapter Twenty-One

Jacob had heard the music in his truck as he drove along the forest road towards the craft market. He changed the station quickly, wanting to avoid the sound, searching for news or sport or even weather, but every station seemed to be playing the same annoying song. He thumped the dial on the radio hard with his fist. It switched back on again. He turned it off firmly. But the music returned, harp strings filling the cab of the truck with a woman's voice, a soft soprano. '*Lorelei*?' he said out loud. He hadn't said her name in some time.

Nia wasn't waiting on the steps in her usual spot. Jacob sighed, then saw Caleb outside the hall, locking up.

'Have you seen Nia?' Jacob shouted over the music.

'They had a fight,' Caleb answered, his back still to Jacob.

'Who did? Fight about what? Where's she gone?'

'She ran off, towards town, Sol thinks. They had a fight about something, he won't tell me any more than that. Believe me I've tried.'

'And you let her go? You just let her run off on her own?' Jacob shouted in disbelief, his eyes scanning the road as the tempo of the music became faster, quicker, more urgent.

'She hit Sol. He was bleeding.'

'Nia did? Nia hit Sol? Are you sure?'

The music stopped.

'That's what he said. Look, let's walk into town. I'm sure we'll find her. Sol tried ringing, but it went to answerphone.'

'Maybe, I don't know… Look, you stay here in case she comes back. I'll find her, OK?' Jacob ran down the road into town.

'I think she went that way,' Caleb called after him, but Jacob didn't need any directions. He didn't need to know which twists and turns his daughter might have taken. The singing grew louder and stronger as he followed his wife's voice and the notes she dropped for him, like clues, in the snow.

Chapter Twenty-Two

Nia crawled along the wet floor on her stomach, the ridges of gravel and stone scraping against her skin. Her body was so numb she almost didn't register the pain. Movement was becoming difficult, but she was aware enough to know that if she didn't keep going, moving, pushing and pulling her body along, she could die.

And she didn't want to die in here, on her own, in the dark. She really didn't.

The ringing was high-pitched. She tried to lift her hand to her ear to push the sound away, but she couldn't concentrate on anything other than moving towards the tunnel entrance. She could hear her mother's singing behind her, accompanied by a repetitive beat which sounded like wings flapping or a dress blowing in the wind, pushing her onwards.

Nia knew just enough about concussion to keep inching closer to the light, to an escape. She tried to talk to herself, to say reassuring things, if only to hear someone's voice, but the words came out in the wrong order, slow and sloppy. She sounded drunk. But the singing didn't stop; her mother's voice rose softly up into the arches of the underpass and fell back down around Nia like a shawl, comforting, encouraging and vital. It was her favourite song, the one about the blackbird.

The beeping was unbearable now, clashing with the scales of her mother's soprano. The beeps were coming quicker and faster, relentless. Nia had to stop, to breathe properly. She lifted her head and saw she was still so far away from the entrance to the underpass. She breathed in and out, the cold catching in her sore throat. Something was vibrating against her hip and Nia forced her hand down to her pocket. Her frozen fingernails scraped and scratched until she managed to pull out her phone. She had turned it down when she was singing and since she'd been attacked she'd completely forgotten about it. There'd been no signal in the middle of the underpass anyway.

The screen wouldn't light up properly when she touched it; the battery symbol was flashing pathetically. It was going to go flat. Going to die. But she wasn't. Nia pushed down hard on the phone symbol, not caring who it would connect with. It rang.

'Nia? *Nia!* Where are you?' It was her father. She tried to shape her mouth, to get the right sound out before her phone cut out.

'Underpass,' she managed. The phone clattered onto the floor as the dim screen light went out.

Two hands wrapped around Nia's body, lifting her off the cold damp ground and carrying her away.

'You're safe now, Nia.'

Nia felt fingers of frost on her face, the heat of the match fading, now a failing flame.

'I just couldn't let you go. I'm so sorry, Nia, sorry for everything.'

Outside the snow had fallen thick and fast; the mountains were white porcelain mounds.

'I've got you, you're safe with me.'

The wind scurried up snowflakes.

'I love you, Nia.'

Woodsmoke and pine needles filled her senses as radiant heat passed from father to daughter.

'I'm so sorry, I was wrong. I can't lose you too. Stay with me, Nia. Stay with *me*?'

Nia forced her eyes open and looked over her father's shoulder down into the underpass as the singing swelled in a grand finale.

'Nia? Are you listening to me? Stay with me!' Her father stopped walking as if unable to continue until she'd answered.

The last match illuminated the shadow of her departing mother, burning almost down to the tip. Nia whispered, 'Yes,' into her father's shoulder. 'Yes, I'll stay with you.'

As the old year began its graceful retreat from the stage, Nia welcomed the new year in, singing the softest of goodbyes to her mother.

And
then
the
match
went
out.